Twisted Pursuit

Iris Frost

Published by Iris Frost, 2024.

This is a work of fiction. Similarities to real people, places, or events are entirely coincidental.

TWISTED PURSUIT

First edition. October 31, 2024.

Copyright © 2024 Iris Frost.

ISBN: 979-8224886173

Written by Iris Frost.

Chapter 1: A Storm on the Horizon

The storm raged outside, the wind howling like a banshee as it lashed against the glass of my apartment. Each crash of thunder felt like a cannon blast, echoing my inner chaos. I stood before the mirror, adjusting the collar of my emerald-green dress, a bold choice meant to capture attention and, perhaps, instill a bit of envy among my political peers. This wasn't just another gala; it was a chance to solidify my standing as a rising star in the chaotic world of Chicago politics.

But the stakes were higher than the typical mingling of the elite. This event had transformed into a battlefield where ambition met avarice. My mind flickered to Grant Hastings, the billionaire developer whose very presence sent a ripple of irritation coursing through me. His plans for the waterfront threatened to swallow our beloved community whole, replacing beloved parks with luxury high-rises. It was infuriating how effortlessly he could charm a room full of well-heeled patrons, all while masking the destruction he left in his wake. His grin was disarming, a casual arch of his lips that seemed to whisper sweet nothings to the uninitiated, but I knew better.

I took a deep breath, steeling myself against the echo of those past encounters—the debates where his smirk had become my personal hell, where his words dripped with the kind of charisma that made him a crowd favorite. Yet beneath that polished exterior, I sensed an unsettling truth. He believed he could trample over anyone who stood in his way. Tonight, I would show him that I wasn't just another obstacle; I was a force to be reckoned with.

As I gathered my belongings—a portfolio filled with community feedback, proposed plans, and the meticulous arguments I'd crafted to counter Hastings' insidious influence—my phone buzzed with a text from Marissa, my campaign manager and best friend.

"Remember, you're not just fighting him. You're fighting for all of us. Go get 'em, girl! ◇❤"

Her support wrapped around me like a warm blanket against the brewing storm outside. I allowed myself a brief smile, one that faded as I glanced out the window. The dark clouds were closing in, heavy and oppressive, and I felt an unsettling kinship with them.

The gala was being held at one of those old-world venues, a sprawling mansion that reeked of privilege. I envisioned the grand entrance, all marble and chandeliers, a perfect backdrop for political maneuvering, whispers of corruption, and the occasional click of heels against the polished floor. It was a place where alliances were forged and broken in the blink of an eye, and tonight, I planned to forge my own.

The drive to the venue felt like a descent into the underworld. The rain hammered against my windshield, blurring the streetlights into swirls of color as I navigated through the Chicago streets. Each drop seemed to echo the doubts pooling in my stomach, but I clung to my resolve. I had come too far to turn back now.

Arriving at the mansion, I stepped into a world drenched in opulence. Guests glided across the marble floor like well-fed swans, their laughter mingling with the haunting notes of a string quartet. My heart raced as I scanned the room for familiar faces and, inevitably, for him. The moment I spotted Grant, standing by the bar, a glass of aged scotch in hand, I felt a rush of adrenaline. He was captivating, his dark hair tousled just so, eyes sparkling with mischief as he shared a joke with a group of influential donors.

"Isn't it charming how some people think they can charm their way into everything?" I muttered under my breath, my fingers curling into fists at my sides.

I needed to maintain my focus. As I made my way through the crowd, I encountered various political figures, each more insufferable than the last. They greeted me with hollow smiles and empty compliments, their eyes drifting over my shoulder, clearly waiting for more prominent personalities to arrive. I plastered on my own polite smile, feeling the weight of their indifference like a chain around my neck.

But then, as if sensing my frustration, Grant turned his gaze in my direction. The corner of his mouth lifted, and for a heartbeat, the room seemed to fade into the background. My heart thudded painfully against my ribs, an unwelcome reminder that I was not just an adversary to him; I was also the target of his undeniable charm. I straightened, shaking off the sensation like a wet dog shedding rainwater, and approached the center of the room, where a podium awaited me.

"Ladies and gentlemen," I began, my voice steady, cutting through the murmur of conversations. The crowd quieted, their eyes shifting from Grant to me. "Thank you for gathering here tonight. I stand before you not just as a politician but as a member of this community, a community that deserves our protection, not our exploitation."

I could feel Grant's eyes on me, assessing, calculating. His presence was a hot brand against my skin, igniting my determination. The whispers started, a ripple of intrigue weaving through the crowd. I pressed on, my heart racing as I recalled every argument I'd ever crafted, every meeting where I'd listened to the fears of my constituents.

"This isn't just about development; it's about preserving the soul of our city. We owe it to our children and our grandchildren to ensure they inherit a Chicago that reflects our values, not just our wealth."

The applause was tentative at first, but it grew, resonating through the room like a tide rising against the shore. I felt emboldened, my words weaving a tapestry of hope and defiance. And in that moment, I caught a glimpse of Grant, his expression inscrutable yet filled with a flicker of respect. But it was fleeting, overshadowed by the storm brewing in his eyes.

As I stepped down from the podium, I was met with a wave of congratulatory pats on the back and insincere compliments. Yet, through the throng, I felt Grant's gaze like a spotlight, a fierce reminder that our battle was far from over. He made his way toward me, a predator closing in on its prey, and despite my resolve, a shiver of anticipation danced down my spine.

"Impressive speech," he said, his voice smooth and laced with that maddening charm. "You certainly know how to stir a crowd."

"Stirring a crowd is easier when you're not hiding your true intentions behind a well-practiced smile," I shot back, my words sharper than I intended.

He chuckled, the sound warm and inviting, but I recognized the challenge in his eyes. "Touché. But tell me, are you really willing to sacrifice progress for the sake of sentiment?"

"Sacrifice? I prefer to think of it as safeguarding our future."

His smirk returned, infuriatingly captivating. "Ah, the noble politician. It's a role you wear well."

As he stepped closer, the scent of cedar and warmth enveloped me, igniting a spark of something utterly confusing. I gritted my teeth, reminding myself of the stakes. I was here to protect my community, not get lost in his dangerously charismatic orbit. The storm outside raged on, but the tempest brewing between us felt just as fierce.

"Don't think for a second that I'll back down," I warned, my voice low and fierce, locking eyes with him.

He raised an eyebrow, amusement dancing in his gaze. "Wouldn't dream of it. After all, what's a good fight without a little electricity?"

In that moment, surrounded by opulence and ambition, I realized that our battle had only just begun. The storm outside mirrored the conflict within me, a thrilling and terrifying dance I couldn't seem to escape.

The air buzzed with anticipation, crackling like the electricity before a storm. As I maneuvered through the throngs of elegantly dressed guests, their laughter mingled with the gentle strains of the string quartet, a backdrop that felt both opulent and suffocating. Each step I took echoed in my mind, a reminder that every word I uttered tonight had to matter. I couldn't allow myself to get lost in the glimmer of chandeliers or the sweetness of champagne. My mission was far too important.

Spotting a cluster of familiar faces—my allies in the fight against Grant—gave me a jolt of courage. They were deep in conversation, eyes bright with the fervor of shared ambition. I approached them, determination simmering beneath the surface. "I hope you all brought your A-game," I said, injecting a lightness into my voice that masked the tension coiling in my gut.

"Of course!" Maria, a fellow council member, flashed a confident smile. "We're not just here to look pretty. We've got work to do." Her fiery spirit was infectious, a perfect counterbalance to my more measured approach.

"Exactly," I said, scanning the room for Grant once more. "We need to rally support and turn the tide against Hastings' plans. If we're going to save our community, we have to strike while the iron is hot."

A chorus of nods confirmed my point, but a new wave of uncertainty washed over me as I caught sight of Grant across the room, effortlessly charming a group of donors. He stood tall, hands animated as he spoke, a predator basking in the attention of his prey. I could feel my heart race, a mix of irritation and undeniable intrigue. It was maddening how his presence alone could unsettle me, like a spark igniting dry grass.

"Focus," I whispered to myself, but even my inner voice sounded shaky.

The evening continued, conversations swirled like the wine in my glass, and I found myself chatting with several supporters who shared their concerns about the development projects looming over our neighborhood. Each story pulled me deeper into the mission that had become my life's work. The stakes were personal; they were my friends, my neighbors, and my community. The thought of losing that—of seeing our green spaces replaced by high-rises—brought a sense of urgency that fueled my resolve.

As I moved through the crowd, I engaged in discussions about community initiatives, weaving a tapestry of connection and shared purpose. Yet, the shadow of Grant loomed large, a constant reminder of the battle I was fighting. I could sense him moving closer, as if the magnetic pull between us was undeniable. My breath caught as he sidled up next to me, the air thickening with unspoken tension.

"Impressive network you've built," he remarked, tilting his head toward the small group gathered around me. "You've certainly gathered the troops."

"Just doing my part," I replied, crossing my arms defiantly. "Not everyone believes in tearing down the fabric of our community for a quick profit."

His eyes gleamed, and I could almost see the gears turning in his mind. "You make it sound so noble, but let's not forget that progress sometimes requires sacrifice."

"Sacrifice?" I scoffed, barely containing my outrage. "You mean the sacrifice of our parks, our history, and our future? That's quite the spin, Grant."

He chuckled, low and rich, and I hated how much I was drawn to the sound. "I'm just saying, change is inevitable. It's how we navigate it that matters."

"We can navigate it by preserving what we have instead of bulldozing over it," I shot back, my pulse quickening. "But I suppose that perspective doesn't line your pockets."

"Touché," he replied, his tone mocking yet playful. "But remember, not all of us have the luxury of clinging to the past."

I opened my mouth to retort, but he raised a finger, interrupting me. "Wait, before you unleash your fiery rhetoric, let's consider a different angle. What if we worked together?"

"Together?" I echoed, disbelief flooding my voice. "What on earth would make you think I'd ever join forces with you?"

"Because," he said, leaning in slightly, his expression shifting to one of unexpected seriousness, "what if we could create something that benefits both the community and, let's say, my business interests? An arrangement that elevates your cause while also allowing for responsible development?"

I narrowed my eyes at him, searching for a hint of insincerity. "And why would you want that? You thrive on conflict."

"Maybe I thrive on the challenge," he suggested, a glimmer of amusement dancing in his eyes. "Besides, I'd much rather have you as an ally than an adversary. You might find that I'm not as villainous as you believe."

The unexpected sincerity in his words caught me off guard. My heart raced, the gears of my mind spinning. Could there be a glimmer of truth hidden beneath his charm? Or was this merely a tactical maneuver, a way to sidestep my relentless pursuit?

"Or perhaps you just want to win me over so I'll stop sabotaging your plans," I replied, tilting my head to meet his gaze, unwilling to show any signs of wavering.

"Who says I want to win you over?" he countered, his smirk returning. "You're the one who seems to be fascinated by me."

"Fascinated? Hardly," I retorted, the words coming out sharper than I intended. "More like intrigued by your sheer audacity."

"Ah, but isn't intrigue a form of fascination?" He leaned against the wall, arms crossed, a confident posture that screamed nonchalance.

"Let's not get carried away. Fascination would imply some level of admiration, and I certainly don't admire the way you bulldoze through everything in your path."

"Fair enough. But you must admit, you're more fun than most of the politicians I deal with."

The playful banter was a welcome distraction, but it was still a dangerous game. "Just because I'm not easily intimidated doesn't mean I'm your friend, Hastings."

"Friend? Who said anything about friendship?" His eyes twinkled with mischief. "I'm merely offering a partnership that could lead to something beneficial. We both know how important this gala is for our reputations."

As I opened my mouth to refute him again, I was interrupted by a loud crash—a glass shattering to the floor nearby, the sudden noise cutting through the tension like a knife. We both turned, the moment broken, and I seized the opportunity to step back. My heart was still racing, and as I glanced around, I realized that the crowd had turned to witness the spectacle.

A couple stood in the center of the commotion, one of them clearly flustered, the other—an older gentleman—looking positively furious. His face was flushed, the remnants of a drink dripping from the table. "You're ruining everything! This is supposed to be a respectable gathering!"

Whispers erupted among the guests, and I couldn't help but feel a pang of empathy for the unfortunate soul at the center of it all. The gala was meant to be a platform for connection, yet here was proof that even the most glamorous events could unravel in an instant.

As Grant and I exchanged glances, the tension shifted from us to the unfolding chaos, a reminder that in politics, one moment could shift the tide. I had come here to fight for my community, and I wasn't about to let a petty squabble derail me.

"Excuse me," I said, stepping away from Grant, my resolve rekindled. "Let's see what's really going on."

He watched me go, a mixture of amusement and intrigue in his eyes, as if I were a puzzle he was desperate to solve. I pushed through the crowd, determined to defuse the situation, my heart pounding with the thrill of the unknown. In the chaos of shattered glass and fraying tempers, I felt a renewed sense of purpose. This gala was my stage, and I would not be overshadowed—not by Grant, and certainly not by a simple mishap.

The glass shards glistened on the polished floor like a field of stars scattered across a dark sky, each piece a testament to the chaos erupting around us. As I navigated through the throngs of guests, I felt the tension shift, the air thick with whispers and uncertainty. I could see the old gentleman gesturing animatedly, his face flushed with a mix of embarrassment and anger, while the other party—a young woman, her dress an eye-catching red—stood frozen, clearly unsure of how to respond.

"Gentlemen, ladies, please," I interjected, stepping into the eye of the storm, my voice clear and authoritative. "What seems to be the issue?"

The crowd hushed, all eyes turning toward me, and in that moment, I could feel the weight of their expectations pressing down like a thunderhead. The old man huffed, his ire barely contained. "This reckless woman bumped into me! Look at my drink! My scotch! A fine drink ruined!"

"An unfortunate mishap," I replied smoothly, flashing a reassuring smile to the red-clad woman, who looked as if she might faint from the attention. "But we're all friends here, are we not?"

She blinked at me, her eyes wide, then rallied, her shoulders squaring as she nodded. "Yes! I'm so sorry—I didn't see you there!"

"Of course, accidents happen." I turned to the man, my smile unwavering. "Perhaps we could all share a toast to the evening and leave this little incident behind us?"

The man frowned, clearly not ready to back down, but the murmurs of agreement from the surrounding crowd seemed to have an effect. The young woman took a deep breath, her cheeks flushed with embarrassment but determination rising to the surface. "I'll buy you a drink! I insist."

Before he could respond, she reached for his arm, pulling him toward the bar, her voice rising above the noise. "Come on, let's get you something to replace that. You deserve it!"

As they moved away, I felt the tension in the room begin to dissipate, the crowd drifting back to their conversations and laughter. I exhaled, feeling like I'd just defused a ticking bomb. "Crisis averted," I muttered to myself, but just as I turned to rejoin my allies, I bumped into a solid chest.

"Impressive," Grant's voice came, smooth as silk, laced with a hint of playful sarcasm. "You really know how to handle a crowd."

"Don't push your luck, Hastings," I said, raising an eyebrow. "I'm still keeping my eye on you."

"Ah, but I can't help but think that maybe, just maybe, we're not so different," he replied, his smile maddeningly charming. "We both thrive in chaos."

"Don't flatter yourself," I shot back, my heart racing despite myself. "You thrive on chaos because you create it."

He held up his hands in mock surrender. "Fair enough. But don't forget, you're not the only one who can play this game."

Our repartee had drawn a few curious glances, and I felt the temperature of the room shift slightly. I needed to maintain my composure, but every fiber of my being was screaming to take the bait, to engage further. Yet, I pushed that desire down; I had bigger battles to fight than my personal war with Grant Hastings.

With a deliberate move, I stepped away from him, scanning the crowd for familiar faces. I spotted Maria and a few other supporters near the hors d'oeuvres table, their laughter a welcome sound amid the simmering tensions. As I made my way toward them, I felt the hum of the room returning to normalcy, but beneath that veneer of civility, the undercurrents of rivalry and ambition still surged.

"Nicely done," Maria said, her eyes sparkling with mischief as I approached. "I thought we were going to witness an old-fashioned duel for a moment."

I chuckled lightly, grateful for the distraction. "Let's hope it doesn't come to that. I'd rather save my energy for the real fight."

"Speaking of which," Maria leaned in, her expression turning serious, "have you heard any whispers about Grant's latest project? I overheard a couple of donors discussing something involving the waterfront again."

My heart sank at the mention. "He's relentless. We need to be prepared for whatever he's plotting. I can't let him succeed."

"Agreed," she said, her brow furrowing. "We should meet after the gala to strategize."

"Definitely," I replied, the determination in my voice hardening. Just as I was about to delve deeper into our plans, a sharp, piercing scream sliced through the air, halting our conversation mid-sentence.

We turned as one, the atmosphere shifting from one of conviviality to palpable fear. The scream had come from the direction of the bar, where several guests were now gathered, a commotion erupting around a figure crumpled on the floor.

"Is that...?" I whispered, my heart racing as I pushed through the crowd toward the unfolding scene. As we neared, the crowd parted like waves, revealing the young woman in red, now pale and trembling, kneeling beside an unconscious man.

"Someone call 911!" she cried, her voice shrill with panic.

I rushed forward, adrenaline surging through me. "What happened? Is he breathing?"

She shook her head, tears streaming down her cheeks. "He just collapsed! I don't know—please, help!"

Kneeling beside the man, I quickly assessed the situation. He was older, his face a shade of ashen gray, the wine glass slipping from his fingers, shattering on the floor next to him. The crowd had thickened again, murmurs of concern and confusion echoing through the room.

"Can anyone get a first-aid kit?" I called out, my voice steady, even as panic threatened to claw at my throat.

As people scrambled, Grant stepped beside me, his earlier charm replaced by a tense seriousness. "What do you need?"

"Check his pulse," I ordered, focusing on the man's chest to see if it was rising and falling. "We need to make sure he's alive before we can do anything else."

"On it," Grant replied, his hands deftly moving to assess the man while I kept watch over the crowd, my heart racing.

"Stay back, everyone!" I commanded, a wave of authority breaking through the tension. "Let us through!"

Just as the first sirens wailed in the distance, a new fear settled in my gut. I could see Grant's face, the determination etched into his features. "We can't let this derail us," he said, his voice low. "Once they arrive, it'll be chaos."

"Right," I breathed, thoughts racing as I tried to maintain my focus. My eyes darted around, seeking out the nearest exit. "We need to keep the crowd calm. They're going to panic."

But just then, another scream pierced the air, and I turned to find another figure crumpling to the floor nearby—a woman I recognized from earlier, her dress swirling around her as she collapsed, eyes rolling back in her head.

"Something's wrong!" I shouted, a chill creeping up my spine. "What is happening?"

The murmurs turned into gasps, chaos unraveling as guests began to panic.

And in that moment, with the storm raging outside and chaos erupting within, I felt a cold shiver of dread settle in the pit of my stomach. Something was very, very wrong.

Chapter 2: Fractured Alliances

The gala stretched before me like a shimmering sea of silk and laughter, the kind of evening where dreams tangled with reality under the glow of crystal chandeliers. Each twinkle in the ballroom felt like a star drawn down from the sky, casting a soft luminescence over the gathering. I wove through the crowd, my heart racing not just from the rhythm of the music, but from the weight of expectation that draped over me like an exquisite yet suffocating gown. I was a puppet in a delicate play, the strings pulled taut by the unseen hands of ambition and obligation.

I took a deep breath, the scent of fresh blooms mingling with the rich aroma of fine cuisine, and steadied myself. My heels clicked against the polished marble floor, a crisp metronome in the symphony of soft murmurs and laughter that filled the space. Guests adorned in elegant attire spun like marionettes around me, their smiles bright but eyes often veiled, secrets hiding behind layers of mascara and velvet. The grand ballroom, with its gilded walls and plush carpets, was a kaleidoscope of colors and emotions, but beneath its glossy surface lay a deeper undercurrent of tension, like the quiet before a storm.

"Ah, there she is," came a voice, deep and mocking. I turned to see Grant, his form effortlessly cutting through the throng of attendees. He moved with the confidence of a man who knew his worth, yet in his blue eyes flickered something that sent a thrill of both irritation and intrigue racing down my spine. The way he smirked suggested that he was privy to a joke only he understood, and I found myself momentarily entranced despite the storm brewing in our recent history.

"Just because you made it through the door doesn't mean you should be gracing us with your presence," I shot back, my tone sharper than intended. He deserved it—he always did. It was our unspoken ritual, our back-and-forth that danced on the line between playful and perilous. I admired his stubbornness, though I'd never admit it. Grant had a way of wearing arrogance like a tailored suit, perfectly fitted to his broad shoulders, making it hard to see the vulnerability beneath.

He stepped closer, lowering his voice so only I could hear. "If you think the gala will save this city from itself, you're sorely mistaken. But then, I'm not surprised. You always did like to dance on the edge of delusion." His words were laced with venom, but there was an unexpected glimmer of sincerity in his gaze.

"Delusion? Or perhaps it's a refusal to accept the status quo?" I retorted, refusing to back down. "This city deserves better than the apathy we've both seen lurking behind these gilded facades."

"You and your lofty ideals," he chuckled, a sound that was at once charming and infuriating. "Dreaming won't protect you from reality, Amelia."

"Reality? Or is it just your reality?" I shot back, my pulse quickening. Our repartee had always been a fine line to walk, each word a carefully placed stone over a turbulent river. But tonight, there was an uncharacteristic weight to his words that lingered in the air between us. Perhaps it was the way he tilted his head, an almost childlike curiosity etched into his features as if he were trying to decode the puzzle that was me.

Just then, the music swelled, and I felt the atmosphere shift, a ripple of something ominous weaving through the fabric of the night. I turned slightly, scanning the room, when I caught a glimpse of a group of men in dark suits huddled together, their hushed tones barely reaching my ears. My instincts kicked in, the gut feeling that had guided me more times than I could count. They were too close, their body language too tense, too secretive.

"Amelia?" Grant's voice sliced through my thoughts, pulling me back to him. "What's wrong?"

"Nothing," I lied, forcing a smile. But my eyes betrayed me, darting back to the group. "Just... I think I heard something."

"Something?" he echoed, his brow furrowing in concern. "What do you mean?"

I hesitated, torn between the instinct to confide in him and the knowledge that our history made him the last person I should trust. But before I could articulate my thoughts, one of the men stepped away from the huddle, glancing around as if scouting for eavesdroppers. My breath caught in my throat. His eyes met mine, and for a fleeting moment, I felt a spark of recognition. The unease settled deeper in my stomach.

"Did you hear that?" Grant asked, his voice low and urgent now.

"What?" I said, trying to sound nonchalant, but my heart raced.

He leaned in closer, his breath warm against my ear. "Whatever you heard, it can't be good."

As we stood there, the tension between us thickening, the elegant facade of the gala faded into the background. I felt the allure of the night wane, replaced by the gnawing uncertainty curling around my thoughts. We were on the brink of something larger than either of us—a potential threat to the very city we both claimed to love, though we expressed that love in vastly different ways.

Our gazes locked, and in that electric moment, I realized that this evening, which had begun as an elegant dance among elite society, had transformed into a precarious game of survival. I could either choose to stand by and watch from the sidelines or dive headfirst into the depths of uncertainty that awaited us, with Grant as the unexpected partner in this dangerous waltz.

The air crackled with the tension of unspoken words as Grant and I stood in the midst of the swirling gala, the once-celebratory atmosphere feeling suddenly charged with apprehension. I shifted my weight, feeling the fabric of my gown swirl around me, a stark contrast to the steel encasing my thoughts. He narrowed his eyes, as if attempting to decode the very fabric of my being. The moment hung suspended, caught in the liminal space between animosity and an inexplicable connection that seemed to tether us despite our past.

"Are we really going to stand here playing coy?" he quipped, a hint of that signature bravado returning to his voice. "I'm not the one hiding behind a facade, Amelia. You're the one with the serious look plastered across your face."

"You have a talent for stating the obvious, Grant," I shot back, but even I could hear the undertone of uncertainty in my voice. It was infuriating, this unbidden effect he had on me. "What's next? A witty commentary on the importance of choosing the right shade of lipstick?"

"Now, that I'd pay to see," he said, a teasing grin breaking through the storm clouds of our conversation. "Though I think you're perfect just the way you are."

That unexpected compliment hung in the air, laced with something deeper than just surface-level banter. It took me by surprise, leaving me floundering for a retort. Instead, I turned my gaze back to the group of men whose furtive whispers had seized my attention moments before. They were still clustered together, their expressions serious, a stark contrast to the glitzy ambiance around us.

"Look," I said, lowering my voice as I gestured discreetly in their direction. "Those men—something isn't right. I overheard them talking about the city, and it sounded... ominous."

Grant's expression shifted, the playfulness evaporating like mist in sunlight. "Ominous? How ominous are we talking? Because last I checked, there's always some level of impending doom lurking at these events."

"Trust me," I insisted, my heart racing. "This felt different. They were discussing plans—something that could affect everyone here."

"Maybe they're just plotting to steal the show," he replied, but his tone lacked conviction. I could see the wheels turning in his mind, his bravado peeling away to reveal a kernel of genuine concern. "Do you know who they are?"

I shook my head, frustration bubbling up within me. "No, but if we don't find out, we could be in real trouble. We need to get closer."

He hesitated for just a moment, the shadows of our rivalry still casting a pall over our interaction. But then, with a resigned sigh that was more of a challenge than an agreement, he nodded. "Fine. But if we get caught eavesdropping, I'm blaming you."

"Noted," I smirked, feeling a rush of adrenaline. "Just follow my lead."

We drifted through the crowd, the music swirling around us like a comforting veil as we approached the group. I could feel Grant's presence beside me, a steady anchor amidst the chaos, though our past had taught me to keep my guard up. I stole glances at him—how the way his jaw clenched when he concentrated added an intriguing intensity to his already captivating features.

We found a vantage point just behind a massive potted plant, its leaves lush and vibrant, providing just enough cover to allow for our clandestine observation. The men's conversation became clearer, the tension palpable.

"...the council won't listen," one of them said, a tall figure with slicked-back hair that glinted under the chandeliers. "But we can't let them decide our fate. Not after what happened last time."

"The mayor's too busy with his gala to notice the ground crumbling beneath us," another chimed in, his voice thick with frustration. "We can't sit back and hope for the best."

The words hung heavy in the air, each syllable more troubling than the last. I exchanged a quick glance with Grant, his brow furrowed as he absorbed the implications of their discussion. "This isn't just idle chatter," he murmured, his voice barely above a whisper. "They're planning something."

"Something that could threaten the very foundation of our city," I added, my pulse quickening. The urgency of the situation gripped me, driving home the reality that we were standing at the precipice of something far larger than a simple gala.

Just as I began to lean closer, intent on catching every word, a commotion broke out on the dance floor. A server had dropped a tray of glasses, the sound shattering the air like a gunshot. The laughter and chatter of the gala surged back to life, drowning out the men's conversation.

"What now?" Grant muttered, frustration evident in his tone.

I straightened, scanning the room for a distraction. "We need to get closer while we still can," I insisted, pulling him along as we skirted the edges of the revelers. As we approached, I spotted a familiar face—a local journalist known for his unyielding dedication to uncovering corruption in the city. He was standing a few feet away, his eyes narrowing as he listened to the men.

"David," I called out, waving him over. His gaze flickered to me, momentarily surprised, but then he hustled over, his expression shifting from confusion to intrigue.

"What are you doing here?" he asked, glancing between Grant and me. "You two look like you're plotting something."

"More like eavesdropping," I admitted, pulling him closer. "Those men—whatever they're discussing, it's serious. We need to find out what's happening before it's too late."

David's eyes widened, and he leaned in, lowering his voice. "I've heard whispers about a faction forming, one that believes the council is mishandling resources. If they're planning something... it could be disastrous."

"Then we need to act," Grant interjected, the familiar spark of determination igniting in his eyes. "Tonight."

I could hardly believe we were on the same page, our past grievances fading into the background. "Agreed. But we need to be careful—if they catch wind of us snooping, it could spell trouble."

"Trouble is my middle name," Grant shot back with a lopsided grin, the tension between us shifting again, now charged with a sense of shared purpose.

"Is that so?" I raised an eyebrow, amusement flickering through the worry gnawing at me. "I always thought it was 'arrogance.'"

"Arrogance is merely confidence in disguise," he quipped, his tone light but his gaze intense. "And right now, we need both."

As the gala continued to pulse around us, the looming threat nestled beneath the surface grew heavier, and the two of us, once rivals, now found ourselves bound by a cause far greater than ourselves. The night had become a precarious dance, and I could feel the rhythm of uncertainty pulsing through the air, urging us onward into the unknown.

The music swelled again, a lush backdrop to the chaos enveloping the gala. Grant and I exchanged quick glances, a silent agreement hanging in the air like a shimmering promise. We had little time, and the walls were closing in around us. The momentary distraction of the broken glasses had drawn the attention of many guests, their laughter ringing hollow amid the growing tension. I could feel the weight of our shared mission settling between us, an unsteady alliance forged in urgency and necessity.

"Stick close," I whispered to Grant, pulling him toward the outskirts of the gathering. He followed, a shadow at my side, his presence both a comfort and a reminder of the jagged edges of our relationship. I led the way through the clusters of elegantly dressed patrons, my heart pounding with a mix of exhilaration and fear. I had to know what they were planning.

David had fallen into step behind us, his eyes flickering with determination. "If they're planning a coup or something equally dramatic, we need to gather evidence," he suggested, glancing over his shoulder as if wary of unseen threats lurking among the opulence.

"Right," I replied, my mind racing. "But how do we do that without arousing suspicion? We can't just stroll up and ask them to spill their secrets."

Grant smirked, a familiar spark igniting in his blue eyes. "Leave that part to me. I've always been good at drawing attention—just not usually the right kind."

Before I could respond, he glanced over at the group of men, who had moved slightly apart, their conversation now hushed but evidently urgent. I watched as one of them, the leader with the slicked-back hair, checked his watch and gestured impatiently, his posture exuding authority. "They're about to break," I murmured, adrenaline surging through me.

"Let's move closer," Grant said, his voice steady despite the chaos swirling around us. We crept forward, weaving through the throng of guests whose eyes sparkled with delight, completely oblivious to the storm gathering just beyond the glimmering lights.

As we drew nearer, the leader's voice cut through the ambient noise, sharp and commanding. "If we don't act soon, everything we've worked for will slip through our fingers. The mayor is too distracted with his little soirée to pay attention to what's happening on the ground."

"What's our next step?" one of the other men asked, his brow furrowed with worry. "We can't risk being exposed."

My heart raced as I leaned in, straining to catch every word. The mention of the mayor sent a jolt of panic through me. "What are they planning?" I whispered, glancing at Grant, who seemed equally transfixed.

"I think we need to find out who else is in on this," he murmured, shifting his weight as if preparing to confront the men directly.

"Wait," I cautioned, grabbing his arm. "We can't go in guns blazing. We need proof first."

Before I could finish my thought, the men abruptly shifted, their attention captured by someone entering the ballroom. A figure glided in, the light catching the sleek fabric of her gown—a striking woman with an air of confidence that rippled through the crowd like an electric charge.

"Is that...?" I began, but Grant's sharp intake of breath cut me off.

"Yes. That's Eleanor Thorne," he said, his voice low, filled with a mix of awe and apprehension. "She's a major player in the city's development projects and has been a vocal critic of the current administration. If she's here, something significant is happening."

The atmosphere shifted as Eleanor moved gracefully through the throng, her presence commanding immediate attention. Conversations quieted, and all eyes turned to her. She appeared to be surveying the room, her sharp gaze lingering on the group of men. I could sense the tension radiating off Grant as he tensed beside me, the rivalry we'd both felt seemingly overshadowed by this new development.

"What do we do?" David whispered, the urgency clear in his tone. "We can't let this moment slip away."

"We need to find out what she wants with them," I replied, my mind racing. "If she's here to confront them, we might be able to leverage that."

Grant nodded, determination igniting in his gaze. "Let's get closer. We can't let this opportunity pass."

As we maneuvered through the crowd, Eleanor stopped just short of the group of men, her voice rising above the murmur of conversation. "Gentlemen," she said, her tone laced with authority, "I've been hearing some unsettling rumors. Care to explain what's going on?"

The men shifted, their earlier bravado faltering under her scrutinizing gaze. "Eleanor," the leader began, a hint of nervousness creeping into his voice. "This isn't the time or place for—"

"Then when is?" she interrupted, her words sharp as daggers. "Because I assure you, whatever you're plotting is not just a simple matter of business. The city deserves transparency, and if you think I won't expose your plans, you're gravely mistaken."

A tense silence fell over the group, the air thick with the weight of her accusation. Grant and I exchanged a look of disbelief. This was the moment I'd been waiting for, yet it also felt like a precarious cliff's edge, ready to plunge into chaos.

Just as I prepared to move closer, a commotion erupted at the entrance. The doors swung open, revealing a team of security personnel who swept into the room, their uniforms stark against the elegant attire of the guests. Whispers spread like wildfire as people turned to watch, the atmosphere shifting again, this time tinged with alarm.

"What are they doing here?" I whispered, anxiety curling in my stomach. "They weren't scheduled to arrive until later."

Grant's eyes narrowed, his intuition kicking in. "They're here for a reason. We need to get out of sight before they notice us."

As we stepped back into the shadows, the reality of our situation crashed down around us. The stakes had risen sharply, and we were now entangled in a web of deception far more complex than we had anticipated. The ballroom, once a shimmering display of elegance, had transformed into a battleground where alliances could fracture at any moment.

I turned my attention back to Eleanor, who stood defiantly facing the men, her resolve unwavering. The tension between them was palpable, thick enough to slice through. I could feel the weight of decisions hanging in the air, each choice fraught with potential consequences.

Suddenly, one of the men stepped forward, a dangerous glint in his eyes. "You have no idea what you're meddling in, Eleanor. You're far out of your depth."

Her expression hardened, but before she could respond, the security team surged forward, their leader barking commands that sliced through the night. "Everyone, please remain calm! We need to ask a few questions regarding an ongoing investigation."

The words sent a ripple of anxiety through the crowd. Gasps mingled with the music, and my heart raced as I realized the true danger we were facing. The men's expressions shifted from confidence to fear, a fracture in their carefully constructed facade.

Eleanor, unfazed, met the security team with a steady gaze, clearly ready to challenge whatever they were about to unleash. My pulse quickened as the realization dawned: we were on the brink of something explosive.

As the tension peaked, a loud crash reverberated through the room, sending glasses shattering to the ground and hearts racing. The doors flung open again, revealing a figure silhouetted against the bright lights, their intentions shrouded in mystery. The air thickened, and I felt the unmistakable grip of dread clutching at my throat.

Before I could take another breath, the figure stepped forward, revealing a face I never expected to see in a place like this. My heart stopped. This was no ordinary guest. This was someone whose presence would tip the balance of power in the city forever.

"Ladies and gentlemen," they declared, voice booming over the chaos, "I think it's time we had a serious discussion about the future of our beloved city."

And just like that, everything I thought I knew began to unravel, leaving me hanging on the precipice of an unknown abyss.

Chapter 3: Secrets Beneath the Surface

The air was thick with tension as I settled into the worn wooden seat at the back of the city council chamber, a place where promises and deceit danced hand in hand under the flickering fluorescent lights. I could feel the familiar grip of anxiety tightening in my chest, a sense that today was not just another day in my slow, unchanging life. No, something was brewing beneath the surface, dark and volatile like the storm clouds gathering overhead, ready to unleash their fury at any moment.

The council members were draped in their tailored suits, their expressions a cocktail of boredom and indignation as they shuffled through the agenda. The mayor, a rotund man with an impressive mustache that quivered with every emphatic gesture, droned on about budget cuts and public safety measures. I leaned back, half-listening, my mind spiraling into the depths of the mystery that had hijacked my thoughts. Grant Reynolds was a name that felt like bitter honey on my tongue, sweet yet laced with a stinging bitterness that reminded me of the times we had clashed. His perfectly coiffed hair and smug smile were hard to forget, but today, he was merely a pawn in a much larger game.

I'd caught wind of whispers, rumors swirling around town about a shadowy figure orchestrating events from the dark corners of our city. It was as if someone had thrown a stone into a pond, and the ripples of discontent were spreading, causing waves of unease among the residents. The council meeting was the perfect breeding ground for conspiracy, where the innocent and the corrupt mingled, each with their own agenda hidden beneath the surface.

As I jotted down notes, my eyes caught Grant's entry. He walked in with an air of arrogance that seemed to radiate from him, his presence demanding attention like a spotlight on a stage. I could hardly believe I was about to engage with him again, but my instincts told me that he might have the key to unraveling the web of lies we were caught in. Just as I was about to mentally prepare for our inevitable clash, he glanced my way, his expression shifting from smug indifference to surprise.

"Fancy seeing you here, Amelia," he said, leaning against the wall, a smirk curling his lips. "I thought you only showed up for the donuts."

I rolled my eyes, crossing my arms defiantly. "And I thought you only showed up for the cameras. What's it like knowing you're the favorite poster boy for bad decisions?"

He chuckled softly, a sound that momentarily disarmed me. "Touché. But maybe today, we'll have to put our animosity aside. I hear there's a storm brewing, and it's not just the weather."

With that, the room fell silent as the mayor called for order. Tension crackled in the air, and I couldn't shake the feeling that something was about to happen. As the meeting dragged on, murmurs of dissent rose like the tide, fueled by residents who felt unheard and overlooked. I could see the frustration on their faces, a mix of anger and helplessness that mirrored my own sentiments.

Then, as if on cue, a figure appeared at the back of the room, a tall silhouette with a hood pulled low over their face. The atmosphere shifted palpably, a collective gasp echoing through the chamber. All eyes turned towards this newcomer, a ghost materializing in the mundane world of bureaucracy. I felt my heart quicken, adrenaline surging through my veins as the shadowy figure stepped forward, the air around them charged with an electric uncertainty.

"I have something to say," the figure announced, their voice cool and resonant, commanding attention without a hint of fear. "You're all being played. Your trust has been exploited for someone's greed."

Murmurs erupted, a blend of disbelief and intrigue that sent a wave of energy through the room. The mayor fumbled with his notes, visibly rattled, while Grant shifted uneasily beside me. I leaned in closer, curiosity piquing my interest. Who was this mysterious speaker, and what did they know that the rest of us didn't?

"Who are you?" one council member shouted, rising from his seat, indignation spilling over like an overflowing cup.

"Someone who cares about this city more than you ever will," the figure shot back, their voice unwavering. "A puppet master is pulling strings behind the scenes. While you argue over budgets, they're setting the stage for chaos."

The room was a cauldron of chaos as people began to shout over one another, fear mingling with anger, creating a tempest of uncertainty. Grant turned to me, his previous bravado fading into concern. "We need to get to the bottom of this," he said, urgency lacing his tone.

"Are you suggesting we work together?" I asked incredulously, every fiber of my being screaming to decline.

"Unless you have a better idea?" His brow furrowed, frustration simmering just beneath the surface.

I hesitated, the familiar heat of resentment bubbling to the surface, but then I took a breath, the gravity of the situation pressing down on me. "Fine. But if you step out of line, I won't hesitate to throw you under the bus."

"Deal," he replied, a flicker of determination igniting in his eyes.

With that, we found ourselves aligned in a battle against the unseen enemy. As the meeting spiraled into disarray, I could feel the threads of our fates intertwining, a reluctant partnership forged in the heat of uncertainty. The storm outside raged on, but within these walls, we were about to uncover the secrets hidden beneath the surface—secrets that could change everything.

The next day, I awoke to the hum of unease that lingered in the air like a half-remembered dream. The morning light filtered through the curtains, casting slanted shadows across my cluttered room, each beam a reminder of the chaos that unfolded the previous night. I had barely slept, my mind a whirlwind of thoughts about the mysterious figure who had disrupted the council meeting and the secrets they hinted at. My instincts clamored for attention, urging me to dig deeper into this web of intrigue that wrapped itself tightly around my small town.

I swung my legs over the side of the bed and groaned at the sight of my reflection in the mirror. My hair resembled a bird's nest after a storm, and my eyes were puffy, betraying the restless night I'd endured. But there was no time for self-pity. I dressed quickly, slipping into a pair of well-worn jeans and a soft sweater that hugged me like a comforting hug. I needed to be sharp today, alert to the whispers of deceit that echoed around me.

My first stop was the local coffee shop, a charming little place that served the best espresso in town, where the baristas knew my order by heart. The aroma of roasted coffee beans wafted through the air, mingling with the scent of freshly baked pastries, a warm embrace that momentarily dulled the gnawing worry in my stomach. I ordered my usual—black coffee with a splash of cream—and settled into my favorite corner table, a strategic spot that allowed me to observe the daily bustle.

As I sipped my coffee, my gaze drifted around the room, landing on a group of patrons engaged in animated conversation. The usual small-town gossip floated on the air, stories of new arrivals and impending weddings punctuated by laughter. But today, beneath that surface chatter, I sensed a current of tension, a shared anxiety that clung to the walls like the remnants of last night's storm.

It was then that I noticed Clara, the town librarian, her brow furrowed in concentration as she scribbled furiously in her notebook. Clara had an uncanny ability to ferret out information, her insatiable curiosity making her the town's unofficial historian. If anyone could help me unravel the mystery of the shadowy figure, it was her. I slid out of my chair, determined to get her attention.

"Clara!" I called, waving her over. She looked up, surprised but pleased, her eyes lighting up with recognition.

"Amelia! What's got you so fired up this morning?" she asked, taking a seat across from me, her pen still poised over the notebook.

"Something's off in town, Clara. I need your help," I said, leaning in. "I heard rumors about a figure manipulating things from the shadows. I think they might be using Grant."

Her expression turned serious, and she leaned back, crossing her arms. "Grant? The charming, infuriating one? What do you mean 'using him'?"

"Exactly that. At the council meeting last night, someone accused the council of being puppets, and I can't shake the feeling that there's a bigger game at play here. We need to dig into it before it explodes in our faces."

"Count me in," Clara said, her voice filled with determination. "I've been hearing whispers too. Let's start with the town archives. There's bound to be something buried in the past that can shed light on this situation."

With our mission set, we headed to the library, a quaint building with creaky wooden floors and the unmistakable scent of old books. I loved this place; it was a sanctuary of knowledge and forgotten stories. Clara led the way, her energy infectious as we made our way to the archives. Dust motes danced in the sunlight streaming through the tall windows, creating a warm ambiance that belied the urgency of our task.

Clara and I rifled through the stacks of files, each piece of paper thick with history. We uncovered stories of past town councils, conflicts, and unresolved disputes, but nothing that tied directly to the current turmoil. My frustration mounted as time slipped away.

"Here," Clara said suddenly, holding up a newspaper clipping from years ago, yellowed and fragile. "This could be interesting. It talks about a controversial land deal that went south. The names listed here... they might connect to what's happening now."

I squinted at the article, the headlines bold and accusatory. "This could be a thread worth pulling. Who knew our quaint little town had such a tangled web?"

As we continued to dig deeper, I couldn't shake the feeling that we were racing against time. The atmosphere in the library had shifted, the once cozy sanctuary now felt like a ticking clock, each second echoing my growing anxiety. Suddenly, Clara gasped, pulling my attention back to her.

"Amelia, look at this!" she exclaimed, pointing to a photograph nestled between the pages of a book. The picture depicted a group of men in suits standing proudly in front of a dilapidated building that once housed our town's main commerce. Among them was a familiar face—the mayor. My stomach dropped as I realized the implications.

"Do you think he's involved?" I asked, my voice barely above a whisper.

"I can't say for certain, but this picture is decades old. If he's still connected to these people..." Clara trailed off, the weight of our discovery hanging heavy in the air.

As if on cue, my phone buzzed in my pocket. I pulled it out, heart racing as I saw Grant's name flashing across the screen.

"Can you believe it?" Clara asked, eyes sparkling with mischief. "The universe is aligning, sending you straight to your nemesis."

"Not helping, Clara," I muttered, but the flutter of anticipation in my chest betrayed my irritation. "I should answer this."

"Definitely. It could be important."

With a resigned sigh, I answered the call. "Grant, what do you want?"

"Amelia, I need your help. There's something I haven't told you," he said, his tone serious.

"What could you possibly have to say that I would want to hear?" I shot back, unwilling to give him an inch.

"Meet me at the old warehouse on River Street. I have information about the figure manipulating everything. I can't talk over the phone. It's too risky."

"Why should I trust you?"

"Because whether you like it or not, we're in this together. If we don't act fast, we might lose everything."

His words sent a chill down my spine, a reminder that time was slipping away. I glanced at Clara, who nodded encouragingly. The pieces were coming together, but we needed to tread carefully in this murky landscape of secrets and lies.

"Fine," I said, determination hardening my resolve. "But if you try anything, I swear I'll—"

"I know, I know. You'll throw me under the bus," he interrupted, a hint of amusement cutting through his urgency. "I'll see you soon."

As I hung up, I felt the weight of the world pressing down on me. Whatever was happening beneath the surface was rising to the forefront, and I was about to dive headfirst into the fray. Clara and I exchanged a look, a mix of excitement and trepidation, as we prepared to confront the chaos awaiting us. The stakes had never felt higher, and with every heartbeat, I knew we were inching closer to uncovering the truth—whether we were ready for it or not.

I stepped into the dimly lit warehouse on River Street, the musty scent of aged wood and rust mingling with the faint remnants of something more sinister—like secrets long buried and best left undisturbed. My heart pounded in my chest, a drumbeat of anticipation and dread. Shadows lurked in every corner, a stark reminder of how little I truly understood about the world unfolding around me.

Grant stood near a window, the slant of moonlight illuminating his profile. He looked more serious than I'd ever seen him, the playful arrogance replaced by an intensity that sent a shiver down my spine. As I approached, he turned to face me, his expression grave.

"Thanks for coming," he said, running a hand through his hair, the gesture surprisingly vulnerable. "I know this isn't your idea of a pleasant evening."

"No, but I have to admit, the prospect of unraveling a conspiracy is quite a bit more thrilling than my usual Netflix binge," I replied, crossing my arms defensively. "So, what's this urgent information you have for me?"

"I wish it were just some gossip, but it's bigger than that," he said, his voice low. "I've been digging into the recent council decisions and realized there's a connection to the shadowy figure we talked about."

"Go on," I urged, curiosity bubbling beneath my skepticism.

"There's a group—call it a syndicate—working behind the scenes, and they're trying to influence our town's development plans. They want to push through some zoning changes that could lead to major commercial expansion, and I think they're using me as a figurehead to get what they want."

The weight of his revelation settled over me like a heavy fog. "But why you? You're not exactly the type people think of as a mastermind."

"Thanks for the compliment," he shot back, a hint of sarcasm creeping into his voice. "I didn't choose this role, trust me. I'm just a pawn, same as you. But someone sees potential in me, or maybe just sees me as expendable."

The honesty in his admission was startling. I had always painted Grant as the antagonist in my story, the embodiment of everything I disliked about political maneuvering. Yet, here he was, exposing himself as just another player in a dangerous game. "So, what's your plan? Just sit back and let them run you?"

"I'm trying to gather more information. I need you to help me," he said, his gaze intense. "We need to confront the mayor."

"Confront the mayor? You really think that's a wise move? He's been in office for ages; he won't take kindly to anyone questioning his authority," I replied, a mixture of dread and exhilaration coursing through me.

"We're not going to just confront him," Grant countered, his eyes glinting with determination. "We're going to expose him."

Before I could respond, the sound of footsteps echoed through the warehouse, heavy and deliberate. Grant's eyes widened, and he gestured for me to stay quiet as we both slipped behind a stack of crates. The footsteps grew louder, and I could feel my pulse quickening, the thrill of danger creeping in as adrenaline surged through my veins.

"What if it's someone from that syndicate?" I whispered, my breath hitching in my throat. "What do we do if they catch us?"

"Stay quiet, and keep your head down. We'll figure this out," Grant murmured, tension crackling between us like an electric charge.

Peering out from behind the crates, I could see two figures entering the warehouse, their silhouettes sharp against the dim light. They moved with a sense of purpose, each step resonating with an authority that made my stomach churn. I could barely make out their faces, but one voice stood out, deep and commanding.

"We need to move quickly. The council is getting suspicious, and if we don't act now, our plans could fall apart," the taller figure said, his words a venomous whisper that sent chills down my spine.

The other nodded, though I couldn't catch a glimpse of his face. "What about the Reynolds kid? He's been sniffing around, asking too many questions."

"Let him sniff. He's just a distraction. We have bigger fish to fry. If he becomes a problem, we'll handle it."

A cold knot twisted in my stomach as realization dawned on me. They were discussing Grant, his life hanging in the balance like a marionette at the end of a string. The gravity of the situation crashed over me, and I glanced at Grant, whose expression mirrored my own shock.

"What do we do?" I whispered urgently.

"Listen," he replied, his voice low but firm. "We need to find out more about their plans. We can't confront the mayor yet; we need evidence first."

"Agreed, but we can't stay here. We're too exposed," I said, my heart racing.

Suddenly, the taller figure turned toward our hiding spot, his eyes narrowing as if sensing our presence. "I think someone's here."

"Run!" Grant hissed, and we bolted, ducking behind another stack of crates as the footsteps grew louder.

Adrenaline surged through me as we dashed toward the back of the warehouse, my heart pounding in rhythm with the frantic cadence of our escape. Just as we neared the exit, I glanced back, my instincts screaming for caution. The two figures were closing in, their voices a low murmur punctuated by the urgency of their task.

"Split up!" Grant urged, shoving me toward a narrow corridor at the far end of the building. "Meet at the diner in ten!"

"No! I can't leave you!" I protested, but he was already moving, determination etched into his features.

"Just go! I'll be fine!" he shouted, disappearing into the shadows.

With one last desperate look over my shoulder, I turned and ran, my breath coming in quick gasps. I could hear the voices behind me growing fainter, and as I burst through the back door into the cool night air, I felt a strange mixture of relief and terror.

I sprinted down the alley, my mind racing with thoughts of Grant and the danger he was walking into. What had we uncovered? Who were those men? And how deeply were they entwined in the fabric of our town? The world around me faded as I focused on the diner ahead, the neon lights flickering like a beacon of hope amidst the uncertainty.

Just as I reached the front door, my phone buzzed violently in my pocket. I yanked it out, heart racing as I saw Grant's name flash across the screen.

"Grant! Are you okay?" I answered, the urgency in my voice echoing the chaos inside.

"Ame—" His voice cut off abruptly, replaced by static and a distant commotion. Panic gripped me as I strained to hear.

"Grant? What's happening?" I pleaded, fear tightening my chest.

And then, the line went dead, leaving me standing in the threshold of the diner, the vibrant world around me fading into a haunting silence. My heart dropped as the gravity of the moment settled in. I had to find him, had to unravel the truth that lay beneath the surface before it swallowed us whole. The stakes had never been higher, and time was slipping through my fingers like sand.

Chapter 4: A Fragile Alliance

The air in Grant's office hummed with a tense energy, the kind that teetered on the edge of electricity and chaos. The city sprawled beneath us, a canvas of lights that twinkled like stars caught in a web of ambition. I leaned back in the sleek leather chair, trying to appear unfazed, but inside, I was a storm of frustration and reluctant excitement. Teaming up with Grant was infuriating; he was arrogant, brash, and utterly infuriating. But the stakes were too high to let my disdain for his audacity blind me to the necessity of our alliance.

"Look, if we're going to make this work," I said, crossing my arms defiantly, "we need to set some ground rules. I can't work with someone who thinks he's the only one with good ideas."

Grant leaned against his polished desk, the light from the city casting a halo around him. He had an air of confidence that could disarm even the most obstinate of opponents. "And I can't work with someone who doesn't know when to take a back seat," he shot back, a smirk dancing on his lips. "It's a partnership, not a power struggle."

I shot him a glare that could have melted steel. "Power struggle? This isn't a game, Grant. We have real people depending on us, and your cocky attitude isn't helping."

"Your righteous indignation isn't winning any points either," he retorted, raising an eyebrow. His eyes sparkled with mischief, a glimmer that sent an unwelcome thrill through me. I hated that I found him charming even as I rolled my eyes.

The banter flowed easily between us, a strange dance of wit and irritation that masked the deeper tension simmering just beneath the surface. As the hours dragged on, our debate morphed from a battlefield into something almost... collaborative. We exchanged ideas, our voices rising and falling in a rhythm that felt almost intimate. Laughter bubbled up unexpectedly, punctuating our heated discussions like confetti in the air.

I caught myself laughing at one of his ridiculous suggestions—a harebrained scheme involving a flash mob to raise awareness for our cause. "What, do you want us to serenade them with show tunes? Because that's a sure way to get us on everyone's bad side."

Grant chuckled, the sound rich and deep. "Hey, it might just work. People love a spectacle. It distracts them from the mundane."

"Or gets us thrown out of every venue in town." I shook my head, a smile tugging at the corners of my lips despite my better judgment. "We're not here to entertain, Grant."

"True," he said, his expression shifting slightly, a hint of seriousness creeping into his playful demeanor. "But maybe entertaining them is exactly what we need to do to make them care."

That caught me off guard. Beneath the bravado and sarcasm, I glimpsed a layer of vulnerability that made me question everything I thought I knew about him. I had only ever seen the polished exterior, the man who exuded success like a cologne. But in that moment, I sensed the weight of his ambition, the relentless drive that pushed him to succeed, even if it meant risking everything.

"Okay, fine," I conceded, leaning forward, intrigued despite myself. "Let's say we ditch the flash mob idea. What else do you have in mind?"

As the night wore on, we delved deeper into our brainstorming, an unexpected chemistry crackling in the air. I watched him as he spoke, animated and passionate, his hands gesturing wildly as if he could mold our ideas into something tangible with sheer force of will. There was a fire in his eyes, a fervor that captivated me even as I reminded myself to stay cautious.

At some point, the discussion shifted from strategies to our lives, our motivations, and the paths that led us here. "So, what's the deal with you and this project?" he asked, leaning back, arms crossed. "What's in it for you?"

I paused, feeling the weight of his gaze. "Honestly? I want to make a difference. I've watched too many people get lost in the system, and I refuse to let that happen on my watch."

He nodded, a flicker of respect passing between us. "I get that. My father..." He hesitated, a shadow crossing his features. "He was always so consumed by his work that he lost sight of what mattered. I don't want to end up like that."

A moment of silence enveloped us, heavy with shared understanding. It was a small crack in the armor we both wore, revealing the insecurities that lay beneath our bravado. I couldn't help but admire him, not just for his ambition, but for the weight he carried. There was more to Grant than I had ever realized, layers of complexity that made him a puzzle I suddenly wanted to solve.

"Hey, if we're going to do this," I said, breaking the tension with a wry grin, "we need to get some caffeine in here. Otherwise, we're going to end up planning that flash mob after all."

"Now you're talking," he said, a genuine smile breaking through. "Coffee is the lifeblood of all great ideas."

As we transitioned from brainstorming to ordering takeout, the tension between us shifted again. The laughter came easier, the jabs less pointed. There was something exhilarating about collaborating with someone who challenged me, even if I hated to admit it. The delicate thread that bound us felt both exhilarating and dangerous, a fragile alliance forged in the fires of our shared goal.

By the time the coffee arrived, I was fully immersed in the rhythm of our partnership. There was a tension that crackled in the air, a mix of ambition, frustration, and an undeniable spark of attraction. I could feel it—the unspoken chemistry lurking just beneath the surface, threatening to unravel all the carefully constructed walls we had both built around ourselves.

The steam from the coffee cups curled lazily into the air, mingling with the faint scent of leather and the metallic tang of a city pulsing with life just beyond the walls of Grant's office. As we settled back into our rhythm, I couldn't shake the feeling that this fragile alliance might actually work. With every sip, I felt the caffeine ignite my senses, sharpening my focus and dampening the remnants of the skepticism that had clouded my mind earlier.

"Alright, if we're serious about this," I said, stirring my coffee with a flourish that belied my excitement, "let's lay our cards on the table. What's your grand plan for this charity event?"

Grant leaned back, his eyes narrowing thoughtfully. "I think we need to create something that doesn't just raise money but also inspires people. We're not selling tickets to a dull fundraiser; we're crafting an experience. Something unforgettable."

I cocked an eyebrow, intrigued despite myself. "Unforgettable? Like how? Flash mobs and show tunes?"

He chuckled, the sound rich and contagious, and I found myself laughing along, surprised at how easily the tension dissolved. "Okay, maybe not that extreme. But what if we set it in a unique venue—somewhere that evokes a sense of wonder?"

"Such as?"

"A rooftop garden," he suggested, his voice gaining momentum. "Picture this: an urban oasis under the stars, surrounded by greenery, with string lights weaving through the branches. We could have live music, local food trucks... even a charity auction with experiences, not just things. Get local businesses involved, make it a community event."

The idea hung in the air between us, tantalizing and vivid. I could already envision the atmosphere—laughter, conversations weaving through the warm night air, the city skyline forming a breathtaking backdrop. "That could work," I admitted slowly, a smile creeping onto my lips. "But we need to ensure we have a solid marketing strategy. Otherwise, it's just another party."

Grant nodded, his expression serious now. "You're right. We need a hook. Something that makes people feel they're part of something bigger than themselves."

"Now you're talking," I said, leaning forward, the excitement igniting within me. "How about partnering with a well-known local artist? We could have them create something live during the event—a mural or an installation that reflects our cause. It would draw people in and give them a reason to stay."

"I like it," he said, a spark of approval lighting his eyes. "And it could serve as a conversation starter, a way to connect with attendees on a personal level."

As we mapped out our plan, each idea seemed to propel us forward, threading an invisible connection between us that felt both thrilling and disconcerting. The more we collaborated, the more I could feel the lines between professional and personal begin to blur. Every time his hand brushed against mine while we reached for the same notebook, an electric shock would pulse through me, igniting a confusion I couldn't quite shake.

"So, what about you?" he asked suddenly, breaking my concentration. "What do you do when you're not saving the world?"

I hesitated, unsure of how much I wanted to reveal. "I'm not exactly saving the world," I said lightly. "I work a nine-to-five like most people, wrangling budgets and organizing chaos. But in my spare time, I volunteer at a local shelter. I guess it's my way of trying to make a dent in the universe."

"Volunteering? You? I never pegged you for the altruistic type," he teased, his grin widening.

I shot him a playful glare, unbothered by the slight sting in his words. "You don't know me very well, Grant. I can be a saint when I need to be."

"Is that so? Care to share your superhero backstory?" He leaned in, genuinely curious.

I rolled my eyes, but there was a warmth spreading through me. "I grew up in a neighborhood where people looked out for one another. I learned early on that everyone has a story worth hearing, and sometimes, just listening can make a difference."

His expression softened, and I saw something flicker in his gaze, a connection building between us. "That's actually admirable," he said quietly. "Not everyone has that perspective."

Before I could respond, the phone on his desk buzzed loudly, shattering the moment. He glanced at the screen and sighed. "Duty calls," he said, his tone lightening as he swiped to answer. "What's up, Dave?"

I busied myself by sipping my coffee, the brief glimpse of vulnerability evaporating under the bright light of practicality. I couldn't let myself get swept away by whatever chemistry was brewing between us. We had a mission, and any distraction could unravel our hard work.

As Grant spoke, I watched him, noting how his entire demeanor shifted. The playful banter evaporated, replaced by a serious, no-nonsense side I hadn't seen before. "Yeah, we're still on track. I'm meeting with a few potential partners this week. If you have leads, send them over," he said, the authoritative tone cutting through the casual atmosphere we'd just created.

I felt a pang of envy mixed with admiration. He was a master of wearing different hats, seamlessly slipping from collaborator to leader. It reminded me of my own struggles to balance my dual roles as a volunteer and a corporate drone.

After a brief exchange, Grant hung up and returned his attention to me. "Sorry about that. Now, where were we? You were about to divulge your secret life as a saint, right?"

I chuckled, relieved to return to our previous banter. "Well, that's my cover story. The truth is, I binge-watch reality TV like the rest of the world. It's a guilty pleasure."

"Ah, a fellow connoisseur of mindless entertainment. You're truly a woman of many layers," he remarked, his smile teasing yet warm. "So, what's your poison? The Real Housewives? Survivor?"

"Actually, I'm more of a cooking competition gal," I admitted, leaning back in my chair. "There's something about watching people craft culinary masterpieces that I find mesmerizing. And let's be honest, it makes me feel like I'm achieving something without leaving my couch."

Grant laughed, the sound infectious, and I couldn't help but join in. "So, if this charity thing fails, we can always open a pop-up restaurant, right? Just think of the possibilities!"

"Only if you promise to wear a chef's hat," I shot back, unable to resist.

"Deal." He grinned, the moment stretching comfortably between us, filled with warmth and unspoken possibilities.

As we continued to weave our banter into the fabric of our partnership, I felt the sense of collaboration deepen, each idea an echo of our shared ambitions. With every strategy we developed, the line between duty and desire blurred further, creating a tension that thrummed beneath the surface, alive and electric. This unexpected alliance was growing into something I hadn't anticipated—a thrilling partnership that danced on the edge of chaos, and I couldn't help but wonder where it would lead us next.

As the night deepened, the glow of the city outside painted shadows across the walls of Grant's office, making the space feel both intimate and charged. With each idea we exchanged, a delicate dance unfolded between us, a mixture of frustration, camaraderie, and something else—something thrilling that twisted in my stomach. The world outside faded into an indistinct blur, and all that remained were the two of us and the ambitious project that lay ahead.

"So, we've settled on the rooftop garden, a local artist, and a culinary showdown," I mused, glancing over our hastily scribbled notes. "Now we just need to figure out how to actually get people to show up."

Grant leaned back in his chair, an expression of mock contemplation etched on his face. "Perhaps we should throw in a few goats. People love goats. They'll flock to the event just for the chance to snap selfies."

"Are you serious?" I laughed, shaking my head. "This is a charity event, not a petting zoo."

"Right, right. No goats. But we could always offer free drinks." He waggled his eyebrows suggestively. "Nothing like a little liquid courage to loosen wallets."

"Is that your go-to strategy?" I teased, relishing the playful banter that had grown so natural between us. "Just ply everyone with booze until they throw money at us?"

"Hey, it worked for me in college," he shot back, a grin spreading across his face. "But I'll admit, I was just trying to impress someone."

"Let me guess—did you serenade her with show tunes?" I couldn't resist throwing in another jab.

"Close," he said, feigning seriousness. "I attempted to cook her dinner. Spoiler alert: I nearly set the apartment on fire."

I snorted, picturing Grant, the polished businessman, grappling with a kitchen disaster. "Now that I can't unsee."

"Why do you think I stick to negotiating deals and charming people in meetings?" he countered, his tone playful yet revealing a deeper truth. "Let's just say I'm better with words than with knives."

"Good to know," I replied, meeting his gaze. "I'll keep my takeout menus handy, just in case."

But amid the laughter, a shadow flickered across his features, and for a brief moment, I felt the weight of the world pressing down on us both. The stakes were high; the success of our charity event felt like a tightrope walk, and I could sense that underneath his bravado lay the same anxiety I grappled with.

"Seriously, though," he said, shifting the mood, "we need a solid plan. If we want this to work, we should start reaching out to sponsors and artists right away. The sooner we lay the groundwork, the better our chances."

"Agreed," I said, tapping my pen against the notebook. "If we can secure a few influential sponsors, we can leverage their networks. We'll need to create buzz on social media, too—get people talking."

Grant's eyes lit up, and I could see the gears turning in his head. "What if we create a teaser campaign? Something cryptic that builds anticipation. Maybe we could even stage a flash mob in the city to draw attention to our cause—"

"Okay, hold on," I interrupted, unable to contain my laughter. "Are you really serious about the flash mob? Because if you are, I'm going to need more coffee and possibly a therapist."

"Alright, no flash mob," he said, raising his hands in surrender, but the twinkle in his eye betrayed his amusement. "But the teaser idea could work. We could unveil the event in stages, building excitement without giving away too much too soon."

"Now you're speaking my language," I said, feeling a swell of enthusiasm. "Let's keep it mysterious. We could use social media to drop hints—engage our audience without revealing the whole picture."

"Right. Create an air of exclusivity," he added, his eyes gleaming with energy. "Let's make them feel like they're part of something special. Something worth their time and money."

As we continued to flesh out our ideas, the laughter faded into a comfortable silence, filled with the rustle of papers and the click of pens against notepads. I could feel the chemistry between us shifting, morphing from light-hearted teasing to a more profound connection. It was exhilarating, but I also felt a flicker of anxiety—this bond was new, and it had the potential to complicate everything.

"Let's not forget the logistics," I said finally, breaking the spell that hung in the air. "We'll need a timeline, a budget, and to figure out how to rally volunteers. It's a lot of moving parts."

"True," he replied, his demeanor shifting back to business mode. "But we can handle it. Together."

The weight of those words settled between us like a promise, and I couldn't help but feel a thrill at the idea of collaborating with him. We were a chaotic symphony, each note distinct yet harmonizing in unexpected ways.

As we prepared to wrap up for the night, Grant leaned back in his chair, a satisfied grin on his face. "You know, I'm glad we're doing this. I didn't expect it to be so... enjoyable."

"Neither did I," I admitted, the sincerity in my voice surprising me. "I thought it would be a complete nightmare, honestly."

He raised an eyebrow, the challenge evident in his gaze. "So, I've changed your mind?"

"Maybe a little," I replied, fighting the smile tugging at my lips. "But don't let it go to your head."

"Too late," he shot back, his grin infectious. "I can't help it if I'm a charming genius."

Just as I opened my mouth to retort, his phone buzzed again, this time more insistently. "Excuse me," he said, glancing at the screen. "It's my assistant. She wouldn't call unless it was urgent."

He answered quickly, his voice shifting to a professional tone, but the slight crease in his brow told me that something was off. My heart raced, the atmosphere suddenly thickening with tension as he listened intently.

"Yeah, I understand," he said, his tone firm yet laced with concern. "I'll be right there." He hung up, his eyes locking onto mine with a gravity that sent a jolt through me. "I have to go. There's been a situation with one of our potential sponsors."

"What kind of situation?" I asked, my instincts kicking in.

"It's complicated," he replied, his jaw tightening. "But I need to handle it immediately. Can you... Can you hold down the fort here? Keep working on the plan?"

"Of course," I said, though my heart thudded in my chest. "Just... be careful, okay?"

He nodded, his expression serious as he gathered his things. "I will. And I'll call you as soon as I know more."

As he rushed out, I felt an unsettling mix of worry and adrenaline coursing through me. What could have happened? The atmosphere we had built moments ago felt fragile, shattered by the unexpected urgency. I sat in the quiet of his office, surrounded by our notes, the weight of uncertainty pressing heavily on my shoulders.

And just as I reached for my phone to start drafting a plan, a notification pinged on Grant's computer—a message blinking urgently across the screen. I hesitated, a flicker of temptation sparking within me. It was his work email, and part of me knew I shouldn't look. But something deeper urged me to open it, the pull of the unknown too strong to resist.

I clicked, and as the words filled the screen, my breath caught in my throat. The revelation that stared back at me sent chills down my spine, a sudden twist that changed everything I thought I knew about our mission and our fragile alliance.

Chapter 5: Unraveling Threads

The moon hung low that evening, a silver coin casting its glow over the polished marble floor of the grand hall. It was a venue fit for royalty, draped in lavish silks and filled with laughter that felt both hollow and intoxicating. As I adjusted the cuff of my silk blouse, I stole a glance at the crowd. Laughter bubbled from groups clustered around tables adorned with extravagant floral arrangements, their hues deep and rich, mimicking the expensive wines in crystal glasses. Somewhere in this glittering sea of wealth and deception lay the answers I sought, but the thrill of the chase was quickly becoming intertwined with an entirely different sensation—an electric charge that sparked with every glance I exchanged with Grant.

Grant was a tempest in tailored clothing, his presence commanding attention without uttering a single word. He moved with the confident grace of a man who belonged to the shadows, and I found myself both intrigued and unsettled. His dark hair, tousled just enough to appear effortlessly charming, framed a face that seemed chiseled from stone. But it was his eyes, piercing and inscrutable, that ensnared me. They held secrets I was desperate to uncover, and yet, as we navigated the throng of mingling guests, my heart warned me to tread carefully.

We wove through the crowd, blending in with those who danced on the fringes of legality. Each handshake and polite smile masked ulterior motives; it was all a delicate ballet of subterfuge. The fundraiser was ostensibly for a charitable cause—education for underprivileged children—but the air crackled with unspoken threats. I could feel it in my bones, a primal instinct telling me that beneath the laughter and luxury lay a labyrinth of lies. It wasn't just the money that attracted the sharks; it was the power, the connections, and the blood that stained the hands of the highest bidders.

"Keep your wits about you," Grant murmured, his breath warm against my ear as we sidled past a cluster of affluent donors, their laughter a dissonant melody to my heightened senses. "We're looking for a man named Weston. He's reputed to be the linchpin in this operation."

"Right, and here I thought we were just here for the hors d'oeuvres and fine wine," I replied, my voice laced with mock sarcasm. Yet, the thrill of being part of something so perilous sent a rush through my veins, the kind that made me feel alive.

He quirked an eyebrow, a playful smirk dancing on his lips. "Well, I'd hate to disappoint you, but we might have to forego the shrimp cocktails if we want to get to the bottom of this."

We shared a moment—a fleeting connection that made the world around us fade into insignificance. But then reality crashed in like a winter storm, reminding me of the precarious position we were in. I had learned the hard way that trust was a luxury I couldn't afford, especially in a game where betrayal was the norm.

As the night wore on, we gathered scraps of information, snippets of conversations that led us closer to the truth. Yet, it wasn't until we found ourselves momentarily alone in a dimly lit alcove, away from prying eyes, that the air shifted between us.

"Do you ever stop to think about the kind of people we're dealing with?" I asked, my voice dropping to a whisper. The shadows danced around us, as if echoing my unease. "These are people who would destroy lives for their own gain."

He stepped closer, the scent of sandalwood and something distinctly him enveloping me. "It's not just about the money for them. It's about power, control. They think they can play god with people's lives."

His words hung in the air, heavy and foreboding, and I felt the walls I had built around my heart begin to crack. I was drawn to him in a way I hadn't anticipated—his passion, his conviction, it ignited a flicker of something I had thought extinguished long ago. But the gnawing doubt remained. Could I really trust him?

Just then, the crowd surged, pulling me back into the cacophony of laughter and clinking glasses. I caught sight of a familiar face across the room, one that sent a chill spiraling down my spine. Dressed in a tailored suit that screamed affluence, Weston stood amongst his peers, his laughter booming like thunder. He radiated confidence, his presence magnetic yet sinister. The man was a wolf in sheep's clothing, a master manipulator who thrived in the shadows.

"Grant," I hissed, urgency threading through my words as I tugged at his sleeve. "That's him. That's Weston."

His gaze shifted, intensity sharpening his features as he surveyed the scene. "We need to get closer," he replied, his voice steady. "Let's see what he's up to."

Navigating through the throng, we moved like specters, invisible yet keenly aware. My heart raced, each beat matching the pulse of the gathering. As we drew nearer, I could overhear snippets of conversation, the sinister undertones revealing a darker narrative. There were whispered plans, promises exchanged like currency, and I felt a knot tighten in my stomach.

Then it happened—a fleeting moment when our eyes met. Weston's gaze locked onto mine, and for a heartbeat, I felt the weight of his scrutiny pierce through the chaos. It was as if he could see right through the mask I wore, a terrifying realization that sent shivers racing down my spine.

"We should go," I breathed, instinctively pulling Grant's arm. The atmosphere shifted, tension thick enough to cut through, and I could feel the urgency crawling up my spine.

"Not yet," Grant said, his expression resolute. "We're so close. Just a little longer."

I opened my mouth to protest but was interrupted by a sudden commotion. A glass shattered, the sound slicing through the air like a warning bell. In that instant, chaos erupted. People screamed, scattering like leaves caught in a storm.

"Stay close!" Grant shouted over the din, his hand gripping mine tightly as we maneuvered through the chaos. My heart thundered in my chest, a frantic beat of adrenaline coursing through me.

As we raced for the exit, I couldn't shake the feeling that this was just the beginning. The truth was weaving itself into a tapestry of danger and desire, and I was caught right in the middle, teetering on the precipice of trust and treachery. The stakes had never been higher, and as the crowd surged around us, I knew I had to decide whether to leap into the unknown or retreat back into the safety of my carefully constructed walls.

The chaos of the fundraiser echoed in my ears, a cacophony of shouts and breaking glass melding into a symphony of disarray. My pulse raced, thrumming like a war drum as we barreled through the crowd. I clutched Grant's hand, feeling the warmth of his grip as we dodged frantic guests who were now scrambling for the exits. Fear and excitement tangled within me, each heartbeat a reminder that we were deep in hostile territory, where shadows whispered secrets I was desperate to unveil.

"Are we seriously running for our lives in designer shoes?" I quipped breathlessly, attempting to inject humor into the madness, but the weight of reality was palpable. Grant shot me a sidelong glance, his lips curving into a half-smile that was both reassuring and infuriating.

"I'd recommend stilettos next time, darling," he teased, pulling me closer as we maneuvered around a toppled table. "They're much better for sprinting."

We emerged into the cool night air, the chaos of the fundraiser fading behind us. The street was illuminated by streetlamps casting a soft glow over the cobblestones, the world outside a stark contrast to the opulence we'd just escaped. I drew in a breath, filling my lungs with the crisp scent of autumn, trying to ground myself amidst the swirling adrenaline.

"What was that back there?" I finally asked, my voice steadier now that we were outside. "You think Weston tipped someone off?"

Grant's expression shifted, his playful demeanor replaced by a grim determination. "It's possible. Weston's not one to take chances. He knows we're onto him."

The weight of his words settled over us like a dark cloud. I couldn't shake the feeling that we had crossed an invisible line into something far more dangerous than I had anticipated. "So, what's next? Are we supposed to go home and forget we saw him? Pretend this was just a bad dream?"

"No," he said, shaking his head firmly. "We need to confront him. Now that we've seen the depth of his connections, there's no turning back."

The thought of facing Weston again sent a chill through me, but beneath that fear lay an undeniable thrill. The hunt was intoxicating, and a part of me reveled in the chase. "Right, because running into a snake pit sounds like a fabulous idea."

"I promise I'll be your charming snake charmer," he quipped, an easy grin breaking through the tension. "Just keep your wits about you. We'll gather what we can from his network, then we'll retreat to reassess."

Our plan took shape as we drove through the city, the glow of streetlights illuminating our path while the muffled sounds of nightlife thrummed around us. I glanced at Grant, his profile a mix of intensity and allure, and I found myself pondering the layers of his character. He was like an enigma wrapped in charisma, and I couldn't help but wonder what his past concealed.

"What's your story, Grant?" I asked, my curiosity piqued. "What made you dive into this world?"

He took a moment, eyes focused on the road ahead. "Let's just say I've seen enough to know that not everything is as it seems. Some people play games for fun; I play for keeps."

His words hung between us, heavy with unspoken truths. The shadows of his past were alluding me, and I felt an odd compulsion to dig deeper. "So, you're saying you have your own reasons for being here, just like me?"

"Something like that," he replied, glancing at me with a hint of vulnerability behind his bravado. "But that's not what's important right now."

We arrived at a dimly lit bar tucked away in a narrow alley, its entrance concealed behind a thick curtain that promised secrecy. A low hum of jazz floated through the air, mingling with the scent of aged whiskey and worn leather. The atmosphere buzzed with whispered conversations, each voice a thread in the web of intrigue.

As we entered, I could feel the tension in the room shift slightly, a subtle acknowledgment that we were newcomers in a space filled with familiar faces. I scanned the crowd, searching for any sign of Weston, my heart pounding like a war drum once more.

"Stick close," Grant murmured, his hand brushing against my back, sending an unexpected jolt through me. "We're looking for information, not trouble."

"Easy for you to say," I shot back, unable to resist a cheeky grin. "You seem to thrive on chaos."

"Only when it's entertaining," he replied, a spark of mischief in his eyes.

We navigated through the maze of bodies, sidling up to the bar where a grizzled bartender polished glasses with a rag that had seen better days. "What'll it be?" he asked, eyeing us with a blend of curiosity and suspicion.

"Two bourbons," Grant replied smoothly, and I marveled at how effortlessly he commanded attention.

As the bartender poured, I leaned in closer to Grant, lowering my voice. "What's our plan? You didn't bring me here just for the ambiance."

His gaze flicked around the room, calculating. "We need to gather intel on Weston's movements. There's always someone willing to talk for the right price."

"Or the right drink," I added, taking a sip of my bourbon, savoring the warmth that spread through me.

Grant chuckled, his eyes glinting. "You catch on quickly."

We drifted to a quieter corner, the low light creating an intimate bubble around us. I caught snippets of conversation that only heightened my curiosity. Words like "deals," "transactions," and "risky business" floated around, but I couldn't make sense of it all.

"I overheard a couple of guys talking about a shipment," I said, leaning closer to Grant, my voice a conspiratorial whisper. "Something big is coming in soon."

"Good. That's the kind of lead we need," he replied, a note of excitement threading through his tone.

Just then, a sharp laugh cut through the air, drawing my attention. I turned to see a woman with striking red hair and an elegant dress that clung to her like liquid gold, her smile both alluring and predatory. She was engaging in animated conversation with a group of men, each of them hanging onto her every word.

"Who's she?" I asked, intrigued.

"Lila Hayes," Grant said, his voice laced with caution. "She's one of Weston's closest associates. If anyone knows something, it's her."

"Then we should talk to her," I suggested, my heart racing at the prospect of unearthing more truths.

"Careful," Grant cautioned, his eyes narrowing slightly. "Lila doesn't play nice. She'll smell desperation a mile away."

"Good thing I've got a PhD in deception," I replied, a confident smirk crossing my lips.

As we approached Lila, the room felt charged with potential. I could see the flicker of recognition in her eyes as we neared, and I fought the urge to step back. Grant's presence was reassuring, but I couldn't ignore the instinct that warned me of the unpredictable nature of the game we were playing.

"Lila, darling," Grant said smoothly, slipping into his charming persona. "Mind if we steal you away for a moment?"

She raised an eyebrow, amusement dancing in her gaze. "Only if you bring something interesting to the table."

I took a breath, summoning every ounce of courage. "We have questions, and I think you might have answers."

"Questions are for the curious," Lila replied, her smile sharp. "What makes you think I'm inclined to share?"

Grant stepped closer, his charm radiating. "Because I can assure you, our interests align more than you think."

The air crackled with tension as Lila studied us, her gaze flicking between Grant and me. "Alright, color me intrigued. But understand this: trust is a currency I don't spend lightly."

As she leaned in closer, I could feel the stakes rising, the web of intrigue tightening around us. Whatever lay ahead, I knew one thing for certain: this was only the beginning, and the truth we were seeking might just be darker than we had ever imagined.

The atmosphere crackled with tension as Lila leaned in, her interest piqued by the glimmer of intrigue in our eyes. "You two clearly aren't just here for the ambiance," she remarked, her tone laced with playful skepticism. "So, spill it. What makes you think I have anything worth sharing?"

Grant exchanged a glance with me, his expression a mixture of confidence and caution. I felt the weight of the moment, as if the very air we breathed was charged with unspoken truths. "Let's just say we're looking for something a bit more substantial than idle chatter. Information about Weston's upcoming shipment would be a good start."

Lila's laughter tinkled like delicate glass, but her eyes remained shrewd, scanning us for weaknesses. "And why should I help you? I have no reason to trust either of you, particularly not with a name like Weston floating around."

"Because," I interjected, mustering every ounce of bravado I could find, "the stakes are higher than you think. We know what's at risk, and we're willing to pay for the right intel."

She tilted her head, clearly intrigued but still skeptical. "Is that so? And what exactly are you offering? You look like you're fresh out of a college lecture."

"Looks can be deceiving," Grant countered smoothly, stepping forward with an easy charm. "I may not wear a three-piece suit, but I have resources that can help you—if you're willing to play ball."

Lila considered us for a moment longer, a flicker of curiosity darting behind her calculated exterior. "Alright. Let's say I'm interested. But understand this: the information you seek comes at a price, and it's not just about cash."

"Define 'price,'" I replied, a sharp edge creeping into my tone as I matched her gaze.

"Connections, favors, loyalty," she said, her smile turning wicked. "And sometimes, blood."

A chill crept up my spine at her words, but I knew we had to press on. "What kind of favors?" I asked, steeling myself for whatever game she was about to lay out.

She took a sip of her drink, her eyes glinting with mischief. "Let's just say there are some in this room who are far too interested in our dear Weston's affairs. If you want to find out what he's hiding, you'll need to make the right friends and the right enemies."

My stomach twisted at the thought of playing a game that could turn dangerous, but it was a risk I was willing to take. "And how do we start?"

"By catching the attention of the right people," Lila replied, her smile widening. "There's a gathering next week at the docks. Think of it as a meet-and-greet for the movers and shakers in this business. Show up, and make a lasting impression. If you're as clever as you seem, you'll find the right connections there."

"And if we don't?" I challenged, my heart racing with a mixture of anticipation and dread.

"Then you'll find yourself with more questions than answers," she replied, her tone playful yet ominous. "And I can assure you, nobody enjoys the company of the curious who can't pay their dues."

I glanced at Grant, gauging his reaction. He nodded subtly, a spark of determination in his eyes. "We'll be there," he said, his voice steady. "But if we're to dance with these sharks, we need to know what we're truly up against."

Lila's gaze flickered between us, and for a heartbeat, I could see her weighing her options. "Fine. I'll give you something to chew on. Weston has been working on something big—something that could rattle this entire city's power structure."

"Something like what?" I pressed, leaning in.

"Like a network of influence that reaches far beyond these walls," she replied, her voice dropping to a conspiratorial whisper. "You find that network, you find Weston's Achilles' heel."

The revelation hung in the air, heavy and laden with possibility. "And how do we find this network?" I asked, curiosity gnawing at me.

"You'll need to gather intel from the insiders," she said, her smile morphing into something more serious. "Trust me, it's a slippery slope. Once you're in, you may not come out unscathed."

"Nothing worth having comes without a cost," Grant remarked, his eyes locked onto Lila's. "And we're willing to pay it."

Lila's expression shifted slightly, a flicker of admiration glinting in her eyes. "Good. Just remember, in this game, loyalties shift faster than the tides. Today's friend could be tomorrow's enemy."

With that, she waved her hand dismissively, signaling the end of our conversation. "If you want to know more, keep your ear to the ground. I'll be watching."

As we turned to leave, I felt the weight of her gaze on my back, a reminder that the world we were stepping into was fraught with danger. Outside the bar, the cool air wrapped around us, but it felt thick with anticipation.

"Did that feel like a bad idea to you?" I asked, half-joking, but the seriousness of our predicament loomed large.

"Every great adventure starts with a leap into the unknown," Grant replied, his confidence unwavering.

"Is that your mantra?" I shot back, half-serious.

"Not a bad one, is it?" he quipped, his grin infectious.

We walked a few paces in silence, the night enveloping us like a velvet cloak, rich and dark. But beneath the surface, I could feel the undercurrents of tension and excitement swirling around us, each step taking us deeper into a world I hadn't anticipated but felt undeniably drawn to.

"Tell me something," I said suddenly, breaking the comfortable silence. "What's your stake in all this? What drives you to chase down these shadows?"

Grant paused, his expression momentarily shifting to one of contemplation. "Let's just say I have my own reasons for wanting to bring Weston down. Things he's done, people he's hurt. It's personal."

The weight of his words hung between us, and I realized that I was inextricably linked to his mission, whether I wanted to be or not.

"And what happens if we find him? If we discover what he's been hiding?"

"Then we take him down together," he said firmly, determination etched into his features.

The confidence in his voice was intoxicating, but it did little to soothe the gnawing anxiety in my gut. I had my own reasons for being here, reasons that were tangled up in layers of distrust and desire.

Just as we turned the corner to head toward the parking lot, the sound of hurried footsteps echoed behind us. I spun around, instinctively stepping closer to Grant, our bodies brushing together in an electric moment that sent shivers down my spine.

A man burst into view, breathless and disheveled, his eyes wide with urgency. "You have to listen to me!" he exclaimed, nearly collapsing against the brick wall for support. "They're coming for you. They know what you're looking for!"

A chill swept through me as dread settled in the pit of my stomach. "Who's coming?" I demanded, my heart racing anew.

"The people you're dealing with... they're not what they seem. Weston has eyes everywhere, and if he suspects you're onto him..." His voice trailed off, the fear evident in his gaze.

"Then what?" Grant pressed, his posture shifting into something protective.

Before the man could respond, a sharp noise echoed down the alley—like the clicking of a gun being loaded.

"Run!" I shouted, and we dashed away, adrenaline propelling us forward, leaving behind the man who had tried to warn us. As we sprinted through the darkened streets, I couldn't shake the feeling that the web was tightening around us, and the real game was only just beginning.

Chapter 6: Shadows in the Night

The night had a way of swallowing sounds, amplifying the pulse of my own heartbeat as I pressed deeper into the shadows of the city. Each step echoed like a whisper of caution, caution that I chose to ignore. I had always been the sensible one, the careful planner who wouldn't dare stray from the well-lit paths of my life. But tonight, I was following the scent of danger, a sweet and acrid perfume that twisted through the air like smoke from a dying fire.

Grant was a few paces ahead of me, his silhouette slicing through the darkness. The streetlights were dim, flickering like the last gasps of a fading star, and I felt a chill skitter down my spine—not just from the cold, but from the palpable tension that hung between us. I was acutely aware of his presence, a steady force in this chaotic tempest. It was the kind of awareness that made my heart race and my breath hitch, and I cursed the stupid romantic notion that dared to linger. He was my partner in this mess, nothing more, even if he did seem to glow under the moonlight like some improbable knight who had wandered out of a fairytale.

"Keep your head down, and don't look anyone in the eye," he murmured, glancing back at me with a mixture of concern and urgency. His voice was gravelly, rough around the edges, yet it held a smoothness that calmed the storm inside me.

"Thanks for the pep talk," I shot back, trying to inject humor into the situation, though my throat felt dry and tight. "Next time, I'll remember to ask for a safety manual, too."

He smiled, and the corners of his eyes crinkled, transforming the tense atmosphere into something almost bearable. But the smile faded as we approached the alleyway. It was dark and narrow, a snaking path that could lead to salvation or a one-way ticket to disaster. I took a deep breath, the air thick with the scent of damp asphalt and the underlying hint of something metallic.

The moment we stepped into the alley, I felt it—the weight of unseen eyes watching us. The hairs on my arms stood at attention, prickling with a mix of anxiety and awareness. I wasn't just hunting for clues anymore; I was part of a bigger game, one with stakes that were deadly serious. This was not the carefully curated life I had designed for myself, full of board meetings and coffee breaks. This was raw and visceral, a pulse that beat in tandem with the city itself.

"Stay close," Grant instructed, his voice low, almost conspiratorial. The way he said it sent an electric thrill through me, sparking something I had been trying to suppress. I wanted to be close to him, not just for safety but for something deeper that I couldn't yet articulate.

"Where exactly are we headed?" I asked, trying to sound nonchalant while my heart raced like it was competing in the Olympics.

"A tip from one of my contacts. If we're lucky, we'll find something that leads us to the truth." His eyes darted around, alert, focused. I was struck by how determined he looked, as if the weight of the world rested on his shoulders—and for a moment, it felt as though I shared that burden.

As we reached the end of the alley, the faint glow of neon lights beckoned us from the other side. It was a small bar, the kind that looked like it had seen too many nights and too many stories unravel. We pushed through the door, and the noise hit us like a wave. Laughter and music intertwined in a cacophony that felt both welcoming and dangerous.

"Wait here," Grant instructed, glancing back at me with that same intensity that made my breath catch. I nodded, but a part of me wanted to follow him, to slip into the shadow of his presence. Instead, I leaned against the bar, surveying the room. It was a tangled web of faces—some familiar, some not—each one a potential ally or enemy in this game we had unwittingly joined.

I ordered a drink, the cool glass feeling solid in my hand, and tried to shake off the growing sense of dread. I was in way over my head, and I knew it. But with Grant at my side, I felt a strange sense of strength, as if the chaos outside could not touch me as long as we were together.

The tension in the air was thickening. I could sense something brewing, an undercurrent of danger that twisted around my thoughts. Just then, Grant returned, his face a mask of determination, but with a hint of something else that I couldn't quite decipher.

"We need to move," he said abruptly, his voice laced with urgency.

"Why? What happened?"

"Someone's onto us," he replied, his eyes scanning the room like a hawk searching for prey. My stomach dropped, and an icy tendril of fear curled around my heart.

"Are you sure?"

"Trust me. We can't stay here."

I nodded, adrenaline surging through my veins. We slipped out the back, moving like shadows through the darkened streets. I was hyper-aware of every sound—the scuff of shoes on pavement, the distant wail of a siren, and the ever-present thrum of the city's heartbeat.

As we turned a corner, the adrenaline surged higher, and I felt that sweet mix of fear and excitement pulsing through me. It was exhilarating, yet terrifying, a potent reminder of just how far I had strayed from the comfort of my ordinary life.

"Where to now?" I asked, trying to keep my voice steady.

"Just keep moving," he urged, and I could see the determination in his eyes, a fire that mirrored my own.

The night stretched out before us, uncertain and dark, but as I ran beside him, I felt a rush of certainty: I was ready to confront whatever shadows lay ahead. With Grant by my side, I would face the lurking dangers that threatened to engulf us both.

We sprinted through the moonlit streets, each shadow shifting like a whispered secret. My lungs burned as we weaved through the tangled web of alleyways and side streets, the city pulsing around us. Every distant siren and flickering streetlight heightened my senses, as if the night itself conspired against us. I focused on Grant, his sturdy form ahead of me, a beacon in the encroaching darkness.

"Do you even know where we're going?" I called out, struggling to keep pace with him. The adrenaline surged through my veins, igniting my instinct to flee, but there was an exhilarating thrill that kept me rooted beside him.

"Trust me," he replied, glancing back with a fierce intensity that sent shivers down my spine. "I have a place in mind."

"Does it come with a complimentary welcome mat, or just more danger?" I retorted, trying to inject humor into the suffocating tension. But as we turned another corner, I felt the weight of his gaze, a mix of reassurance and urgency that grounded me, even in our reckless flight.

The air thickened with the scent of rain-soaked concrete as we ducked into a narrow passageway, the sound of our footsteps swallowed by the shadowy embrace of the walls. The passage opened into a small courtyard, illuminated by a flickering bulb hanging overhead. It felt like a forgotten world, caught between the bustling city and the secrets lurking in the night.

"Here," Grant said, breathing heavily as he motioned toward a door half-hidden behind a stack of crates. It was unmarked, the paint peeling in patches, revealing the rough wood underneath. "This is it."

"Charming," I quipped, eyeing the door with skepticism. "Are you sure it's not a portal to the underworld?"

Grant smirked, the tension in his shoulders easing slightly. "Only if you're planning on summoning something. Besides, you should know by now that I have a penchant for the unconventional."

"Unconventional doesn't quite capture it," I replied, trying to catch my breath. "More like 'dangerously unpredictable.'"

"Don't worry. I'll keep you safe," he assured me, the seriousness of his tone grounding me. It was a promise laced with layers of meaning, and I felt a warmth blossom in my chest, mingling with the adrenaline coursing through my veins.

The door creaked as Grant pushed it open, revealing a dimly lit room that smelled of stale beer and something spicy, like old incense. A battered couch sat against one wall, and mismatched furniture cluttered the space. Despite its disarray, there was a certain charm in its chaos, as if it held stories of all who had sought refuge within these walls.

"Welcome to my hideaway," he said with a flourish, stepping inside. I followed, my heart racing as I took in the environment. "It's not much, but it's safe."

"Safe? Right." I chuckled, crossing my arms as I leaned against the doorframe. "If by 'safe' you mean a cozy little den of misfits, then sure."

He shot me a look, half-amused, half-serious. "It's better than the streets. Besides, we need to figure out our next move. I have a lead on a contact who might know something about our situation."

"Your situation, you mean," I corrected, though I knew the truth. I was in this with him now, whether I liked it or not. The reality settled over me like a thick blanket, both comforting and suffocating.

Grant rummaged through a box in the corner, pulling out a few items. "I didn't plan for a late-night escapade, but there are some essentials here." He held up a flashlight, a roll of duct tape, and a map that looked like it had seen better days.

"Essential survival gear, huh? I feel so much safer already," I teased, taking the flashlight from him and clicking it on. The beam sliced through the gloom, illuminating the dusty corners and cobwebs that decorated the room. "What's next? A how-to guide on self-defense?"

He grinned, the light reflecting off his eyes in a way that made my heart flutter. "Not a bad idea. You could probably teach a seminar on how to get into trouble."

"Ha! And you'd be the poster boy," I shot back, but my laughter faded as the reality of our situation crashed back in. "So, what's the plan? We can't just sit here and wait for trouble to find us."

Grant's expression shifted, his humor fading as he unrolled the map on the table. "We need to find this contact, someone who can help us connect the dots. He's a little... unconventional, but he's reliable."

"Unconventional seems to be the theme of my night," I muttered, peering over his shoulder at the map, trying to make sense of the scribbles and markings. "And where exactly do we find this reliable source?"

"He works out of a bar in the lower part of the city," Grant explained, tracing a line on the map with his finger. "It's not the safest area, but he has connections. If anyone knows what's happening, it'll be him."

"Great. So we're heading back out into the jaws of danger. How romantic," I replied, rolling my eyes but feeling a spark of determination flicker to life.

"Don't worry, I've got your back," he said, his tone low and serious. There was a weight to his words, a promise that resonated deep within me.

"Just keep your hands to yourself this time," I teased, but the truth lingered unspoken between us. There was an undeniable connection simmering under the surface, a thread woven through our banter that hinted at something more than mere partnership.

We gathered what we needed, the atmosphere crackling with anticipation as we prepared to step back into the fray. With one last glance around the dimly lit hideaway, I felt a strange sense of calm settle over me. The night was fraught with danger, but I wasn't alone anymore. With Grant by my side, I was ready to face whatever lay ahead, even if it meant diving headfirst into the chaos.

"Let's do this," I said, a newfound resolve filling my voice.

He nodded, his eyes locked onto mine, a fierce intensity there that sent a thrill racing through me. "Together."

And with that, we stepped back into the world outside, ready to chase shadows and confront the darkness lurking just beyond our reach.

The night enveloped us as we stepped into the city's underbelly, a labyrinth of secrets veiled in darkness. Each flicker of light cast eerie shadows that danced along the cracked pavement, drawing us deeper into the heart of danger. I felt the pulse of the city thrum beneath my feet, a reminder that we were not just wandering aimlessly—we were intruders in a world that thrived on chaos.

"Are you sure about this place?" I asked, casting a wary glance around the dimly lit street. The bar loomed ahead, its neon sign flickering like a warning beacon. It had the kind of reputation that sent shivers down the spines of even the most seasoned locals.

"Trust me. This is where we'll find him," Grant replied, his confidence a steady anchor in the rising tide of uncertainty. I nodded, unwilling to let my nerves bubble to the surface. The truth was, despite the mounting tension, a part of me was excited, a thrill coursing through me that I couldn't quite suppress.

We pushed through the bar's heavy door, the music and laughter spilling out like a secret invitation. The interior was a cacophony of life, a jumble of mismatched tables, faded posters, and the intoxicating aroma of cheap beer and spicy wings. It felt like stepping into a different time, a place where the world's troubles faded, if only for a moment.

"Keep your eyes peeled," Grant said, scanning the room as we stepped inside. "He should be around here somewhere."

"Great. So we're hunting for a ghost in a haunted house?" I quipped, trying to inject levity into the situation.

"Something like that," he replied, a faint smile tugging at his lips. "But more of a ghost with connections."

As we navigated through the crowd, I could feel the weight of stares upon us, a mixture of curiosity and suspicion. I shifted closer to Grant, feeling a strange sense of comfort in his presence. Each time our shoulders brushed, an electric jolt surged through me, reminding me of how much I wanted to lean into that connection.

"There he is," Grant said suddenly, stopping short. I followed his gaze to a man sitting alone in a booth, hunched over a drink like he was sharing secrets with it. His beard was wild, his clothes a patchwork of styles that screamed 'I-don't-care' while simultaneously whispering 'I know too much.'

"Are we sure he's not just a patron with a penchant for bad fashion choices?" I whispered, uncertainty creeping in again.

"Trust me," Grant insisted, moving toward the booth with purpose.

As we approached, the man looked up, his eyes sharp and assessing. "You're a long way from home," he remarked, his voice gruff but tinged with curiosity.

"Eli," Grant greeted, extending a hand, which Eli regarded with a mix of wariness and intrigue. "We need to talk."

"About what?" Eli replied, leaning back, clearly unimpressed. "I don't do favors for free."

"Let's just say we're in a bit of a bind," Grant said, his tone low and steady. I watched, feeling the tension radiate between them. "We need information. Fast."

Eli studied us for a moment, then smirked, his eyes flickering to me. "You're the one who looks like she's stepped out of a safer reality. What's your angle, sweetheart?"

"Just here to listen," I retorted, surprising myself with the sharpness in my voice. "But if you're smart, you'll answer his questions before the night gets a lot more complicated for all of us."

Eli chuckled, a sound that held no warmth. "Complicated, huh? I like a little chaos with my drinks." He took a slow sip from his glass, making a show of enjoying the moment. "Alright, what's got you both running around in the dark?"

Before Grant could respond, a loud crash erupted from the bar, drawing every eye to the entrance. The door swung open with a force that rattled the frame, and a group of men surged in, their expressions fierce and menacing. They scanned the room like wolves searching for prey, and my stomach dropped as I realized they were not just patrons; they were trouble incarnate.

"Time to go," Grant said, his voice barely a whisper as he grabbed my arm, urgency igniting his every movement.

"Wait, what about—" I started, but he pulled me back, his eyes locked onto Eli, who had gone pale as the realization of the newcomers sank in.

"Eli!" Grant shouted over the rising tension in the bar. "We need that information now!"

Eli stood up, his bravado melting away. "You have to get out of here! They're looking for you!"

"Who?" I asked, panic clawing at my throat.

"Just go! This isn't the place for you!" Eli pushed back, fear etched into his features.

Before I could process his words, Grant was pulling me toward the back exit, adrenaline fueling our flight. The bar erupted into chaos, shouts and the sound of glass breaking ringing in my ears as the men advanced, their intentions clear.

"Stick close," Grant urged as we rushed through the narrow hallway leading to the back alley. My heart raced, a frantic drumbeat against the backdrop of the chaos behind us.

"We can't let them catch us!" I shouted, my voice tinged with panic.

"I know!" he replied, determination hardening his features. We reached the door at the end of the hall, and just as he swung it open, the air shifted—a dark figure stepped into the doorway, blocking our escape.

Time seemed to freeze for a heartbeat as I recognized the figure, my breath catching in my throat. The dim light illuminated a familiar face, one that had haunted my thoughts and dreams, yet now stood before me with a predatory smile.

"I've been looking for you two," he said, his voice smooth and deadly, sending chills racing down my spine. "And it seems you've led me straight to you."

The tension thickened, a live wire crackling in the air as I glanced at Grant, whose eyes narrowed in recognition. The game we were playing had just escalated, and as the shadows closed in around us, I couldn't shake the feeling that we were no longer the hunters but the hunted.

Chapter 7: A Fractured Heart

The chill of the evening air wrapped around me like a shroud, biting at my skin as I stood across from Grant on the cobblestone street. A slanting moon cast silver shadows, illuminating the tension etched into his features. I could hardly recognize the man I had grown to trust, the one whose laughter echoed in my mind even in the heaviest of moments. Tonight, however, his expression was a fortress, impenetrable and cold.

"What do you mean, you don't care?" I shot at him, my voice trembling with a mix of disbelief and anger. The words slipped out sharper than intended, jagged edges catching on the fraying threads of our relationship. The street was empty, save for the distant hum of late-night traffic, but our argument felt like a storm ready to explode.

"Why should I?" he retorted, his eyes narrowing. "This was never meant to be anything more than what it is." Each word felt like a pebble thrown, intended to hit me squarely in the chest. I struggled to swallow down the rising tide of hurt that threatened to overwhelm me.

"This was never just a fling for me, Grant!" My voice was louder now, reverberating against the stone walls of the surrounding buildings. "I thought you understood that."

He stepped closer, the anger in his gaze mingling with something else—a flicker of regret, perhaps? But it was gone as quickly as it appeared, replaced by the hardened resolve I had come to loathe. "You're imagining things, Lily. We both are. We were caught up in the moment, but reality is waiting for us outside this little bubble we've created."

Reality. That single word hung between us like a guillotine, ready to drop. I could feel the cracks widening in the fragile foundation we'd built, each unspoken truth like a ticking clock. "You don't get to decide what's real for me," I snapped, my heart racing. "You don't get to dismiss everything we've shared."

His jaw tightened, and for a moment, the cool night air was charged with something almost electric. He glanced away, breaking the intensity of the moment, and I seized the opportunity. "You're afraid, aren't you? Afraid of what this could be. Afraid of me."

"Don't flatter yourself," he shot back, but his voice lacked conviction. There was a tremor beneath the surface, an undercurrent of something deeper that he wasn't ready to face. The vulnerability in his eyes did not escape my notice, and for a split second, I thought he might finally let down his guard.

"Then why do you keep pulling away?" I pressed, stepping into his space, closing the distance that felt insurmountable. The moonlight caught the contours of his face, making him look both fierce and impossibly vulnerable. "You say you don't care, but your actions tell a different story. What are you really so afraid of?"

He inhaled sharply, the air thick with the weight of our unacknowledged feelings. I could see him grappling with my words, each second stretched into eternity. "It's not that simple," he muttered, frustration evident in his tone. "You don't understand what I have to lose."

"And you think I don't?" I was surprised at the fierceness that bubbled up inside me. "You think I haven't had my heart ripped apart before? I've fought for everything I have, just like you. And I won't let you push me away when I can see the truth lurking beneath your bravado."

At that, he fell silent, his gaze drifting to the ground. The weight of his thoughts hung heavy, and I sensed the shift in him—a recognition that maybe, just maybe, there was something more than animosity simmering beneath the surface. "You think you know me, Lily, but you don't. I've been hurt too. Maybe more than you."

I took a step back, the revelation momentarily stunning me. "What do you mean?"

His eyes met mine, vulnerability crackling in the air between us. "Trust isn't easy for me. It's like walking a tightrope over a chasm. One slip, and everything falls apart." He paused, swallowing hard. "When you come from where I do, letting someone in can feel like inviting a tornado into your home."

"And you think I'm a tornado?" I asked, half-teasing, trying to lighten the mood despite the gravity of our conversation.

He cracked a smile, but it didn't reach his eyes. "You might be a whirlwind."

"Then let me be your whirlwind," I implored, my heart racing. "What's the worst that could happen?"

"Everything," he whispered, his voice barely audible above the rustle of leaves. The moment hung in the air, thick with tension and unspoken desires. "Everything could fall apart."

"And what if it doesn't?" The question slipped out, a challenge more than a plea. "What if we could build something strong enough to withstand anything? Something real?"

He hesitated, the flicker of hope dancing behind his guarded exterior. "You make it sound so easy."

"Nothing worth having ever is," I replied, stepping closer again, my heart pounding in my chest. "But it's worth the risk. Isn't it?"

In the fragile silence that followed, I saw the storm behind his eyes—conflict battling desire, fear battling something else entirely. And as we stood there, teetering on the edge of a precipice neither of us had been willing to acknowledge, the air crackled with unspoken possibilities.

"I need time," he finally said, his voice steadier. "Time to figure out what I want. What we want."

"Then take it," I said, my heart aching with the weight of uncertainty. "Just know that I'll be here. No matter what."

With those words, the night air shifted, and I felt something fragile and beautiful stir between us—a promise wrapped in hope and uncertainty. As he turned away, I felt the distance grow, but not without the lingering touch of possibility—a fragile thread that could bind us closer together or pull us apart entirely. And in that moment, standing under the vast expanse of the starry sky, I realized that love, like trust, was a precarious dance, balancing between what was known and what remained unspoken.

The sun hung low in the sky, casting long shadows that stretched across the pavement like tendrils of a lingering tension. I leaned against the cool brick of the café wall, absently stirring my coffee as the familiar aroma swirled around me. Each sip felt bittersweet, mirroring the conflict that churned in my chest. My mind replayed the confrontation with Grant, each moment echoing painfully. Did he even realize how close we had come to something real? How quickly we had teetered on the edge of a connection that could shift everything between us?

A playful laugh drew my attention, and I glanced up to see Claire, my best friend, approaching with her usual effervescent energy. She was a whirlwind of sunshine, her hair bouncing as she wove through the afternoon crowd, oblivious to my turmoil. "Hey, stranger! Did you forget about our coffee date, or have you been sulking like a moody poet?"

I forced a smile, though it didn't quite reach my eyes. "More like a drama queen. You know, the kind that contemplates the existential weight of their love life over lattes."

Claire perched on the edge of the table, her expression a blend of concern and amusement. "Well, if it's drama you need, I'm your girl. Spill the tea! Is it Grant? Is it bad? Tell me you didn't scare him off with all that honesty. You know how guys can be with feelings—like cats and baths."

"Honestly?" I sighed, raking my fingers through my hair. "I think I scared him off. He made it pretty clear he doesn't want to get involved. Too much baggage or something."

"Ugh! Men and their emotional walls," she scoffed, rolling her eyes dramatically. "What is it with them? You know, my ex used to say he was a 'work in progress.' I should have taken that as a cue to run, but instead, I thought it was charming. Spoiler alert: It wasn't."

I chuckled, appreciating her ability to find humor in my mess. "I thought I had him figured out, but he keeps pulling away. And just when I think we're making progress, he puts up his defenses like some kind of emotional fortress."

Claire leaned in, her eyes sparkling with mischief. "Maybe he just needs the right incentive to let you in. You know, like a well-placed cupcake or a well-timed hug."

"A cupcake?" I raised an eyebrow, amusement bubbling up. "You really think Grant is the type to crumble at the sight of frosting?"

"Trust me, a cupcake can work wonders. Or a dance-off. Something unexpected to shake things up." She flashed a grin, clearly enjoying the idea.

"Great, because nothing says romance like a dance-off in the middle of a crowded street." I shook my head, laughing. "What's next, a serenade under a streetlamp?"

"Now you're talking!" she chirped. "But let's be real. You need to confront him again. Show him you're not afraid of his baggage. You can't let him hide behind those walls forever."

Her words hung in the air, igniting a spark of resolve deep within me. Perhaps it was time to take charge of this situation instead of waiting for him to figure it all out. I wanted Grant, and not just as some fleeting summer romance. I wanted the real deal, all of him—flaws and fears included.

After finishing my coffee, I thanked Claire for her unwavering support and made my way toward the park where Grant often jogged. The sun had dipped below the horizon, leaving behind a cascade of purples and oranges that painted the sky. I spotted him in the distance, his familiar silhouette cutting through the dusky light, moving with a grace that belied his earlier tension.

Taking a deep breath, I approached him, my heart pounding in my chest. I would not let this moment slip away. As I drew closer, he slowed, his expression shifting from surprise to a mix of apprehension and curiosity.

"Lily," he greeted, his voice low and cautious. "What are you doing here?"

"I came to talk." I matched his intensity, determined not to back down. "We need to sort through this mess we've made of things."

His brow furrowed, and for a moment, I feared he might retreat again. "Do we? I thought we established that this—whatever this is—can't go anywhere."

"Maybe you established that," I countered, refusing to let him sidestep the truth. "But I can't walk away without trying. You're not the only one with fears, Grant. I've been hurt too, but that doesn't mean I'm willing to throw in the towel. Not without a fight."

"Lily—"

"Let me finish," I interrupted, raising a hand. "You've put up these walls, and I get it. I really do. But you're not the only one who's afraid of getting hurt. You think I'm just some naive girl chasing after a fantasy?"

He opened his mouth to respond, but I pressed on, unwilling to let him silence me. "I'm willing to face whatever is holding you back. I won't be the one to push you away."

The tension between us crackled, thickening the air as he stared at me, assessing my resolve. I could see the gears turning in his mind, and for a fleeting moment, I thought I caught a glimpse of something—longing, perhaps? "I don't know how to be what you want me to be," he finally admitted, his voice softening.

"I'm not asking for perfection," I said, my heart racing. "Just be you, and let me be me. If we can't face our fears together, then what's the point?"

His expression softened, vulnerability flickering in his eyes. "You're asking for a lot."

"And I'm willing to give a lot in return," I shot back, emboldened by the truth of my feelings. "But you need to meet me halfway. I want to understand you, Grant—your past, your fears. I'm not here to judge. I'm here to be your partner in whatever this is."

He fell silent, the weight of my words hanging between us like a fragile thread. Finally, he stepped closer, his gaze unwavering. "You make it sound so easy, yet here I am, struggling to let anyone in."

"Then let's struggle together," I said, my heart swelling with hope. "You don't have to do this alone. None of us do."

As the last remnants of daylight faded, an unspoken understanding formed between us, delicate yet powerful. Perhaps we were both navigating through a labyrinth of emotions, but for the first time, I felt we were no longer lost. Instead, we stood at the cusp of something extraordinary—a chance to uncover the depths of each other's hearts.

The night deepened around us, the streetlights flickering on one by one, casting a soft golden glow that illuminated the shadows where our words hung heavy in the air. I could see the war raging within Grant, the internal battle that mirrored the storm in my heart. It was palpable, a tension that crackled with the electricity of possibilities and fears unspoken.

"I'm not used to this," he finally said, his voice low, almost a whisper. "This... whatever it is between us."

"Neither am I," I admitted, my heart racing. "But does that mean we should run away from it? Because I'm not willing to do that. I refuse to let fear dictate what we could become."

He ran a hand through his hair, a gesture of frustration mingled with something akin to admiration. "You make it sound so simple. But it's not just fear, Lily. It's complicated. I have things in my past—things I'm not proud of."

"Don't we all?" I shot back, my voice steadying with determination. "You think I haven't made mistakes? You think I don't carry my own baggage?"

He looked at me, a flicker of surprise crossing his features. "That's different."

"Is it?" I challenged, stepping forward, my heart thundering in my chest. "You're not the only one with scars, Grant. We can't hide behind our pasts forever. What's the point of even trying if we're both just going to keep our walls up?"

"Maybe it's safer that way," he murmured, his eyes searching mine as if looking for a way out. "What if we hurt each other?"

"Then we learn and grow. Isn't that what life is about?" I countered, my breath quickening. "And who says we have to do this perfectly? I'm tired of playing it safe. I want to feel something real, even if it's messy."

For a moment, I thought I saw a flicker of understanding in his gaze. The tension shifted slightly, a crack forming in the wall that had been built between us. "You're so stubborn," he said, a hint of a smile breaking through his brooding facade.

"Guilty as charged," I said, matching his smile. "But stubbornness can be a virtue, you know. It means I don't give up easily."

He laughed, a rich sound that warmed the chilly air between us. "You're impossible."

"Maybe, but I'd like to think I'm worth the trouble," I replied, my heart fluttering at the unexpected intimacy of the moment. I stepped closer, drawn in by the magnetic pull of our shared vulnerabilities.

"We both have fears, but I refuse to let them define us. Can you meet me halfway?"

As the words left my lips, a silence settled, heavy with anticipation. The world around us faded, leaving only the two of us standing at the crossroads of fear and hope. I could feel the weight of the moment pressing down, the potential for something extraordinary lying just beyond the veil of uncertainty.

Grant's gaze softened, and for an instant, I thought he might take that leap with me. "Okay," he said finally, his voice a mix of resignation and resolve. "But you have to promise me that if it gets too intense, we'll talk about it. No running away, no shutting down."

"I promise," I said, my heart soaring with relief. "Let's just take it one day at a time. We can figure this out together."

He stepped even closer, the warmth radiating from him pulling me in like a moth to a flame. The space between us felt charged, electric with unspoken words, and I couldn't help but wonder if this was the moment where everything changed.

Before I could lose myself in his gaze, the sudden blare of a horn shattered the serenity. We both turned to see a car speeding down the street, headlights glaring like a predator stalking its prey. My stomach dropped as I caught sight of the driver—a familiar face with a sneer that sent a chill down my spine.

"Lily!" The voice cut through the night like a knife, pulling me from the spell I was under. I turned to see David, my ex, leaning out of the passenger window with a look of disdain that made my heart race for all the wrong reasons.

"What the hell are you doing here?" I snapped, my stomach knotting at the sight of him. "You shouldn't be here!"

"Just checking in on my favorite drama queen," he retorted, the smirk on his face oozing arrogance. "You look cozy with your new boyfriend."

"David, this isn't your business," I shot back, anger bubbling up inside me. I could feel Grant tense beside me, his protective instincts kicking in.

"Isn't it?" David's eyes glinted with malice. "You think you can just move on? Like I didn't mean anything to you? You're just going to forget about me that easily?"

"Forget about you? It's been months! I've moved on!" I felt my composure fraying as his taunts cut deeper.

"Oh, is that what you're calling this?" he gestured dismissively at Grant. "A rebound? You really think he's going to stick around when things get tough?"

"Get out of here, David," Grant interjected, stepping in front of me, a wall of strength and fury. "You're not welcome."

I felt a rush of gratitude mixed with dread. Grant was standing up for me, but I could see the storm brewing in David's eyes—a dangerous mix of jealousy and possessiveness.

"Who do you think you are?" David shot back, his tone dripping with contempt. "You don't know anything about her."

Grant's jaw tightened, but I sensed the tension in the air shifting again, thickening like fog rolling in from the sea. "And you don't get to dictate who she spends her time with," he replied, each word measured and calm, yet the anger simmering beneath the surface was palpable.

David's laugh was harsh, mocking. "You really think you can protect her from me? I know her better than anyone. You're just a placeholder."

I felt my breath hitch in my throat. The words struck a chord, reverberating in the air like a cruel echo. "You don't know me at all!" I shot back, anger fueling my voice. "I'm not a placeholder for anyone. Not for you, and certainly not for him."

But even as I said it, I could feel the ground beneath us shifting. The darkness around us felt more threatening, the shadows stretching, twisting like serpents ready to strike.

David grinned, an unsettling glimmer in his eyes. "We'll see how long this little fairy tale lasts, Lily. People like you don't get happy endings."

Before I could respond, he slammed the car door and sped off, leaving behind a trail of dust and dread. The air grew heavy with unspoken fear, and I felt a chill creeping up my spine.

Turning to Grant, I saw the flicker of concern in his eyes mirrored by my own. "You okay?" he asked, his voice low, the intimacy of our moment shattered like glass.

"I'm fine," I said, but even I could hear the tremor in my voice. "It's just—"

"Lily," he interrupted, stepping closer again, but this time the warmth felt different, laced with uncertainty. "I'm not letting this go. Not after what he said. You mean too much to me."

"Then we need to face this together," I insisted, my heart racing again, not just from fear but from something deeper, something that pulled us closer despite the danger. "We can't let him control what we have."

Grant nodded, determination shining in his eyes. But even as he spoke, I felt a nagging doubt whispering in the back of my mind—was I strong enough to weather this storm? Would we truly be able to rise above the chaos, or would the shadows from our past drag us both down?

Before I could voice my fears, the air grew thick again, crackling with tension, and I knew the battle was far from over. But as long as we faced it together, maybe, just maybe, we could emerge on the other side unscathed.

Yet as the echoes of David's words faded into the night, I couldn't shake the feeling that the real storm was just beginning, and the shadows were closing in fast.

Chapter 8: Reckoning

The wind howled through the narrow alleyways of Riverton, carrying with it the damp scent of impending rain. I stood with my back pressed against the cool stone wall of the old clock tower, my heart racing in tandem with the frantic ticking echoing above. The air was charged with a tension that felt almost tangible, like static electricity buzzing at the edge of my skin. Just a few blocks away, the warmth of the Café Lume beckoned—a sanctuary filled with the aroma of fresh coffee and baked pastries, where laughter echoed and the world seemed oblivious to the shadows creeping at its fringes. But I wasn't looking for comfort today; I was hunting the truth.

Grant leaned against the opposite wall, his posture relaxed yet his eyes darting with purpose, scanning the street for any sign of the threat that loomed over us. I admired that about him—the effortless way he carried himself, like a coiled spring ready to launch into action. Just a few weeks ago, I would have laughed at the absurdity of this moment, the idea of being trapped in a web of conspiracy alongside a man who had once been a thorn in my side. Yet here we were, bound by secrets and unspoken feelings, two unlikely allies facing a darkness that threatened to consume us.

"Are you sure we're ready for this?" I asked, breaking the silence that had settled between us. My voice felt too loud, too raw against the backdrop of the dimly lit alley.

His gaze flickered to mine, and for a heartbeat, the world around us faded into the background. "We don't have a choice. If we don't confront this now, it'll only get worse." He paused, the weight of his words sinking in. "Besides, I'd rather face it with you than alone."

I swallowed hard, the gravity of his statement wrapping around my heart like a vice. The feelings I'd been wrestling with—confusion, attraction, fear—swirled together in a chaotic dance. Grant had become more than just a partner in this unraveling mystery; he was a distraction from the suffocating doubts clawing at my insides. Yet, the question remained: could I trust him?

As if sensing my inner turmoil, he took a step closer, his voice a low murmur. "You're stronger than you think, you know. We'll figure this out together." His confidence was a lifeline, and I found myself clinging to it, even as the shadows loomed larger around us.

We made our way through the labyrinth of backstreets, the faint light of the café fading behind us, replaced by the oppressive darkness that lay ahead. Each step felt like a countdown, the seconds stretching out as we approached the abandoned warehouse where the syndicate was rumored to meet. My heart pounded in my chest, an insistent reminder of the stakes involved.

As we neared the entrance, an unsettling sense of foreboding washed over me. I glanced at Grant, who had transformed into a determined figure, his jaw set, eyes blazing with resolve. "Remember, we stick to the plan. In and out," he said, his voice steady despite the tension crackling in the air.

"Right, in and out. Just like a bank heist," I replied, my attempt at levity falling flat against the gravity of the moment. The corner of his mouth twitched, but we both knew there was little room for humor.

I pushed the heavy door open, the creak echoing ominously in the silence that followed. Inside, the warehouse was a cavernous shell, shadows pooling in the corners like secrets waiting to be uncovered. Dust motes danced in the slivers of moonlight that filtered through the cracked windows, adding an ethereal quality to the grim surroundings.

We crept deeper into the space, the distant sound of muffled voices rising and falling like a heartbeat. The tension was palpable, and I could feel the adrenaline coursing through my veins, propelling me forward despite the dread coiling in my stomach. With each step, I reminded myself of the reasons we were here—the lives that hung in the balance, the future we could forge if we succeeded.

"Do you think they know we're coming?" I whispered, glancing back at Grant. The way he studied me, his brow furrowed with concern, sent a shiver of unexpected warmth through me.

"Let's hope not," he replied, his voice low and steady, though I could sense the tension beneath the surface. "Stay close."

We rounded a corner and found ourselves in a large open area. My breath hitched as I took in the sight before us—a gathering of men and women, their silhouettes stark against the dim light. They were the very embodiment of danger, cloaked in shadows and secrecy, plotting their next move like spiders weaving a web.

Grant shifted slightly, positioning himself protectively at my side. "We need to get closer," he said, his voice barely above a whisper.

As we inched forward, the conversation grew clearer. I caught snippets of their plans—talk of power, of control, of a city teetering on the edge of chaos. My stomach twisted at the implications. This was no ordinary gang; they were a force intent on reshaping the world around us.

But in the midst of this chaos, I felt a spark of clarity ignite within me. This was not just about exposing their plans; it was about standing up for what was right. I had fought for my dreams, clawed my way through the darkness of doubt, and now, with Grant beside me, I could feel the weight of that fight surging back to life.

Suddenly, a voice cut through the air, sharp and accusatory. "We know you're here! Come out and face us!"

The room went deathly silent. Every head turned in our direction, and I could feel my heart leap into my throat. It was time. No more hiding in the shadows; we had to confront the reality of our choices.

Grant's hand found mine, squeezing it with a reassuring grip as we stepped into the open. The atmosphere crackled with anticipation, the air thick with danger. As I looked into the faces surrounding us, I felt a swell of defiance rise within me. We would fight not just for our future, but for the world we wanted to build—a world illuminated by love rather than fear.

"Let's settle this," I called out, my voice steady despite the storm raging inside me. "We're not backing down."

And as the words left my lips, I realized they were more than just a declaration; they were a promise. A promise to myself, to Grant, and to the lives we were determined to protect.

A low murmur rippled through the gathering, a palpable shift as the group turned to assess our presence. Faces hardened, tension thick enough to slice through. I could see the uncertainty in their eyes morph into anger, like a storm gathering on the horizon, dark and menacing. But with Grant's hand firmly clasped in mine, I felt a spark of courage igniting in my chest, urging me to stand taller, to lean into the chaos instead of shying away from it.

"Surprise! We've come for the big reveal!" I declared, summoning every ounce of bravado I could muster. The words hung in the air, a mix of challenge and humor, deflating the tension for just a heartbeat. Grant shot me a look, half amusement and half disbelief, but the corner of his mouth quirked up, just enough to remind me that we were in this together.

"Nice one," he murmured, his voice low and warm, the sound wrapping around me like a favorite sweater on a chilly day. But the laughter was short-lived as a man stepped forward from the shadows, a hulking figure with a scar that traced a menacing path down his cheek.

"Who do you think you are?" he growled, his voice gravelly and low, echoing ominously through the vastness of the warehouse.

"Just two people with a serious aversion to organized crime," I quipped, unable to resist the urge to challenge him. There was something exhilarating about standing here, daring to face the very villains we had been hunting.

He advanced, the weight of his presence drawing the others closer, as if the shadows themselves conspired to swallow us whole. "You have no idea what you're getting into. This isn't a game."

"Funny, because it feels like one," I shot back, fueled by adrenaline and a surge of reckless defiance. The thrill of confronting danger ignited something deep within me—an ancient fire that pushed me forward. "But let me guess, you think you're the hero of your own story? Spoiler alert: you're not."

The crowd shifted, some exchanging glances that hinted at doubt, perhaps considering my words. It was a tiny crack in their facade, a chink in the armor that Grant and I could exploit.

"You want to play?" the scarred man said, his eyes narrowing as he attempted to regain control of the situation. "Fine. But understand this: you have no allies here. We're everywhere, and we don't take kindly to interference."

Grant stepped in front of me, the protective gesture sending a wave of warmth through my chest. "We're not here to make friends, but to end this." His voice was a steady force, cutting through the mounting tension like a knife. "You're the ones who've underestimated us."

The scarred man scoffed, an ugly laugh escaping his lips. "Underestimating you? Oh, sweetheart, this isn't about underestimating. This is about you playing a dangerous game against forces you can't even begin to comprehend."

His words hung in the air, taunting and threatening. But beneath the bravado, I could sense a flicker of uncertainty. Perhaps he had begun to realize that we weren't just pawns in his twisted game. We were something more—resilient, determined, and resolute in our quest for justice.

"Then let's not waste any more time," I said, the conviction in my voice surprising even myself. "We've come to expose you, and we're not leaving without the truth."

"Expose us?" he echoed, laughter mingling with derision. "You think you can just waltz in here and demand truth like it's a free sample at the market?"

"Free samples are nice, but I'd settle for a good story," I replied, a playful smirk gracing my lips despite the gravity of the moment. "You're the one with the dirty little secrets, and I'm just dying to hear all about them."

The crowd shifted again, a wave of uncertainty rippling through the ranks. I could see their eyes darting between their leader and us, questioning, pondering. This was our moment to capitalize on their hesitation, to turn the tide in our favor.

The scarred man glared at me, a mixture of anger and confusion. "You have no idea who you're dealing with. You think love can conquer all? This is a war, and war is not won with feelings."

I exchanged a glance with Grant, who nodded slightly, a silent agreement passing between us. "No, it's not," I countered, my voice steady. "But love gives us strength. It empowers us to fight against the darkness."

"And sometimes," Grant added, stepping forward with an intensity that sent a shiver down my spine, "it gives us the clarity to see our enemies for who they really are."

In that instant, the air crackled with energy, a potent mix of fear and defiance. We were not just here to confront them; we were here to challenge their very foundation. The scarred man's bravado began to falter, the arrogance in his stance wavering as he faced the strength we exuded.

"You think you can intimidate me with your little theatrics?" he spat, yet the tremor in his voice revealed his faltering confidence.

"No theatrics here," I said, my voice cutting through the haze of tension like a knife. "Just truth. And you're about to face the consequences of your actions."

The crowd's restlessness was palpable, and I sensed the tide shifting in our favor. Grant's hand tightened around mine, his touch both grounding and electrifying. I could feel the heartbeat of the moment thrumming beneath our feet, urging us forward, demanding we seize the opportunity.

Suddenly, a loud crash echoed from the far side of the warehouse, the sound reverberating like a thunderclap. The crowd jumped, startled, and we exchanged a glance, adrenaline spiking. "What was that?" I whispered, scanning the dimly lit room for any sign of movement.

"Reinforcements?" Grant suggested, his voice low as we instinctively moved closer, our shoulders brushing, igniting a warmth that battled the chill of danger enveloping us.

"Or a distraction," I murmured, my heart racing as the shadows danced around us. Just as I turned to refocus on our adversaries, I caught a glimpse of someone slipping through the back entrance, their face obscured in the darkness.

"Look out!" I shouted, instincts kicking in as I pulled Grant back just as a figure lunged toward us, their intentions shrouded in malice.

We stumbled back, caught off guard, but not unprepared. As the figure lunged, Grant's reflexes kicked in, and he grabbed my arm, pivoting to shield me. I felt the rush of air as the attacker's momentum carried them forward, crashing into the pile of crates behind us with a loud thud.

The crowd erupted into chaos, shouting and scrambling as the unexpected confrontation sent shockwaves through their ranks. I barely had a moment to gather my thoughts before the figure began to rise, shaking off the impact and revealing a familiar face—one I had never expected to see here.

"Daniel?" I gasped, disbelief swirling within me as the pieces clicked into place.

His eyes narrowed in anger, but there was something else beneath the surface—fear, desperation, perhaps even regret. "You shouldn't be here," he spat, brushing debris from his jacket as if it could somehow erase the consequences of his actions. "You don't know what you're involved in."

"But I do know," I retorted, feeling the ground shift beneath my feet as the world I thought I understood crumbled. "You're in way over your head."

As Daniel advanced, I felt a surge of protectiveness for the lives we were fighting for, for Grant beside me, for the future we were desperately trying to reclaim. This was no longer just about our confrontation with the syndicate; it was about confronting the demons we had all been wrestling with, whether they were rooted in past grudges or the relentless pursuit of power.

The stakes had never been higher, and as Daniel drew closer, I steeled myself for the fight ahead. In that moment, surrounded by chaos, I knew one thing for certain: we would confront this darkness together, and whatever the outcome, we would emerge transformed.

"Daniel, what are you doing here?" I managed to choke out, a strange mix of disbelief and anger bubbling to the surface. My heart raced as I took a step back, assessing the situation unfolding before me. This wasn't just an old acquaintance; Daniel had been a friend once, a trusted ally in our misguided escapades. Now, he stood here, poised like a coiled spring, and the unspoken tension in the air was nearly unbearable.

"I could ask you the same," he replied, his voice low and gravelly, the hint of a smirk playing at the corners of his mouth. "But it seems you've already waded into the deep end without a life preserver. Bold move, but foolish."

"Foolish?" I echoed, incredulous. "You're the one who has clearly lost his way! Aligning yourself with these—" I gestured around at the seedy crowd that had formed, watching us with hungry eyes. "These people? Do you even realize what you're getting into?"

"Do you?" he shot back, stepping closer, the shadows deepening the lines of his face. "You have no idea what I'm a part of, what this all means. You think you can just barge in here and fix things? You're naive, Maya."

Before I could respond, a murmur swept through the crowd, and suddenly, a glint of steel caught my eye. My stomach dropped as a knife glimmered in the dim light, raised threateningly by one of the syndicate members who had been lurking in the background.

"Back off, Daniel!" Grant commanded, his body positioning itself protectively in front of me. The bravado in his voice was like a blanket, warm and reassuring, even as the chaos around us threatened to engulf us.

I took a deep breath, grounding myself in the moment. "We're not the ones in danger here, Daniel," I said, forcing my voice to remain steady. "You are. You're making a choice that could cost you everything."

His eyes flickered for just a moment, a shadow of doubt crossing his face. "And what do you suggest? That I walk away from the power, from the influence? This is a game, and I'm not losing."

"A game?" I laughed, the sound ringing hollow in the air. "You think this is just a game? You're playing with lives, Daniel. Your own included."

The tension escalated, and I could see the flicker of anger mixed with confusion in his expression. He glanced toward the syndicate members who were shifting restlessly, their hands itching at their sides, anticipation thrumming in the air.

"Are you really willing to throw all of this away for some misguided sense of morality?" he asked, his voice dropping to a conspiratorial whisper. "What have you got to gain? You think your love story with Grant is worth it? You're dreaming if you think that will protect you."

"Love is worth more than power," I shot back, heart pounding in my chest. "It's worth the risk. It's worth fighting for."

With that, I stepped away from Grant's protective stance, the sudden distance between us feeling like a chasm, and faced Daniel head-on. "I'm not here to save you, Daniel. I'm here to stop you."

In that moment, chaos erupted. The syndicate members surged forward, and instinct kicked in as Grant pulled me back, shielding me from the impending onslaught. "Stay close!" he urged, his voice firm, filled with determination.

I felt the adrenaline coursing through my veins as the first punch was thrown, the sound of flesh hitting flesh reverberating in my ears. Grant tackled the closest attacker, their bodies crashing against a stack of crates with a loud thud. I barely had time to process the scene before another figure barreled toward me, and I sidestepped, using the momentum to shove them away.

"Nice moves!" Grant shouted, a hint of admiration shining through the chaos as he took down another opponent, his movements fluid and practiced.

"Years of practice!" I quipped back, exhilaration flooding my system as I launched myself into the fray. I never would have imagined I could feel so alive in the midst of danger, the thrill of combat igniting a fire within me that I hadn't known existed.

Daniel watched from the edge of the chaos, his expression shifting from disdain to something that resembled concern. "You're making a mistake, Maya!" he called out, but I was beyond his reach, beyond the point of caring what he thought.

The warehouse erupted into a cacophony of grunts, shouts, and the sound of bodies colliding, a symphony of chaos that propelled me forward. I fought with a purpose, driven by the memories of what we had once shared, of the friend I had believed in. But those days felt like a lifetime ago, overshadowed by the choices he had made.

"Don't get too cocky!" Grant yelled, throwing a punch that landed squarely on an opponent's jaw. "We're still outnumbered!"

"Always the pessimist," I shot back, ducking under a swinging arm and countering with a swift kick that sent another attacker sprawling. "But I'm feeling lucky!"

As the fight escalated, I caught a glimpse of the knife-wielding syndicate member advancing towards Grant. "Behind you!" I shouted, but the warning was lost amid the din of battle.

In a split second, time slowed. I lunged forward, adrenaline surging through me as I reached out, grasping for Grant's arm, desperate to pull him away from the oncoming danger. But the attacker was faster, swinging the blade with a ferocity that left no room for error.

"No!" I screamed, the world narrowing to the point of impending collision.

In a blur of movement, Grant spun around just in time, dodging the knife's arc and countering with a deft maneuver that knocked the weapon from the attacker's grip. But it was too close. Too dangerously close.

With the knife clattering to the ground, the tide of the battle shifted again, the syndicate members retreating slightly, uncertainty creeping into their ranks. It was a fleeting moment of victory, but it was enough for us to regroup, to reassess.

"Are you okay?" Grant panted, catching his breath as he glanced at me, concern etched across his face.

"I am now," I replied, though my heart still raced from the brush with danger. "But we need to keep moving. We can't let them regroup."

Just as I turned to lead the charge, the warehouse doors burst open, and the sound of heavy footsteps echoed from the entrance.

My stomach dropped as I caught sight of a new group pouring in—more syndicate members, their faces twisted in malice, intent on reinforcements.

"Great, just what we needed," Grant muttered, his eyes darting around for a way out.

"This way!" I yelled, grabbing his hand and leading him toward a side exit I had noticed earlier. The sound of chaos behind us became a distant roar as we sprinted through the narrow corridor, adrenaline fueling our escape.

But as we neared the door, a figure emerged from the shadows, blocking our path. "Going somewhere?" Daniel's voice was smooth, but beneath it lay a current of danger, his expression unreadable as he loomed in front of us.

The weight of the moment crashed down, and I felt the air thicken with tension. "Daniel, move!" I demanded, my voice trembling with urgency.

"Not until we talk," he replied, his eyes locking onto mine with an intensity that sent a shiver down my spine.

"Now is not the time for this!" Grant interjected, stepping protectively in front of me. "Get out of our way!"

But Daniel held his ground, and in that charged moment, the gravity of our choices hung precariously in the air. It was a standoff, a culmination of everything that had led us to this point—love, betrayal, the echoes of a friendship shattered.

"Choose wisely, Maya," Daniel said, his voice low and laced with a challenge. "You may not like what you find on the other side."

Before I could respond, the ground beneath us trembled with the sound of approaching footsteps, a warning of impending danger. The choice was upon us, and with it, the very fabric of our fate.

Chapter 9: The Weight of Shadows

The fallout from our confrontation hangs in the air, heavy as the mist that rolls in from the sea, shrouding everything in an uncertain gray. I find myself navigating the twisting alleys of both politics and my own heart, where the shadows of betrayal threaten to swallow me whole. Grant's betrayal cuts deeper than I care to admit, leaving jagged edges in its wake, and as I sit at my cluttered desk, a fortress of papers and half-empty coffee cups surrounding me, I can almost hear the echo of his laughter from that fateful night. It taunts me, teasing out the unresolved tension that sits like a coiled snake beneath my skin.

The dim light of my study casts an orange glow over the pages of my notes, illuminating the scattered remnants of my research on our adversary, a man who hides his true nature beneath a polished veneer. Jonathan Mercer—a name whispered in corners, accompanied by wary glances and hushed voices. I'd heard the stories, of course, but the chilling details I've uncovered paint a far more sinister picture. He doesn't just play the game; he rewrites the rules with blood-stained hands and a calculating smile.

As I sift through the wealth of information, the shadows seem to grow thicker, wrapping around me like a suffocating blanket. I pull my sweater tighter, its familiar texture grounding me amid the chaos. Each snippet of intelligence I gather weaves a more intricate web, threading together the factions that dance around Mercer like moths to a flame. It's a delicate dance of power and deceit, and I'm caught in the crossfire, unsure of who to trust.

With every passing hour, the weight of this new knowledge settles heavily on my shoulders. It's not just the weight of responsibility; it's the weight of fear—fear for myself, for those I care about, and for what's to come. My thoughts dart back to Grant, that unpredictable spark who has somehow burrowed himself into the very fabric of my existence. I hate him for his betrayal, yet a flicker of warmth surfaces, igniting memories of shared laughter and whispered secrets in the dark.

When the opportunity arises to infiltrate one of Mercer's hidden meetings, it feels both like a risk and a necessity. This could be the moment that changes everything, a chance to uncover the depths of his malevolence. Grant insists on joining me, and though I want to refuse him, to cast him aside like a worn-out shoe, I realize I can't do this alone. Our connection, fraught with tension and unspoken words, still pulses between us like a live wire.

The night of the meeting arrives, cloaked in shadows and secrets. We slip into the gathering disguised as part of Mercer's entourage, our identities wrapped in layers of deception. The venue is a dilapidated warehouse on the outskirts of town, its crumbling façade a stark contrast to the opulence promised by Mercer's dealings. Inside, the air buzzes with a mix of anticipation and menace. The flickering fluorescent lights cast long shadows, and I can almost taste the tension, thick and acrid, in the air.

As we weave our way through the crowd, I can feel Grant's presence beside me, a steadying force that both comforts and unnerves me. His profile is sharp, eyes scanning the room with the intensity of a predator on the hunt. I catch a glimpse of the man himself—Mercer—standing at the front, his voice smooth and commanding, a dark melody that seems to wrap around the assembled crowd like a silken noose. The way he moves is mesmerizing, each gesture deliberate, exuding a confidence that is both intoxicating and terrifying.

"Is this what power looks like?" I murmur to Grant, barely above a whisper.

He leans in closer, his breath warm against my ear. "Power can be intoxicating, but it's also fragile. One wrong move, and it all comes crashing down." There's a flicker of something in his eyes—determination mixed with a hint of vulnerability. It catches me off guard, and for a moment, I find myself wanting to believe in the man standing next to me.

The meeting unfolds like a carefully choreographed dance, with Mercer playing the role of both conductor and star. His words paint a picture of ambition and ruthlessness, weaving a narrative that captivates his audience. Yet beneath the surface, I sense the undercurrents of treachery, the alliances forged not in trust but in fear. I exchange glances with Grant, the air between us crackling with unspoken thoughts. There's a connection here that we can't ignore, an understanding that transcends our past conflicts.

"Do you think he knows we're here?" I ask, my voice low, barely audible above the growing murmur of the crowd.

"Not yet," Grant replies, his gaze steady on Mercer. "But he will. They always do."

I shiver, the realization sending a chill through me. This isn't just a game; it's a battlefield, and we're mere pawns in a much larger scheme. The thrill of danger courses through my veins, mingling with the remnants of fear. The atmosphere thickens, heavy with impending doom as Mercer's speech crescendos, and I feel a palpable tension building around us, wrapping its fingers around my throat.

Just as I start to question the wisdom of this venture, a sudden commotion erupts on the other side of the room. A voice rises above the din, sharp and accusatory. "You think you can play us against each other, Mercer? You underestimate the power of unity!" The words hang in the air, charged with an electricity that demands attention.

I turn to Grant, eyes wide with shock. "This wasn't part of the plan."

"No, but it's just the distraction we need." His voice is low and urgent, and I can sense the adrenaline pumping through him as he takes a step closer, his body instinctively shielding mine.

And in that moment, as the chaos unfolds, the past fades into the background. We're not just two people with a history; we're allies bound by a shared purpose, standing against the looming darkness of Jonathan Mercer. As the tension escalates and shadows deepen, I realize that our journey has only just begun.

The chaos unfurls like a dark flower, petals twisting and tangling, revealing the depths of uncertainty that lurk within every whisper and glance. The air crackles with tension, a mix of fear and excitement that sends shivers racing down my spine. I can hardly catch my breath as I peer around the dimly lit warehouse, the flickering lights casting ghostly shadows that dance against the cracked concrete walls. Mercer stands at the center, an architect of disarray, his voice smooth and persuasive, but the hostility emanating from the opposing faction shifts the energy like a storm brewing on the horizon.

"Who the hell do you think you are?" A man with a voice like thunder cuts through the tension, his stance wide and defiant. He steps forward, fury etched into every line of his face, and I can see the glint of something sharp hidden in his jacket. "You think you can toy with our lives like we're pawns in your little game? We're not afraid of you!"

Mercer's eyes narrow, darkening like a sky just before the rain, but his smile remains polished, unsettlingly charming. "Fear is not what I seek. I offer power, opportunity—a chance to rise above the rest. If you're too blind to see it, that's your loss." He glances around the room, gauging his audience, and I can feel the palpable shift in the crowd as loyalty wavers. This isn't just a meeting; it's a tempest, and I'm caught in the eye of it, bewildered and entranced.

Grant's hand brushes against mine, grounding me as I catch his eye. The familiar heat radiates between us, an unspoken understanding that our fight is as much against Mercer as it is against the feelings swirling in my heart. "We need to blend in, find out what we can," he whispers, his breath warm and laced with determination. The urgency in his voice makes my heart race; the stakes are high, and there's no turning back now.

As the confrontation escalates, I spot a narrow hallway leading to what looks like an office, partially obscured by a curtain of shadows. "Let's see what Mercer's hiding," I say, my voice steady, despite the flutter of nerves in my stomach. Grant nods, and we maneuver through the crowd, ducking under tense exchanges, the energy palpable like a live wire.

Once in the hallway, we press our backs against the cool wall, momentarily shielded from the chaos outside. My heart pounds in my chest as I pull my phone from my pocket, its screen lighting up the dim space. I quickly scan for any signals—no luck. "Of course, he'd have this place rigged," I mutter, frustration bubbling just below the surface.

"Just as well," Grant replies, his voice low and conspiratorial. "No one can overhear us." He leans closer, and the proximity sends a jolt through me, igniting something that had been simmering beneath the surface. "What's the plan, genius?"

I smirk at his playful jab, even though my mind is racing with possibilities. "We find evidence. Anything that can expose Mercer for what he truly is. But we need to be quick."

With a shared nod, we glide into the office, the air thick with the scent of old leather and something acrid that I can't quite place. Papers are strewn across the desk, a chaotic testament to the man's ambitions. The faint glow of a computer screen illuminates the room, casting eerie shadows that dart across the walls.

Grant steps toward the desk, rifling through the papers with a practiced ease. "This is a treasure trove," he mutters, scanning the documents, while I keep a lookout by the door. My pulse quickens as I catch snippets of words—"illicit trades," "covert alliances," and "terms of engagement." Each phrase fuels the fire within me, igniting a fierce determination to uncover the truth.

"Look at this," Grant says, his tone suddenly serious. He holds up a printed email, the sender's name grayed out but the contents unmistakably damning. "Mercer is arranging shipments—dangerous shipments. If we can get this to the right people..." His words trail off as the weight of what we've stumbled upon settles over us like a thick fog.

Before I can respond, the sound of footsteps echoes down the hallway, heavy and deliberate. My heart races as I lock eyes with Grant. "We need to go. Now." I grab his arm, urgency pushing me forward, but he hesitates, eyes flicking to the document in his hand.

"We can't leave empty-handed," he insists, voice low and intense. "This could change everything."

A part of me understands his resolve; we're on the precipice of something monumental. Yet another part screams at me to run, to escape this web before it ensnares us completely. "We'll find more later. We have to get out before they realize we're missing."

Reluctantly, he shoves the document into his jacket pocket, and we slip back into the fray, hearts pounding in sync. The confrontation is still raging, voices rising like a cacophony of discord. We navigate the chaos, trying to blend in as much as possible, but an electric charge hangs in the air—a sense that change is coming.

Then, without warning, Mercer's voice cuts through the noise, sharper than glass. "Enough! Let's not waste time with trivial disputes. We're here to make a deal." The crowd quiets, every gaze riveted on him, their hostility momentarily quelled by the promise of his words.

I exchange a glance with Grant, tension coiling tightly between us. "We need to hear what he's proposing," I whisper, inching closer. As we move forward, I can feel the intensity of his presence beside me, a strange comfort amid the storm.

Mercer's words flow like honey, enticing and sticky. He offers power and protection, painting a picture of opportunity that makes eyes gleam with avarice. "Join me, and you will thrive. Resist, and you will be crushed beneath my heel."

I can't help but admire his charisma, a dangerous mix of charm and menace that could sway even the most stalwart hearts. As he speaks, I feel Grant's hand find mine, a small act of defiance that sends warmth racing through me.

Just as I start to believe we might witness a pivotal moment, the warehouse door slams open with a loud bang, sending a gust of wind through the space, stirring up dust and unease. A figure steps into the light, silhouetted against the darkness, and my heart drops into my stomach. The newcomer's presence sends a ripple of shock through the crowd, tension snapping like a frayed wire.

"Jonathan Mercer!" the figure calls, voice ringing out with authority. "Your time is up."

The room falls silent, every eye trained on the new arrival, and I can feel the collective breath being held. In that moment, the stakes shift yet again, the balance of power teetering precariously on the edge. The unexpected twist sends my mind racing, and I find myself wondering if the tides are about to change, if perhaps the shadows that have enveloped us might finally recede.

The air crackles with a palpable tension, a thick haze of uncertainty settling over the room like an unwelcome guest. The newcomer stands boldly in the doorway, a silhouette framed by the chaos, and as the crowd parts in a mix of awe and dread, I strain to see who it is. A flash of recognition hits me, and my breath catches in my throat. This wasn't just any outsider; it was someone I had never expected to see here—someone whose very presence could shift the tide of this dangerous game.

"Officer Lila Evans," she announces, her voice cutting through the tension like a knife through butter. She strides forward with purpose, her eyes gleaming with fierce determination. "I'm here to bring you down, Mercer. Your reign of terror ends tonight."

Whispers ripple through the room, uncertainty mixing with excitement. The air is thick with the scent of impending conflict, and I feel Grant's grip tighten around my hand, our fingers intertwined like a lifeline in a storm. "She's a cop?" he mutters, incredulous.

"More like a storm chaser," I reply, my heart racing as I study Lila's steely expression. She's not here to play nice; she's here to dismantle everything Mercer has built. "But this could get messy."

Mercer's expression shifts, the cool facade cracking just enough to reveal the chaos roiling beneath. "You think you can waltz in here and ruin my plans? You underestimate me, Officer Evans. My reach extends far beyond this room."

"I've got a few friends who would disagree," Lila retorts, her voice steady and unwavering, the authority behind it sending a thrill of hope coursing through me. "This is not just about you anymore. You've made enemies of the wrong people."

I catch Grant's gaze, the electricity between us now tinged with urgency. "We need to stay close to her. She might be our best shot," I whisper, my voice barely above a breath. He nods, the tension still palpable, but a sense of clarity settles in.

Mercer smirks, the kind of smile that feels like it belongs on a wolf. "Friends? You think they can save you? This is my territory, and you've just wandered into the lion's den."

"Funny you should mention lions," Lila replies, her tone wry, the confidence in her posture unwavering. "Because I'm more of a hunter."

The words hang in the air, heavy with the promise of confrontation, and the crowd seems to hold its collective breath, waiting for the first move. Tension thickens like a taut string, ready to snap. I can almost feel the electric buzz of adrenaline flowing through the room, igniting dormant fears and desires.

Mercer's gaze hardens, and he takes a step forward, the atmosphere shifting like a storm cloud gathering overhead. "You think this ends well for you, Lila? You're playing a dangerous game."

As if on cue, the lights flicker ominously, plunging us into a dim half-light. The whispers rise again, panic flickering in the eyes of those who have followed Mercer. I feel the pulse of fear ripple through the crowd, igniting a frantic energy that sends shivers down my spine. "We should get ready to move," I urge, my voice low but urgent.

But before we can react, Mercer pulls a sleek phone from his pocket, his expression triumphant. "I have a few surprises of my own lined up," he says, tapping furiously at the screen. "And you, my dear, are about to discover just how much power I truly wield."

The crowd shifts nervously, some eyes darting toward the exits, while others remain riveted to the unfolding drama. The lights dim further, and I catch a glimpse of shadows moving in the corners, dark figures emerging as if summoned by Mercer's call.

"Stay close," Grant murmurs, and I can feel the warmth of his body pressed against mine, a comforting anchor amid the impending storm. "Whatever happens, we're in this together."

I nod, my heart racing as I scan the room for exits, the growing sense of dread clawing at my insides. The air crackles with danger, and I can feel the shift as the crowd begins to panic, their loyalty wavering like a candle in a draft.

"Enough of this theatrics!" Lila shouts, stepping forward with defiance. "You may have your thugs, but you're outnumbered. Surrender now, and this can end without bloodshed."

Mercer's laughter echoes through the room, a chilling sound that raises the hair on the back of my neck. "You really think I'm afraid of a few uniformed wannabes? I have more than enough resources to ensure my survival."

Before anyone can react, he gestures sharply, and the shadows coalesce into menacing figures, their faces obscured but their intentions clear. A feeling of dread washes over me as they fan out, surrounding Lila and us like a pack closing in on its prey.

"Get down!" Grant yells, his voice booming over the rising chaos. Without thinking, I duck, pulling him down beside me just as shots ring out, sharp and jarring. The chaos erupts as people scream, shoving each other in a frantic scramble for safety.

I can feel the heat of the gunfire and the frantic energy of the crowd pressing against us. Grant's arm wraps protectively around my waist, shielding me as we roll to the side, seeking cover behind a toppled table. The world feels like it's moving in slow motion, each heartbeat echoing in my ears as I struggle to focus on the immediate reality.

"Is this what they meant by a 'hostile takeover'?" I quip, trying to lighten the grim atmosphere, even as adrenaline surges through my veins.

Grant glances at me, a mix of concern and admiration in his eyes. "If we survive this, I'm going to need a better sense of humor."

The noise escalates, shouting mingling with the sound of chaos, and I peer around the table, searching for a way out. Lila stands tall, directing the chaos with a fierce determination, but I can see the weight of the situation bearing down on her.

"Head for the back! We need to regroup!" she shouts, her voice cutting through the din like a beacon.

But before we can move, the door bursts open again, this time slamming into the wall with a deafening crack. A new figure steps through, and my heart drops as recognition dawns. It's someone I thought I'd never see again, someone whose presence could change everything.

"Get away from her!" the figure yells, stepping into the light, their eyes blazing with defiance.

Before I can react, the room shifts again, and the tides of conflict surge once more, leaving me breathless as I stand on the precipice of a truth I can scarcely comprehend. The weight of shadows bears down, and the reality I thought I understood unravels in an instant, leaving me teetering on the edge of a cliff, unsure of what will happen next.

Chapter 10: The Heart's Dilemma

Every corner of my apartment seemed to vibrate with the remnants of the night before, where laughter echoed and fleeting touches lingered like whispers in the air. I stood in the middle of the living room, the sun spilling through the sheer curtains, dust motes dancing lazily in the golden light. Grant's deep laughter was still a palpable memory, resonating within me, and I could almost feel the warmth of his presence wrapping around me like a favorite blanket. My heart fluttered unsteadily, caught between the exhilaration of those moments and the weight of the reality that threatened to drag me down.

I wandered over to the kitchen, where the remnants of our hasty breakfast still lay strewn across the counter—two mismatched plates, a half-empty bottle of orange juice, and a trail of crumbs from the toast I had burned in my flustered state. Every mundane detail seemed to echo the turmoil within me. I poured myself a cup of coffee, savoring the rich aroma that filled the air, a grounding comfort amid my swirling thoughts. As I stared into the dark liquid, I could see reflections of my uncertainty staring back at me. What was happening between Grant and me?

I had always prided myself on my emotional clarity, an unshakable anchor amidst the chaos of life. But now, my thoughts were a jumbled mess of longing and fear, each feeling vying for dominance. I leaned against the cool counter, heart racing, trying to piece together the fragments of the night. The way Grant's fingers had brushed against my arm while reaching for the syrup, sending a jolt through me. Or the way his gaze had lingered just a heartbeat too long, an unspoken promise hanging between us.

But then, reality would crash down like a wave of cold water. We were bound by a purpose far more significant than our burgeoning feelings. The shadow of our enemy loomed large, a sinister presence that threatened to rip us apart if we dared to let our guards down. I took a sip of coffee, wincing at the bitterness, the heat barely registering against the chill of dread creeping into my bones.

As the day wore on, the sun dipped lower in the sky, casting elongated shadows that seemed to mimic the tension coiling in my chest. My phone buzzed on the table, and I snatched it up, half-hoping it would be a message from Grant. Instead, it was just a reminder for the team meeting later. I had been trying to avoid the thought of it, knowing full well that the enemy would be a topic of discussion—plans to strategize, ways to gather intel.

But what if we had gotten it all wrong? What if our perceptions were tainted by our fears and prejudices? I bit my lip, pacing the floor as I wrestled with the thought. The tangled web of our lives had become increasingly complex, with threads of loyalty and betrayal interwoven into every decision we made. The darkness of our mission could not eclipse the light I felt around Grant, and that contradiction was a dangerous game to play.

By the time I arrived at the meeting, a storm was brewing inside me. The conference room was stark, with white walls and a polished table that reflected the fluorescent lights overhead. My colleagues filed in, their faces etched with concern, and I felt my heart race as I scanned the room for him. Grant was leaning against the far wall, arms crossed, a knowing smile playing on his lips when our eyes met. Just seeing him sent a shiver down my spine, igniting every nerve in my body, and I fought the urge to rush to his side.

"Let's get started," our team leader said, a frown marring her features. The atmosphere felt heavy, and I could sense the tension rippling through the group as we delved into the agenda. Reports of our enemy's movements had increased, and we needed a plan that would not only protect us but also allow us to get closer to the truth.

"Maybe we should consider a diversion," Grant suggested, his voice cutting through the tension. "Draw them out instead of waiting for them to make the first move." His gaze flicked to me, a spark of something—hope?—shining in his eyes.

"Or we could reinforce our current position and wait," another team member countered, skepticism etched on her face. "Rushing in blindly is a recipe for disaster."

The conversation spiraled into a heated debate, opinions flying around the room like errant arrows, each one aimed at finding the truth. But the more we discussed our strategy, the more I felt the weight of my own indecision. I wanted to fight, to contribute, but the closer I got to the heart of our enemy, the more my own heart ached with fear.

Finally, the conversation shifted to a point where I could no longer contain myself. "What if we're not looking at this from the right angle?" I blurted out, the words spilling forth like a dam breaking. The room fell silent, all eyes on me, and I felt my cheeks flush under their scrutiny. "What if our enemy isn't just a threat we can strategize against? What if there are layers we haven't even considered?"

Grant met my gaze, his expression a mixture of surprise and admiration, and for a fleeting moment, the chaos around us faded. It was just the two of us, connected by an invisible thread that seemed to pulse with unacknowledged possibilities. But then reality crashed back in, heavy and suffocating, as murmurs of confusion rippled through the group.

The meeting ended in a haze of unresolved tension, and as we filed out, I found myself walking beside Grant. The air between us was charged, a potent mix of unresolved emotions and lingering doubts. "You had a point," he said, his voice low, tinged with respect. "Maybe we're letting our fears cloud our judgment."

I nodded, the truth of his words settling over me like a soft blanket. But even as I felt the warmth of his presence beside me, the nagging fear gnawed at my insides. I wanted to delve deeper, to explore what lay beneath the surface of our interactions, yet the risk was immense. Just as I gathered my thoughts to respond, the lights flickered ominously overhead, plunging us into a momentary darkness that felt like a metaphor for everything I feared.

The flickering light ignited a spark of uncertainty, a reminder that shadows could conceal more than mere doubts. And as we stepped into the unknown, I couldn't shake the feeling that our hearts were on a collision course, a heart's dilemma fraught with the potential for love and the peril of loss.

The following morning, the sun poured in with a relentless brightness, illuminating every corner of my apartment, as if trying to highlight the turmoil swirling within me. I stumbled into the kitchen, still half-asleep, my mind caught in a web of confusion and longing. The coffee maker gurgled and sputtered, a comforting backdrop to my chaotic thoughts. I poured myself a cup, the rich aroma momentarily distracting me from the reality that awaited. Today was a day for clarity, I told myself, though my heart had other ideas.

Outside, the city hummed with life, the sounds of morning traffic blending with distant laughter and the occasional bark of a dog. I let the noises wash over me, a reminder that the world kept spinning, regardless of the storms raging in my heart. Grant had been my anchor, yet every glance we exchanged during yesterday's meeting felt like it could either tether me to him or drag me under. I took a tentative sip of coffee, hoping it would ground me, but instead, it seemed to ignite a storm of thoughts.

"Hey, coffee addict," Grant's voice broke through my reverie, rich and warm like the drink in my hand. I turned to find him leaning against the doorframe, an easy grin stretching across his face, as if he'd just stepped out of a magazine shoot rather than my chaotic kitchen. The sight of him sent a jolt of recognition through me, a reminder that beneath the layers of tension and uncertainty, something genuine flickered between us.

"Don't you have a job?" I shot back, attempting to inject levity into the moment while my heart raced. "I mean, do you really think it's appropriate to just waltz into my space uninvited?" The words slipped out before I could think better of them, a playful challenge that hinted at the chemistry we shared.

He shrugged, his casual confidence radiating. "Thought I'd check in on my favorite coffee connoisseur. Besides, someone has to make sure you're not burning down the kitchen." His eyes sparkled with mischief, and I couldn't help but laugh, the tension in my chest easing just a fraction.

"Touché," I replied, rolling my eyes, but the flutter of warmth in my stomach betrayed my amusement. We fell into a comfortable banter, our exchanges tinged with the underlying tension that had defined our interactions recently. As we settled into a rhythm, it became apparent that we were playing a game, each of us trying to navigate the uncharted waters of our relationship while cloaked in humor and lightheartedness.

"So, what's the plan for today?" he asked, leaning closer as if sharing a secret. The warmth of his proximity sent a shiver down my spine, igniting a fire that simmered just beneath the surface.

"Maybe I'll bake cookies," I offered, half-joking. "You know, something sweet to balance out all this tension." I gestured vaguely around the kitchen, where my anxiety hung like an unwelcome guest.

"Cookies, huh? That sounds dangerously tempting. What flavor?" His playful tone was laced with sincerity, and I felt my cheeks flush.

"Chocolate chip, of course. It's classic for a reason," I replied, a smile creeping onto my lips. "What about you? Are you just going to stand there and look pretty, or are you planning to help?"

"I can't resist a challenge," he said, a hint of mischief lighting up his eyes. "Count me in."

We set to work, our movements synchronizing like a well-rehearsed dance. The kitchen filled with laughter as we measured and mixed, flour dusting the countertops like a light snowfall. I tossed him a playful smirk when he nearly dropped the bag of chocolate chips, a moment that felt so ordinary yet utterly profound in its simplicity.

"How is it," I began, stirring the dough with fervor, "that we can strategize against an enemy with calculated precision but can't seem to make cookies without nearly creating a disaster?"

He leaned against the counter, arms crossed, an amused expression on his face. "Maybe the stakes are too high. The cookies could change everything." His voice dripped with mock seriousness, and I couldn't help but chuckle.

"Right, because cookies have the power to change our fates," I said, rolling my eyes but relishing the lightness of our conversation. "Next, you'll be telling me that chocolate is the key to world peace."

"I mean, have you tasted it?" He feigned incredulity, and I felt a surge of affection for this man who had somehow slipped past my defenses, igniting a spark I didn't know I was capable of feeling.

The warmth of the kitchen enveloped us, but as the dough began to take shape, my mind drifted back to the reality we were trying to escape. The dark clouds of our situation loomed large, threatening to engulf us both. Just as I was about to voice my thoughts, the shrill sound of my phone cut through the atmosphere like a knife, shattering the moment.

I glanced at the screen, my heart sinking as I read the message. It was from our team leader, a call to action that I could no longer ignore. I hesitated, looking back at Grant, who was watching me with an intensity that made my heart race.

"What is it?" he asked, his tone shifting from playful to serious.

"Just a reminder about the mission briefing," I replied, trying to keep my voice steady, but the words felt like stones lodged in my throat. "I think we should... I should..." I trailed off, uncertain.

"Are you okay?" He stepped closer, his gaze searching mine, and I could see the concern etched into his features, the way his brow furrowed slightly.

"I just don't know how to balance this—" I gestured between us, feeling the tension pull tight like a bowstring. "The mission and this... whatever this is between us."

He nodded, understanding washing over his face. "I get it. But maybe we don't have to choose. What if we can focus on both?"

I took a deep breath, appreciating his optimism, yet dread coiled in my stomach. "It's not that simple, Grant. If we don't keep our heads in the game, we could lose everything."

"Or maybe we'll find something worth fighting for," he said softly, his words lingering in the air like the sweet scent of cookies baking in the oven.

Just then, the oven timer dinged, and I jumped, the sound jarring me from my thoughts. "Cookies!" I exclaimed, rushing over to the oven, my heart racing not just from the adrenaline of the moment but from the intensity of our conversation.

Grant watched as I carefully pulled the tray from the oven, the warm scent enveloping us like a comforting embrace. "See?" he said, a hint of triumph in his voice. "Sometimes you have to take a risk for something sweet."

I looked at the perfectly golden cookies, a moment of clarity piercing through the haze of uncertainty. Maybe he was right; maybe it didn't have to be an either-or situation. With the sweet aroma surrounding us, I realized that perhaps the balance between duty and desire was something we could navigate together, as long as we didn't lose sight of what truly mattered.

"Let's take these to the meeting," I said, the idea forming in my mind like the cookies baking in the oven. "Maybe we can sweeten the mood a bit."

Grant's eyes sparkled with enthusiasm. "Now that's a plan I can get behind."

As we shared a conspiratorial smile, the walls of anxiety I'd been erecting began to crumble, the prospect of facing the storm ahead feeling just a little less daunting with him by my side. With the weight of our unspoken connection lingering in the air, I felt a surge of hope, even as the shadows of our situation loomed large. The journey ahead would be fraught with challenges, but for the first time, I didn't feel like I was facing them alone.

The meeting room buzzed with energy, a mixture of anxiety and determination filling the air. As we walked in, the tray of freshly baked cookies felt like a delicious distraction, the warm scent a balm for the tension that hung over us like a storm cloud. Grant and I exchanged conspiratorial smiles, and I could sense the spark of something burgeoning between us, igniting the air.

"Cookies?" our team leader raised an eyebrow, glancing at the tray as if it were a peace offering amidst an impending war. "Is this your secret strategy to win us over?"

"Absolutely," I quipped, setting the tray down on the conference table with a flourish. "Sugar and chocolate chips—what better way to soften the harsh realities we're facing?"

As the team gathered around, taking their share of the cookies, the atmosphere shifted ever so slightly, laughter threading through the discussions about our enemy's latest movements. I watched as Grant engaged with the others, his charm effortlessly lighting up the room. Yet, beneath the laughter, my heart raced with the weight of our situation. I couldn't shake the feeling that each moment of levity was borrowed time.

"Alright, team, let's focus," our leader said, her tone serious as she outlined the new intel. "We've received reports that our enemy is making moves in the eastern sector. We need to strategize our next steps."

I settled into my seat, the sweet taste of chocolate lingering on my tongue but quickly overshadowed by the looming shadows of our mission. Every detail seemed to ripple with significance, but amid the strategic chatter, my mind wandered to Grant. He leaned forward, engaged, his brow furrowed in concentration, and I could see the determination etched into his features.

"Grant, what do you think?" our leader prompted, pulling me back into the present.

He glanced up, his hazel eyes meeting mine for a fleeting moment before he spoke. "I think we need to consider a two-pronged approach. While we gather intelligence, we can create a diversion to draw their attention away from our main target."

"Risky," another team member chimed in. "Diverting resources could backfire."

"Or it could provide the opening we need," Grant countered, his voice steady and confident. "We have to take calculated risks if we want to get ahead."

As the debate unfolded, I felt a rush of pride swell within me. Grant was captivating in his conviction, and I could sense a shift in the room as others began to rally behind his suggestion. My heart swelled with affection, but the underlying fear clawed at me. Every strategic move brought us closer to danger, and I feared what might happen if our enemy caught wind of our plans.

By the time the meeting concluded, I felt drained yet energized, a conflicting whirlwind of emotions surging through me. Grant stepped closer as the others filtered out, his presence a comforting weight beside me. "You did great in there," he said, a genuine smile breaking across his face.

"Thanks, but you're the one who had everyone wrapped around your finger," I replied, trying to keep the conversation light even as my heart raced with unspoken words.

"We make a good team," he said, his gaze steady, searching. "And we could be even better if we let ourselves explore...this." He gestured between us, a hint of vulnerability peeking through the confidence.

"Yeah, but what if—" I began, but he interrupted, his expression earnest.

"What if we could figure it out together? We're already navigating this mission side by side; why not see where it leads us?"

The weight of his suggestion hung in the air, electric and terrifying. I wanted to grasp at the promise of what could be, but the shadows of doubt loomed larger. "I just don't want to lose focus. Our mission is paramount."

He took a step closer, his voice dropping to a whisper. "And what if our connection makes us stronger? What if it's the very thing that keeps us grounded in all this chaos?"

I hesitated, my heart pounding with the tantalizing possibility of exploring something real with him. But the truth clawed at me, reminding me of the looming danger that could tear us apart. Just as I opened my mouth to respond, my phone buzzed insistently in my pocket, interrupting the moment.

I pulled it out, my stomach dropping as I read the message. "We need to meet. Urgent." It was from one of our field agents, and the urgency in the words sent a chill through me.

"Everything okay?" Grant asked, concern flickering in his eyes.

"It's from the team," I said, feeling a knot tighten in my stomach. "They need us to meet immediately."

"Let's go," he said, determination flickering in his gaze. We hurried out, the camaraderie of our previous moments fading, replaced by the weight of the unknown that awaited us.

As we entered the briefing room, the atmosphere was tense, the air thick with unspoken fears and unresolved tensions. Our field agent stood at the front, his face pale as he addressed the group. "We've got a problem. We received intel that the enemy is onto us. They've started targeting our positions, and we need to act fast."

A murmur of concern rippled through the group, but I felt my focus sharpen. I glanced at Grant, who met my gaze with a determined nod. "What do we know?" he asked, his tone steady as he pushed back against the tide of anxiety.

"Not much," the agent replied. "But we've identified a potential mole within our ranks. Someone is feeding them information."

The revelation hit me like a slap to the face, my mind racing with possibilities. "What do we do?" I asked, my voice steady even as my heart raced.

"We need to figure out who we can trust," the agent said, scanning the room. "And we need to do it fast. If we don't cut this off at the source, everything we've worked for could be in jeopardy."

A ripple of shock washed over us, and as I exchanged glances with Grant, a chill settled deep within me. The enemy wasn't just an external threat; it was lurking among us, waiting to strike when we least expected it.

"What if it's someone close to us?" I blurted out, my thoughts spiraling. The very idea made my skin crawl.

"We have to be vigilant," Grant replied, his voice firm but his expression betraying a flicker of fear. "We'll figure this out together."

As we strategized, I felt the tension in the room increase, each suggestion weighed against the very real possibility of betrayal. The stakes were rising, and with every passing moment, the darkness closed in tighter around us.

As the meeting wrapped up, a sense of urgency gripped me. The team dispersed, but Grant lingered by my side, concern etched across his face. "We need to watch our backs," he said softly, the gravity of our situation settling heavily between us.

"I know," I replied, feeling the weight of the world on my shoulders. "But how can we trust anyone if there's a traitor among us?"

He reached for my hand, a grounding gesture amidst the chaos. "We'll find a way," he said, determination shining in his eyes. "We just have to stay one step ahead."

Just then, the lights flickered ominously overhead, plunging the room into momentary darkness. A collective gasp filled the air, followed by the frantic flickering of fluorescent bulbs. Heart racing, I grasped Grant's hand tighter, a reflex born of instinct and fear.

When the lights returned, a deafening explosion echoed outside, rattling the windows and sending a jolt of panic through the room. I stumbled back, the ground shaking beneath me, my mind racing with the realization that our worst fears had just become reality. The enemy was here, and we were standing in the eye of the storm.

As chaos erupted around us, I met Grant's gaze, the intensity of the moment forging a connection deeper than any words could express. "We have to move," I shouted, adrenaline surging through me, propelling us forward as the world around us crumbled.

But just as we reached the door, a shadowy figure emerged from the chaos, blocking our escape. My heart raced as I recognized the familiar face, the betrayal etched in their eyes, leaving me frozen in place as the truth crashed over me like a tidal wave. The enemy had infiltrated our ranks, and everything I thought I knew was about to unravel.

Chapter 11: The Approach of Darkness

The wind whispered through the trees, a soft rustle that seemed to echo my own mounting unease. I laced up my running shoes with a mix of determination and dread, my heart thrumming like a restless bird against the cage of my ribs. The cool evening air brushed my skin, invigorating yet chilling, reminding me that the world was a tangle of shadows as the sun dipped below the horizon. Each step outside felt like an invitation to the unknown, and as I ventured into the twilight, the creeping sensation of being watched settled over me like an unwelcome shroud.

My nightly runs had always been my sanctuary, a chance to escape the chaos of my thoughts and the mounting pressure of my responsibilities. I could lose myself in the rhythm of my feet pounding against the pavement, the familiar path stretching ahead like a promise of freedom. But now, with every echoing footfall, I felt an unsettling presence lurking in the periphery, just out of sight but ever so palpable. It was as if the darkness had teeth, ready to bite into my solitude and drag me into its depths.

Grant, with his quiet intensity and unwavering support, sensed my anxiety like a well-tuned instrument. He had become a steadfast companion on my runs, insisting on joining me in the evenings after the sun had retreated completely. I welcomed his presence, the solidity of his form next to mine a balm against the unease that gnawed at my insides. Together, we raced through the dusky streets, our breaths mingling in the crisp air, the sound of our footfalls harmonizing in an oddly comforting cadence.

"Do you ever think about what's out there?" I asked one night, my voice barely a whisper as we navigated a particularly dark stretch of road. The streetlights flickered above us, casting long, dancing shadows that felt like hands reaching out to pull us into the abyss.

Grant's response was measured, his gaze fixed ahead as if searching for answers in the night. "You mean besides the usual suspects—ghosts, monsters, and the occasional raccoon?" His half-smile was teasing, a light spark in the growing darkness.

I chuckled softly, grateful for his humor even as my heart raced with unease. "Right, because that's all we need—an army of raccoons plotting world domination."

His laughter warmed the air between us, but it quickly faded as we continued running, the silence settling back around us like an unwelcome blanket. We pushed ourselves harder, the adrenaline sharpening our senses, making us acutely aware of the slightest rustle in the bushes or the distant hoot of an owl. With each run, our connection deepened, a tangible thread weaving between our shared breaths and unspoken fears.

The nights were becoming increasingly fraught, though, with every run filled with an inexplicable tension. I was haunted by late-night phone calls—muffled voices on the other end, hang-ups before I could respond. Shadows flitted through my peripheral vision when I was home, a fleeting suggestion of movement that sent my heart into a frantic dance. Each time I turned to face the nothingness, I was met with silence, yet the sensation of being watched clung to me, a persistent ghost that refused to let go.

"Let's change the route," Grant suggested one evening, his brow furrowed in that endearing way that made him seem both fierce and protective. "We could try the park instead. It's busier."

"Sure, let's do that," I agreed, although I couldn't shake the feeling that it wouldn't matter. The shadows could be anywhere, lurking in the spaces where the light failed to penetrate, waiting for the moment to pounce.

As we ventured into the park, the sounds of laughter and the chatter of other runners filled the air, a refreshing change from the oppressive silence of the streets. Families picnicked on the grass, their happiness a stark contrast to the weight I carried in my chest. Yet, even among the throng of people, my instincts screamed at me that something wasn't right. The laughter felt too bright, the lights too vivid, as if they were a façade hiding darker truths just beneath the surface.

"Are you okay?" Grant's voice cut through my swirling thoughts, his eyes searching mine with an intensity that sent a thrill of warmth through my veins. "You've been quiet."

"Just thinking," I murmured, trying to sound nonchalant. "About how people can seem so carefree while..." I trailed off, not wanting to burden him with my spiraling fears.

"While the world outside our bubble is a mess?" he finished for me, his expression softening. "I get it. It's hard to keep running when the shadows loom large."

I met his gaze, feeling a surge of gratitude for his understanding. "It is hard. But I can't let it stop me. I won't."

He nodded, his determination mirroring mine. "We'll face it together. Just know that you're not alone in this. I've got your back."

We fell into a comfortable silence, the park lights illuminating our path as we rounded a bend. Yet, in that quiet, I felt an unmistakable chill—the hairs on the back of my neck prickled, and I turned to see a figure watching us from the edge of the trees. My breath caught in my throat, and for a fleeting moment, I wondered if the shadows had finally come to claim me.

The figure stood at the edge of the trees, silhouetted against the soft glow of the park lights. It was just a dark shadow, but it sent a shiver racing down my spine. My heart pounded a frenetic rhythm, each beat echoing in my ears like a warning bell. I instinctively took a step closer to Grant, his presence grounding me as fear swirled in my gut like a tempest.

"Did you see that?" I whispered, nodding toward the looming shadow. The laughter and chatter of the park faded into a distant murmur, swallowed by the sudden tension that thickened the air around us.

Grant squinted into the darkness, his jaw tightening. "Yeah, I did. Let's keep moving."

We picked up our pace, but I could feel my breath hitching in my throat, the earlier adrenaline morphing into something more primal. I didn't want to look back, but curiosity gnawed at me, a dark little worm burrowing deeper into my thoughts. What if the figure was someone I knew, a friend playing a prank? Or worse, what if it wasn't? My mind spiraled, conjuring images of lurking threats and sinister plots.

As we rounded a bend, I finally dared to glance over my shoulder, half-expecting to see the figure following us. The trees stood stoic, their branches rustling in the night breeze, but there was no one there. Just a deceptive stillness that felt somehow charged, like the silence before a storm.

"I think we should go back," I suggested, my voice shaky, almost a plea.

"Just a little further," Grant replied, his tone calm yet insistent. "Let's finish our loop and then we'll head home. Together."

I wanted to argue, to demand we turn back right then and there, but his confidence was like an anchor, keeping me steady in the rising tide of my panic. I nodded, forcing myself to breathe, counting each inhalation as we pressed on, the cool air stinging my lungs.

We continued our run, the rhythm of our feet hitting the pavement a steady metronome against the quiet. I focused on the sound, willing it to drown out my fears, but the feeling of being watched persisted, a gnawing itch between my shoulder blades. The park, once a sanctuary, had transformed into a maze of shadows and unspoken threats.

"Let's sprint the last stretch," Grant announced, his eyes alight with a challenge. He took off ahead of me, and for a moment, I was caught off guard by the sudden surge of energy in him. My competitive spirit ignited, and I sprinted after him, feeling the wind whip through my hair as I pushed myself harder.

We flew down the path, laughter bubbling up between gasps of breath, but just as quickly as it had come, my joy faded. My instincts screamed at me again, a piercing alarm that resonated deep within. I glanced over my shoulder once more, and there, just at the edge of the trees, the shadow reappeared, closer this time, creeping toward the light like a hungry predator stalking its prey.

"Grant!" I shouted, panic lacing my voice.

He turned, his expression shifting from playful to serious in an instant. "What? What is it?"

"There's someone behind us!" I pointed, my heart racing faster than my feet had moments before.

But as he turned, the figure melted back into the darkness, as if it had never been there at all. "I don't see anyone," he said slowly, uncertainty creeping into his tone. "Maybe it was just a trick of the light."

"No," I insisted, my voice rising with urgency. "I felt it. I know I'm not imagining this."

His brow furrowed, concern etching deeper lines on his face. "Alright, let's get to the car. I'll walk you home."

We resumed our pace, but it felt different now—each step more laden with fear. The moonlight bathed the path in an eerie glow, and I couldn't shake the sense that the darkness was alive, waiting for just the right moment to pounce. The last thing I wanted was to show Grant how rattled I was, but my skin prickled with the weight of unseen eyes.

"I'm sorry," I said as we jogged, the words tumbling out before I could stop them. "I didn't mean to freak out. It's just... everything has been so overwhelming lately."

He glanced at me, his expression softening. "You're allowed to feel that way. It's a lot to handle. We're in a dangerous situation, and it's okay to be scared. You don't have to pretend with me."

A warmth spread through me at his understanding. "Thanks. It's just hard to admit I'm scared. I hate feeling vulnerable."

"That's the first step to being brave," he replied, his voice steady and reassuring. "Facing what scares you. You're not alone in this."

We arrived at my car, the old sedan a beacon of familiarity amidst the encroaching night. I fumbled with my keys, my fingers trembling slightly as I tried to unlock the door. Grant stood close, his presence a protective shield against the suffocating darkness.

Just as I swung the door open, a sharp sound cut through the night—a rustling from the nearby bushes, followed by a low, guttural growl that made my stomach drop. My heart thudded in my chest, and I froze, the key dangling from my fingers.

"Stay behind me," Grant instructed, stepping closer, his body a solid barrier between me and the source of the sound.

"What is it?" I whispered, my voice barely audible over the pounding of my heart.

"Just stay quiet," he said, his gaze locked on the shadows.

Suddenly, a figure lunged from the underbrush, not a monstrous creature but a scraggly dog, ribs protruding beneath its matted fur. It barked once, a desperate sound that echoed the fear I felt inside. Relief flooded through me, but it was quickly overshadowed by a fresh wave of tension as I realized how close the darkness had come, how easily fear could take shape in the form of a nightmare.

Grant relaxed slightly, crouching down to approach the dog, his movements slow and deliberate. "Hey there, buddy," he murmured, coaxing the animal closer with a gentle tone. The dog seemed wary but curious, its eyes darting between Grant and me. "You look like you need a friend."

As he reached out a hand, I felt a warmth bloom in my chest, seeing his kindness in action, a reminder that not all shadows held malice. I stepped forward cautiously, the tension in my shoulders easing slightly. "What do you think? Should we take him home?"

Grant chuckled softly, the sound a balm against the lingering dread. "You really want to add a stray dog to your chaotic life right now?"

"Why not? I could use a distraction," I said, a grin breaking through my earlier tension.

"Alright, but only if he can keep up with our runs," he replied, eyes twinkling.

The dog, sensing the shift in the air, stepped forward, tail wagging tentatively, as if he understood that this could be a new beginning. I couldn't help but smile, the warmth of Grant's presence and the promise of companionship weaving a fragile thread of hope in the dark. Even as shadows lurked, this moment felt like a small victory—a reminder that light could still find its way through the cracks.

The scruffy dog stepped closer, its tail wagging with cautious optimism. It was a small creature, scrappy and thin, but there was an undeniable spark in its eyes that hinted at resilience. As I crouched to meet its gaze, I felt an unexpected warmth blooming within me, a flicker of hope amidst the darkness that had begun to suffocate my spirit.

"Looks like we've got ourselves a new running buddy," I said, a teasing lilt in my voice. Grant chuckled, clearly amused by my enthusiasm.

"Only if he can handle the pace. I'm not slowing down for anyone, even if he has the world's saddest eyes," he replied, a mock-seriousness creeping into his tone.

The dog cocked its head, as if considering this challenge. It seemed to sense the lightness in our conversation, and for a moment, the weight of the shadows that clung to me lifted, even if just a little.

"Alright, pup, let's give you a name," I said, tapping my chin thoughtfully. "What do you think about 'Shadow'? You know, for all the company you keep?"

Grant raised an eyebrow, a smirk tugging at the corner of his mouth. "A little on the nose, don't you think? How about something with a bit more flair? Like 'Mystery'?"

"Mystery, huh? I like it." I stood, offering the dog my hand. "What do you think, Mystery? Ready to join the chaos?"

Mystery bounded forward, licking my fingers and wagging its tail even harder. The moment felt pure, a small slice of joy in an otherwise tumultuous world.

We headed back to my car, the night still alive with sounds—the rustling of leaves, the distant laughter of families, and the soft padding of our feet on the pavement. With Mystery now settled into the back seat, I felt an odd sense of normalcy wash over me. As we drove, I glanced in the rearview mirror, catching a glimpse of the scruffy dog as it curled into a tight ball, its little body shivering from the chill in the air.

"Think he'll be alright?" I asked, my voice breaking the silence, but not my resolve.

"Absolutely," Grant said, his tone reassuring. "A little warmth and food, and he'll be ready to conquer the world—or at least keep up with your running."

The banter continued, a soothing balm for my nerves, but as we pulled into my driveway, the sensation of unease returned, wrapping itself around me like a thick fog. I parked and turned off the engine, the sudden silence amplifying the shadows that crept along the edges of my yard.

"Do you want me to come in with you?" Grant asked, his concern evident.

I hesitated. My instinct was to welcome him inside, to have that familiar warmth beside me. But the thought of the strange phone calls, the feeling of being watched—everything swirled in my mind like an unsettling cocktail. "I'll be okay. It's just a little late, and I don't want to impose."

His expression shifted, something deeper flashing behind his eyes. "You're not imposing. I just... I'd feel better if I knew you were safe."

My heart softened at his concern, the warmth between us palpable in the cool night air. "I appreciate that. I really do. But I promise I'll be fine. If something feels off, I'll call you."

"Alright. Just... be careful."

With a nod, I opened the car door, and as I stepped out, the door swung shut behind me with a soft thud that echoed in the night. I waved goodbye to Grant, watching him drive away, the taillights fading into the distance until they vanished entirely.

The house loomed before me, shadows gathering like a hushed audience, waiting for the show to begin. I took a deep breath, summoning my courage as I walked up the path. As I stepped inside, the familiar creak of the floorboards greeted me, but the atmosphere felt different—thick with unspoken tension.

I flicked on the lights, illuminating the cozy space filled with mismatched furniture and half-unpacked boxes. The comforting chaos of my life offered little solace against the creeping dread. I dropped my keys into the bowl by the door and stood still for a moment, scanning the room for anything amiss. The night felt heavier than it should have, the stillness unsettling.

After a few minutes of settling in, I grabbed a blanket and curled up on the couch, turning on the TV in a bid to drown out the silence. But as the screen flickered to life, I couldn't shake the feeling that the walls were closing in around me. The chatter of the news anchor buzzed in the background, but I couldn't focus, my thoughts spiraling back to that lurking shadow in the park.

Then, just as I began to let the warm glow of the television soothe my nerves, my phone buzzed violently on the coffee table, a shrill sound that made me jump. I reached for it, my heart pounding in anticipation of an unknown caller. The number flashed across the screen, one I didn't recognize. Hesitantly, I swiped to answer, my voice steady despite the turmoil inside.

"Hello?"

Static crackled on the line, and for a moment, I thought the call might be a mistake, some misdialed number. Then a voice emerged, low and distorted, as if coming from the depths of a dark abyss.

"Stop looking. You're in over your head."

The words sent a jolt of cold fear racing through my veins. I opened my mouth to respond, but the line went dead, the call abruptly severed as if cut by a knife. My heart thundered in my chest, and I dropped the phone as if it had burned me.

Everything—the strange figure, the unsettling calls, the whispers of danger—flashed in my mind, intertwining like a web I couldn't escape. I stumbled back, pressing myself against the couch as the reality of my situation crystallized in a chilling moment of clarity.

Someone was watching. Someone knew.

I had stepped too far into the dark, and now the darkness was closing in, ready to consume everything I held dear.

Chapter 12: Tangled Paths

A chill swept through the damp air as we approached the warehouse, its weathered facade a grim reminder of neglect and betrayal. The once-vibrant blue paint was now a ghostly hue, peeling like the memories hidden within. I could almost hear the sigh of the structure, as if it held its breath, waiting for the stories it had buried to emerge. Grant walked beside me, his presence both an anchor and a tempest, each step stirring the tension simmering just beneath the surface.

"Are you sure this is the right place?" I asked, my voice a hushed whisper, barely audible over the distant rumble of traffic. It felt odd to be on the fringes of civilization, where streetlights flickered like dying stars, casting long shadows that danced with the wind.

"Unless the intel was wrong, this is where we find the missing pieces." Grant's gaze was locked on the rusted door, its hinges sagging with age. I could see the determination etched across his features, the sharp angles of his jaw set in a firm line that spoke volumes about his resolve.

"Right, the missing pieces," I muttered under my breath, recalling the web of secrets that had brought us to this moment. This wasn't just a hunt for answers; it was a plunge into the dark abyss of our pasts. A past that, unbeknownst to me, was tangled with his in ways I had yet to fully comprehend.

We pushed through the door, its creaking protest echoing in the silence that engulfed us. Inside, the air was thick with dust and the scent of forgotten memories, mingling with the faintest hint of mildew. Sunlight filtered through shattered windows, illuminating motes that danced like lost souls seeking escape.

"Stick close," Grant instructed, his tone more authoritative than I liked. The flicker of irritation flared in me, but I swallowed it down.

It was hard to ignore the way his presence loomed, an undeniable force that both thrilled and annoyed me.

"Believe me, I've got no intention of getting lost in this nightmare," I replied, my voice laced with bravado. "You can keep your gallant rescues for someone else."

He shot me a sidelong glance, a hint of amusement playing at the corners of his mouth. "Trust me, you'd want my gallant rescue if things go south."

The air crackled with a mixture of unspoken words and the tension that had begun to define our relationship. I had never imagined that hunting for answers could feel like a slow dance on the edge of a knife, but here we were, bound together by our shared mission and the weight of our unsaid feelings.

As we ventured deeper into the cavernous space, the shadows swallowed us whole. The echoes of our footsteps were swallowed by the crumbling walls, leaving an oppressive silence that felt more ominous with every step. I couldn't shake the sensation that we were not alone. A cold sweat prickled my skin as we moved past rusted machinery and remnants of a bygone era, the stories of which seemed to whisper through the dust-laden air.

"Over here," Grant called, breaking the stillness. He had found a set of crates, their edges splintered and worn, each one teeming with potential secrets. My heart raced as I rushed to his side, the thrill of discovery igniting a fire within me. We pried open the nearest crate, revealing a cache of documents, faded and yellowed with age.

"This is it," I breathed, the weight of our quest pressing down like a leaden blanket. As we rifled through the papers, I felt the intensity of Grant's focus, his fingers brushing against mine in an electrifying touch that sent shockwaves through me.

"Do you realize what this could mean?" he asked, his eyes wide with revelation. "If we connect these dots, we could expose everything."

"Yeah, or land ourselves in even more trouble," I replied, a sudden flash of caution puncturing my excitement. The world we were tangled in was fraught with danger, and every discovery could lead us closer to enemies lurking in the shadows.

Before I could dwell on the implications, the sound of footsteps echoed from the far end of the warehouse. The air thickened with tension, and instinct kicked in. "We need to move, now!"

Adrenaline surged through me as we shoved the papers back into the crate, our earlier camaraderie evaporating into instinctual survival. We ducked behind a stack of crates, hearts pounding in unison, the urgency of our predicament tightening the space between us.

"Do you think they saw us?" Grant whispered, his breath warm against my ear. I shivered involuntarily at the closeness, my heart racing for reasons beyond mere fear.

"I don't know," I replied, forcing my voice steady, "but we can't stick around to find out."

In the dim light, the figures emerged from the shadows, cloaked in menace and purpose. My stomach twisted as I took in their silhouettes, sharp and defined against the glow of the scattered beams of sunlight. It was as if the past had manifested in flesh, the shadows taking form to confront us.

"Time to go," Grant urged, his hand brushing against my back, urging me forward. In that moment, the world narrowed to just the two of us and the shared desperation coursing through our veins. We raced toward the nearest exit, the shadows pursuing us, relentless and hungry.

The rush of adrenaline made every sense sharpen. I felt alive, acutely aware of every heartbeat, every breath, and every fleeting thought. As we navigated through the maze of crates, the whispers of secrets beckoned from every corner, but survival was the only thought that consumed me now.

A sharp gasp escaped me as a figure lunged from the darkness, and instinctively, I reached for Grant, our fingers intertwining like vines clinging to life. The sensation sparked something deep within, a realization that in this chaotic dance of survival, our unacknowledged feelings were laid bare, raw and undeniable.

"Stay close," he shouted, determination etched on his face as we moved as one, fighting against the tide of uncertainty. In that moment, I realized that whatever lay ahead, we were no longer just two individuals caught in a web of mistrust and hidden desires. We were allies, bound by the chaos that swirled around us, and perhaps, just perhaps, the paths we were tangled in might lead to something greater than mere survival.

The chaos swirled around us, a tempest of shadows and uncertainty as we darted through the labyrinth of crates. The urgency in Grant's voice snapped me back to the present, and I felt the unmistakable pull of adrenaline coursing through my veins, sharpening my senses. Every sound echoed ominously, the creaking of metal and the scuffle of feet signaling that the figures were gaining on us. It was a race against time, and I was determined not to be caught.

"Left!" Grant shouted, grabbing my wrist and pulling me to the side just as a figure lunged toward us from the gloom. The unexpected force of his grip sent a jolt through me, an electric current that both thrilled and terrified. I barely had time to think before I was whisked through a narrow gap between crates, my heart pounding wildly.

"Is this your idea of a cozy escape?" I shot back, trying to infuse levity into our desperate situation. The tension crackled between us, the thrill of the chase amplifying every fleeting touch and exchanged glance.

"Honestly, I'm just trying to keep us alive," he replied, a grin flashing across his face that did little to quell the racing of my heart. "But if you have better suggestions, I'm all ears."

I rolled my eyes, but the tension gave way to a reluctant chuckle. "Next time, maybe try a nice café instead?"

"Noted," he said, pushing through a stack of crates as we barreled deeper into the warehouse. The flickering lights above cast erratic shadows that seemed to dance with malicious glee, echoing the chaos swirling within me. I could feel the weight of our predicament pressing down, but somehow, the banter softened the edges of fear, weaving an unexpected thread of connection between us.

Ahead, I spotted a door partially ajar, a sliver of hope amid the dark. "There!" I pointed, urging him forward. But just as we approached, the air shifted, and from the corner of my eye, I spotted two figures emerging from the shadows, their movements purposeful and deliberate.

"Go! Now!" Grant's voice cut through the air, and without a moment's hesitation, I surged toward the door, my heart racing faster than my feet could carry me.

We burst through the doorway into an adjacent room, a stark contrast to the chaos we'd just left. Sunlight streamed through cracked windows, illuminating dust motes swirling in the air. It felt almost surreal, a calm after the storm that made my heart ache with uncertainty.

"Are we safe?" I asked, panting as we pressed ourselves against the wall, hearts still pounding like war drums.

"For now," Grant replied, his brow furrowed as he peered through the glass. "But we need to keep moving." His voice was steady, but I could sense the tension lurking beneath the surface, like a taut string ready to snap.

"Do you think they'll find us?" I could barely keep the tremor out of my voice. The weight of the unknown pressed down on me, and I hated that I felt vulnerable.

"Let's just say they're not exactly the friendly type," he replied, scanning the area for any signs of danger. "But I won't let them catch you. I promise."

His earnest gaze held mine for a heartbeat longer, the air thick with unspoken words that lingered like smoke in the aftermath of a fire. I felt the warmth of his promise enveloping me, an anchor in the storm of uncertainty.

With a deep breath, I shook off the moment's intensity. "So, what's the plan, Captain Hero?"

"Captain Hero? Really?" He raised an eyebrow, the corner of his mouth quirking up in that infuriatingly charming way that made me want to both laugh and scream. "How about we go with something a bit more subtle, like 'the people who survive?'"

"Fine, but you'd better start leading the way," I shot back, trying to suppress a grin. "You know I have a knack for ending up in trouble."

"I think we both do," he replied, a teasing glint in his eyes. "But let's see if we can find our way out of this particular mess before we go looking for more."

As we moved further into the building, my pulse quickened. I could still feel the echoes of danger vibrating through the air, and the thought of those figures lurking just beyond the door sent a shiver down my spine. I focused on Grant, his quiet confidence grounding me even as the tension wrapped around us like a vise.

We navigated a narrow hallway, dimly lit and lined with peeling posters that whispered stories of a long-forgotten time. My fingers brushed against the frayed edges, and I could almost hear the laughter of the people who once filled this space, lost in their own moments of joy. It was a stark contrast to our reality, where danger loomed like a specter, always one step behind.

Suddenly, Grant halted, raising a finger to his lips. The silence thickened, and my breath caught in my throat. I could hear the faint sound of voices drifting from a room at the end of the corridor. My stomach twisted with anxiety as we pressed ourselves against the wall, the faint light spilling from the doorway illuminating Grant's face, casting it in sharp relief.

"What do you hear?" I whispered, straining to catch the conversation.

"Sounds like they're planning something," he murmured, his eyes narrowing in concentration. "We need to know what."

A sudden burst of courage surged within me, and I nodded, taking a step toward the door. "Let's eavesdrop."

"Are you out of your mind?" he hissed, grabbing my arm and pulling me back. "We need a strategy, not a death wish."

"It's not a death wish if we're careful," I countered, the fire of determination igniting in my chest. "We can't let them outsmart us. We need to know what we're up against."

He hesitated, the tension between us coiling tighter. "Fine. But if things go sideways, you follow my lead. Deal?"

"Deal," I agreed, heart racing at the thrill of the impending confrontation.

As we crept closer to the door, the voices grew clearer, and I strained to hear the words slipping through the crack. My heart raced, fueled by the knowledge that we were on the cusp of uncovering secrets that had eluded us for far too long.

"Tonight's the night," a gravelly voice said, sending chills down my spine. "We strike while they're vulnerable. No more waiting."

Grant shot me a look, his eyes wide with realization. "This is bigger than we thought," he murmured.

"Do you think they're talking about us?" I whispered back, fear threading through my veins like ice.

"Could be. We have to find out how deep this goes."

In that moment, I knew we were caught in a web far more intricate than we had imagined, and the stakes were rising with every passing second. The tension between us surged anew, fueled by our shared fear and determination, a fragile alliance forged in the heart of chaos. As we steeled ourselves for whatever lay ahead, the shadows of the past loomed large, threatening to engulf us whole.

The whispers drifted through the air, weaving a tapestry of treachery that sent a chill down my spine. "They'll never see it coming," the gravelly voice declared, dripping with sinister satisfaction. I shot a glance at Grant, whose eyes were steely with resolve, and the weight of our decision hung heavily between us. We had to know what these shadows were plotting, even if it meant exposing ourselves to danger.

"Are you ready?" I whispered, my heart pounding like a drum in my ears. The urgency of the moment electrified the air, each breath carrying the scent of dust and forgotten stories, mingling with the rising tension.

"Just stay behind me," he murmured, his voice a low growl that stirred something protective within me. We pressed ourselves against the wall, the door frame a thin barrier separating us from whatever fate awaited on the other side.

With a shared nod, we leaned in closer, straining to hear more. "No one's getting in our way this time," another voice chimed in, this one laced with arrogance. "We finish this tonight."

My breath caught in my throat. Whatever plan was brewing was clearly aimed at us—or worse, those we cared about. "We need to warn the others," I said, feeling the urgency in every fiber of my being.

"Shh!" Grant hissed, his eyes narrowing as he gestured toward the doorway. "They're coming out."

Panic flared in my chest as I quickly retreated, dragging Grant back with me. We stumbled into a narrow alcove, just as the door swung open, revealing two figures shrouded in darkness. My heart raced, not just from fear, but from the undeniable thrill of being this close to uncovering the truth.

They stepped out, their voices carrying as they moved past us. "Once we have them cornered, there's no way they can escape," the first voice said, the confidence in his tone sending a shiver down my spine.

"Let's just hope they don't get wise to our plan," the second replied, his laughter echoing ominously. "We can't afford any more slip-ups."

As they walked further down the hall, Grant and I exchanged frantic glances, the weight of their words pressing down like a fog. "We need to get out of here," I whispered urgently, my instincts screaming that we were no longer safe.

But before I could turn to leave, the door creaked open again, and a third figure stepped into the light. My breath caught as recognition washed over me, turning the room into a scene from my worst nightmares.

"Is that...?" Grant's voice trailed off as disbelief twisted his features.

"Yeah," I said, the realization striking me like a lightning bolt. "It's Aaron. He's in on it."

The shadow of betrayal loomed large, and I felt the ground shift beneath me. Just when I thought I had a handle on the chaos, the truth slithered into the light like a venomous snake. Aaron, the very person we had trusted, was part of the danger we sought to evade.

"I knew he was up to something," Grant muttered, his jaw tightening as he clenched his fists. "We can't let him get away with this."

My heart raced, the stakes escalating with every beat. "We need to find a way to confront him, to get him to talk," I urged, feeling the weight of the situation settle heavily on my shoulders.

"Confront him? Are you insane?" Grant's voice was a mix of incredulity and concern. "You don't know what he's capable of."

"I don't care," I shot back, my frustration boiling over. "We can't just let him slip away. We owe it to everyone he might hurt."

"Fine," he conceded, his gaze steadying as he focused on the door. "But we do it my way. We stick together, no heroics."

"I'll hold you to that," I replied, determination hardening my resolve. With a shared breath, we inched back toward the door, ready to face the darkness that had crept into our lives.

Just as we prepared to step out, a loud crash echoed from somewhere in the distance, followed by the sound of frantic footsteps. Panic surged through me as I glanced at Grant. "What was that?"

"Something's gone wrong," he replied, eyes narrowed. "We need to hurry before—"

Before he could finish, the door slammed open with such force that it ricocheted against the wall. I barely had time to react as a figure lunged into the room, their eyes wild with desperation.

"Run!" they shouted, breathless and panicked.

It was Mia, our ally and friend, and the fear etched across her face sent a jolt of dread through me. "They know we're here! We have to move, now!"

Without a second thought, we bolted past her, our hearts pounding in unison as we raced through the winding hallways. The cacophony of shouts and footsteps grew louder behind us, echoing the urgency of our escape.

"Mia, what happened?" I shouted over my shoulder as we sprinted.

"They're everywhere! I barely got away!" Her eyes were wide, shimmering with unshed tears. "They were waiting for us."

Grant and I exchanged a quick glance, the weight of her words heavy between us. "We need to regroup," he said, his voice steady even in the midst of chaos. "Find a secure place where we can plan our next move."

"Good luck finding one of those," I quipped, trying to lighten the mood despite the suffocating dread creeping in. "This place is practically a horror movie set."

"Then let's turn it into an action movie and blow the place up," Grant replied, a hint of a smile tugging at the corner of his mouth, despite the gravity of our situation.

But before I could respond, the sound of pounding feet echoed closer, and I felt a surge of panic. "This way!" I yelled, veering left into a narrow corridor that branched off from the main hallway.

We dashed down the dimly lit passage, our breaths mingling with the dust swirling in the air, the sharp scent of metal filling my lungs. Adrenaline coursed through my veins, sharp and electric, and I could feel the weight of our pursuers closing in on us.

Mia took the lead, her instincts kicking in as she navigated the maze of crates and discarded machinery. "There's a back exit up ahead," she urged, her voice steady. "If we can make it, we might have a chance."

"Just a little further!" I echoed, pushing past the growing sense of dread that threatened to choke me. With every step, I felt the danger coiling tighter, the weight of the unseen enemy pressing down like a vice.

Finally, we reached a heavy door, the metal cold beneath my fingertips as I fumbled for the handle. "It's locked!" I shouted, panic creeping into my voice as the footsteps grew louder, more menacing.

"Stand back," Grant said, and with a swift motion, he kicked the door with all his might. It groaned in protest before giving way, the hinges squealing in agony.

We tumbled through the opening, into a small, dimly lit alley behind the warehouse, the cool night air rushing over us like a balm. But the reprieve was short-lived as we heard the distant shouts of our pursuers spilling out into the night.

"There's nowhere to hide," Mia gasped, glancing around as if seeking refuge among the shadows.

"Then we run," I said, my heart pounding fiercely in my chest. We had to make it to safety, had to uncover the truth before it consumed us whole. But as we sprinted down the alley, the darkness pressed in around us, and the sensation of being hunted clawed at my mind.

Just when I thought we might slip away, the sound of footsteps rang out behind us, and the darkness seemed to congeal, forming into figures blocking our path.

I skidded to a halt, the realization crashing down like a tidal wave. "Grant!" I screamed, feeling the weight of despair settle heavily in my chest. "They're here!"

The menacing shadows closed in, their faces obscured but their intentions clear. My heart raced as the full weight of our peril bore down upon me, the shadows of betrayal and danger merging into a singular force.

As the first figure lunged toward us, my instincts kicked in, and I readied myself for the fight of our lives. But just as I steeled myself to confront the darkness, a familiar voice pierced the chaos, freezing me in place.

"Stop! You don't know what you're doing!"

The figure halted, and for a moment, everything hung suspended in the air, anticipation crackling like electricity. And as the shadows loomed ever closer, I realized that our survival hinged on the very secrets that had brought us together in the first place.

Chapter 13: Echoes of the Past

The air felt thick and heavy as we stumbled away from the chaos that had erupted just moments before. Adrenaline surged through my veins, electrifying every nerve ending, while the echo of shouting voices faded into the background. It was a strange cocktail of fear and exhilaration that left me both lightheaded and grounded. The streetlights flickered, casting long shadows that danced like specters along the cracked pavement, reminding me of my childhood, of the nights spent listening to sirens in the distance, and the pervasive sense of danger that had hung over my neighborhood like a shroud.

Grant moved beside me, his expression a mixture of determination and concern, but in his eyes, I glimpsed something deeper—an understanding that went beyond the superficial. The man who had seemed so invincible just hours ago now bore the weight of unspoken memories, and I felt a pull toward him, an inexplicable urge to peel back the layers of bravado he wore like armor. We ducked into an alley, the gritty scent of garbage and rusted metal assaulting our senses. My heart raced, not just from the escape, but from the connection I could feel forming between us.

"You okay?" he asked, his voice low, almost reverent, as if he feared shattering the fragile silence we found ourselves in.

I nodded, but the truth was more complicated than that. I was okay, but I was also not okay. My past was clawing at the edges of my mind, rearing its ugly head at the most inconvenient moments, ready to swallow me whole. The shadows in this alley felt familiar, yet foreign, and I couldn't help but wonder if they mirrored the shadows of my childhood.

"I grew up in a neighborhood like this," I confessed, the words slipping out before I could stop them. "Every day was a challenge. You never knew when trouble would come knocking."

Grant turned to me, the tension in his shoulders easing slightly as he listened. "What do you mean?"

"It was like living in a war zone. I remember nights when I'd hide under my bed, heart racing, listening to the sounds of shouting and breaking glass. I learned early on that trusting anyone was a gamble."

He shifted closer, the warmth radiating from his body anchoring me as memories flooded back. "What did you do?"

I swallowed hard, the past too vivid, too present. "I learned to be invisible. If you didn't draw attention to yourself, you had a better chance of survival."

A brief silence settled between us, heavy with understanding. "I lost my sister when I was a kid," Grant revealed, his voice barely above a whisper. "She was in the wrong place at the wrong time. Ever since then, I've had this... this weight. It pushes me to protect the people I care about."

The revelation hung in the air, heavy with shared pain. "I'm sorry," I said, feeling the sincerity of my words echoing in the space between us. "I can't imagine how hard that must have been."

"It was everything," he replied, a flicker of vulnerability crossing his features. "But it taught me to fight, to not let fear control me. That's why I'm here, doing this—whatever this is."

His eyes locked onto mine, a fierce intensity sparking between us. For the first time, I saw him not just as a partner in this chaotic adventure but as a man carrying scars I could understand. The distance that had separated us began to dissolve, replaced by a bond forged in shared trauma and a desire for redemption. Just as I thought we were on the verge of something beautiful, the shrill sound of my phone broke the moment like glass shattering against concrete.

I cursed under my breath as I fumbled for my phone, the screen lighting up with a message that made my heart drop. "It's from Leo,"

I muttered, my voice tinged with dread. "He says we need to meet immediately. He thinks the threat is closer than we realized."

"What does he mean?" Grant asked, tension creeping back into his posture as he took a step back, his earlier vulnerability replaced by the cool mask of a strategist.

I shook my head, anxiety twisting in my stomach. "I don't know, but it can't be good."

"Then we need to move." He stepped back into the street, determination radiating from him like a beacon.

As we made our way through the dimly lit streets, the city felt alive with possibilities and peril. My childhood fears tangled with my current reality, creating a knot in my chest that refused to loosen. Every rustle of leaves, every shadow that flitted across our path seemed to carry whispers of what had been and what could be. The echoes of my past weren't just haunting me; they were shaping the decisions I made now, guiding me toward a destiny I was still trying to grasp.

The alley opened up to a street filled with life—music spilled from a nearby bar, laughter mingled with the sounds of clinking glasses, and the scent of something delicious wafted through the air. It was a stark contrast to the darkness that had just enveloped us, but there was no time to appreciate it. My heart pounded in my ears as I followed Grant, the beat synchronizing with the dread pooling in my gut.

"What if Leo's right?" I asked, urgency lacing my words. "What if we're being watched?"

Grant glanced back at me, a glimmer of reassurance in his gaze. "Then we stay one step ahead. We're not children anymore, haunted by shadows. We've survived this long, and I refuse to let our pasts dictate our futures."

His confidence bolstered me, and for the first time since the chaos had erupted, I felt a flicker of hope. Together, we would navigate the labyrinth of danger that lay ahead, drawing strength from the painful lessons we'd learned. Just as we turned the corner, a chilling realization washed over me. The connection we were forging, built on trust and vulnerability, was about to be tested in ways we could never anticipate.

The air hung thick with anticipation, as if the universe itself was holding its breath. I followed Grant through the chaotic streets, where laughter mingled with the distant hum of cars and the clinking of glasses. Each step we took felt charged, reverberating through the damp concrete beneath us, echoing the weight of our revelations. A stray cat darted across our path, pausing for just a moment to eye us with suspicion before disappearing into the shadows.

I couldn't shake the feeling that something was watching us, lurking just beyond the edge of perception. "You'd think they'd find a less conspicuous way to follow us," I said, forcing a lightness into my tone that felt precariously unsteady. "Like hiding in a trash can or something. It's a classic."

Grant chuckled, though his gaze remained vigilant, scanning our surroundings. "Yeah, because nothing says stealth like the smell of old pizza and cat litter."

"Exactly! If only the criminals in this town had a sense of humor." I attempted to ease the tension with a smile, but beneath my laughter lay a current of unease that threatened to rise to the surface.

As we approached the rendezvous point, a small café tucked away on a side street, I felt a strange mixture of hope and dread. It was cozy, the kind of place that promised warm pastries and strong coffee. The glow of fairy lights draped across the entrance created an inviting atmosphere, almost luring us into a false sense of security. But I knew better than to be lulled into complacency; danger had a way of lurking in the most unsuspecting places.

"Let's keep our voices down," Grant murmured as we stepped inside. The café was a sanctuary of soft chatter and the comforting aroma of brewing coffee, but the warmth did little to ease my fraying nerves. "Leo should be here any minute."

I found a small table in the corner, choosing to sit facing the entrance. Grant settled across from me, his fingers tapping a nervous rhythm against the wooden surface. I admired the way his jaw clenched slightly when he was focused, an endearing quirk that made him all the more human in the midst of our chaotic reality.

"So, what's your plan if Leo spills the beans and we find ourselves in deeper than we already are?" I asked, crossing my arms. The thought of being trapped in a web of conspiracies sent a shiver down my spine.

Grant's lips curled into a wry smile. "I thought I'd just wing it. You know, keep it casual. 'Oh, just a little kidnapping and conspiracy; no big deal.'"

"Sounds like a solid plan," I said, my sarcasm cutting through the tension like a knife. "I'll be sure to take notes."

The door swung open, and in walked Leo, his tall frame and tousled hair giving him an air of casual nonchalance that was almost comforting. But the moment his eyes met mine, I felt the gravity of the situation return. He walked briskly toward us, his expression unreadable.

"Sorry I'm late," he said, sliding into the seat beside Grant. "Had a little issue with some of the locals."

"Is it ever a quiet day for you?" I asked, leaning in, curiosity overcoming my unease.

"Not in this line of work," he replied, glancing around as if ensuring we weren't being overheard. "I'm glad you both are okay. I'm not going to sugarcoat this—things are getting messy."

"Messy how?" Grant pressed, his demeanor shifting from casual to serious in an instant.

Leo leaned closer, lowering his voice. "There's a faction that's been watching you two. They're not just random thugs; they're organized and determined to get what they want."

"What do they want?" I asked, dread pooling in my stomach.

"Information. There's something you both stumbled upon, something that links back to a much larger game at play."

"What kind of game?" Grant's eyes narrowed, suspicion etched on his face.

"I can't say too much right now, but it involves powerful people. Those in control don't like loose ends, and you two are starting to look like one."

An icy wave of fear washed over me, settling into my bones. I glanced at Grant, his jaw clenched, a storm brewing behind his eyes. "What do we do?" I asked, my voice steadier than I felt.

"We need to find out how deep this goes," Leo replied, his expression grave. "There's a meeting tonight, and I think it's crucial we attend."

"A meeting? With whom?" I couldn't keep the incredulity from my voice. "We're supposed to just walk into a room full of dangerous people?"

"Exactly," Leo said, the corners of his mouth lifting slightly in amusement. "I thought you liked a little thrill."

"Not the kind that involves potential bodily harm," I shot back, frustration bubbling beneath the surface. "You know, I thought the danger was behind us. I didn't sign up for a field trip into the lion's den."

"Believe me, I'm not thrilled about this either, but we need information, and this could lead us to it."

Grant's gaze was fixed on Leo, his brow furrowed as if weighing the options. "And if this goes south?"

"Then we improvise," Leo replied, a glimmer of mischief in his eyes. "Just like you two always do."

I could feel the tension in the air thicken, a shared apprehension binding us together in this precarious moment. The weight of our circumstances pressed heavily on my chest. I wanted to argue, to resist the path laid out before us, but I also knew that retreating was no longer an option. We had come too far, faced too much, and the thought of walking away now felt like admitting defeat.

With a heavy sigh, I looked between them, steeling myself for what lay ahead. "Fine. Let's do it. But if we end up in a hostage situation, I'm holding you both responsible."

"Deal," Grant said, his lips twitching into a reluctant smile.

As we prepared to leave, I took a moment to breathe in the comforting aroma of coffee and pastries one last time. The world outside was calling, a blend of uncertainty and adventure waiting just beyond the door. I was stepping back into the shadows, but this time, I wouldn't be doing it alone. With each heartbeat, the bond between us strengthened, transforming our fear into resolve, and as we stepped into the night, I realized that we were not just chasing shadows; we were confronting the darkness head-on.

As we stepped out of the café, the city embraced us in its frenetic energy, the sounds of laughter and music mingling with the distant hum of traffic. The night air was crisp, invigorating, almost electric as if it were charged with the secrets we were about to unravel. With each step, I could feel the weight of our mission pressing against my chest like a heavy cloak. Grant walked beside me, a solid presence in the chaos, and I couldn't help but steal glances at him, searching for reassurance in his steely resolve.

"Just so we're clear," I said, trying to mask my apprehension with levity, "if this meeting turns into an episode of a bad crime drama, I'm blaming you two."

Grant chuckled, the sound low and warm, but his eyes remained serious. "No one's planning on getting captured tonight. We're just gathering intel. Think of it as an elaborate scavenger hunt."

"Only this time, the prize isn't a shiny trophy but the possibility of staying alive," I quipped, the irony not lost on me.

"Gotta love a good twist," Leo added, a hint of mischief sparkling in his eyes. "We'll make it out with stories to tell."

We moved through the streets, shadows clinging to our heels like reluctant friends. The streetlights flickered above, creating pools of light that illuminated our path and shrouded the edges in darkness. The city had its own pulse, a rhythm that felt familiar yet foreign, each heartbeat a reminder of what was at stake.

Soon, we arrived at an inconspicuous building that resembled a forgotten warehouse, its façade weathered and nondescript. A neon sign flickered, the words "The Retreat" barely legible through layers of grime and neglect. "Charming place you've picked, Leo," I remarked, eyeing the entrance warily.

"Trust me, it's the kind of charm that doesn't attract attention," he replied, the hint of a smirk dancing on his lips.

We stepped inside, the air shifting immediately from cool night to warm and slightly musky, an aroma that hinted at stale beer and untold stories. The interior was dimly lit, with low-hanging lamps casting a warm glow over small tables scattered throughout. A bar stretched along one side, and a few patrons lounged in booths, absorbed in quiet conversations.

"Let's find a spot where we can observe," Grant suggested, scanning the room with a predator's vigilance.

We settled into a secluded booth at the back, the dark wood offering us a semblance of cover. As we waited, I fiddled with the edge of the table, my mind racing with thoughts of what might unfold. "What's the plan if things go sideways?" I asked, casting a sidelong glance at Leo.

"Stick together and keep your wits about you," Leo replied, his tone serious. "If anything feels off, we leave. No hesitation."

"Easy for you to say," I shot back, feeling the adrenaline surging through me. "You're the one who thrives on danger. I'm just here for the coffee and occasional witty banter."

"Hey, you're doing great so far. You've added a whole new layer of entertainment," Grant teased, his smile cutting through the tension like sunlight through clouds.

Just then, the door creaked open, and a group of three individuals entered, their energy shifting the atmosphere in the room. The leader, a tall figure with slicked-back hair and an air of authority, surveyed the space, his eyes narrowing when they landed on our corner.

"Looks like our guests have arrived," Leo murmured, leaning in closer.

I squinted, trying to discern more about them. "You know who they are?"

"Not personally, but I've seen them around. They're part of the network I've been tracking."

As the group settled at the bar, I couldn't help but feel a tingle of apprehension. The leader spoke with a voice that carried an undertone of menace, every word laced with authority that demanded respect. "Keep your eyes peeled," Grant said, his expression shifting into one of concentration. "We need to hear what they're discussing."

I leaned closer, straining to catch snippets of their conversation. "They're definitely not here for the ambiance," I whispered, glancing at Leo. "What's our next move?"

"We wait," Leo replied, his voice steady. "Just long enough to gather information, then we make our exit."

Minutes ticked by, the atmosphere thickening with tension. The group at the bar seemed animated, gesturing emphatically, their voices rising in intensity. I could feel the pulse of uncertainty thrumming beneath my skin, a mix of anticipation and dread swirling together like a storm on the horizon.

Then, without warning, the leader's voice cut through the din. "We can't afford any mistakes. If they find out we're watching, it'll all be over."

I exchanged glances with Grant and Leo, a shared understanding passing between us. "They're onto something bigger than we realized," I whispered, my heart racing.

"Stay focused," Grant replied, his tone urgent. "We need to know what they're planning."

Just as I turned to listen more intently, the leader's gaze darted toward our booth. My breath caught in my throat as he leaned in, whispering to his companions. A chill raced down my spine, an unshakeable feeling that we had crossed an invisible line, that our presence had not gone unnoticed.

"They're looking this way," I murmured, a mixture of fear and adrenaline coursing through me. "What do we do?"

"Act natural," Leo said, his voice low and steady. "We're just patrons, right?"

But as I forced a smile, I couldn't shake the feeling that the moment was slipping away from us. The air crackled with anticipation, each second stretching out, tension mounting like a coiled spring ready to snap.

Then, without warning, the leader stood up, his eyes locked onto mine with an intensity that made my skin prickle. "You," he called, pointing straight at our booth. "What are you doing here?"

Panic washed over me, my heart pounding against my ribs as I exchanged frantic looks with Grant and Leo. "This isn't good," I whispered, barely able to form coherent thoughts as the room seemed to shrink around us.

"Time to improvise," Grant said, his voice a calm anchor amidst the chaos.

"Wait, what?" I started to say, but the leader was already striding toward us, determination radiating from him like heat from an open flame.

My instincts screamed at me to run, to escape this situation before it spiraled further into chaos, but I was frozen, caught in the spotlight of his piercing gaze. "I suggest you start talking," he said, a dark smile curling at the corners of his lips. "Or this little chat is going to get very interesting."

In that moment, every nerve in my body ignited with fear. This was it—the tipping point where everything we had risked collided with the harsh reality of the danger we faced. As the leader leaned closer, the world outside faded, the weight of our predicament pressing down on me like a vise.

"Let's see how well you play the game," he said, and as the shadows closed in around us, I realized that the stakes had never been higher.

Chapter 14: Beneath the Surface

The air crackled with an energy that sent shivers down my spine as I stepped into the dimly lit café, the familiar scent of freshly brewed coffee and warm pastries enveloping me like a comforting embrace. This was where it all began, where our investigation had sparked over cups of bitter espresso and pastries dusted with powdered sugar. I slid into a corner booth, the plush red leather chafing against my jeans, and waited for Grant. He was always late, as if he thrived on the suspense of my impatience.

Tonight, the café pulsed with an undercurrent of urgency that matched my own racing heart. A couple at the next table whispered animatedly, their eyes darting as if they were sharing secrets meant only for the shadows. Outside, the city thrummed with life, neon lights reflecting in puddles left behind by the afternoon rain, creating a kaleidoscope of colors that danced on the pavement. Yet inside, my focus narrowed to the flickering flame of the candle in front of me, its light casting playful shadows on the wall, mirroring the turmoil brewing in my mind.

As I traced the rim of my coffee cup, my thoughts spiraled back to the last few days—an investigation that had taken a dark turn, leading me down a rabbit hole of secrets tied intricately to my family's past. There was something unsettling about it, a connection that felt like an invisible thread binding me to the sinister figure haunting our steps. A figure who seemed to know more about my family than I did, and with every piece of information I unearthed, the chill of familiarity deepened, wrapping around me like a cold, unforgiving shroud.

The door swung open, and a gust of wind swept through the café, momentarily stealing the warmth from the room. Grant walked in, his silhouette framed by the bright lights outside, a tall figure radiating confidence and just a hint of mystery. His dark hair was tousled, and a smirk danced at the corners of his lips as he approached me, his brown eyes sparkling with mischief. "You look like you've been plotting world domination," he teased, sliding into the booth across from me. "What's on your mind?"

I rolled my eyes, but I couldn't help the smile that tugged at my lips. "Just the usual, you know, unraveling my family's dark secrets and chasing shadows. No big deal."

"Sounds thrilling," he replied, leaning back with an exaggerated nonchalance that only made the tension in my chest tighten. "Tell me more."

"Let's just say I've stumbled upon some old letters," I said, lowering my voice as if the words themselves could conjure the lurking darkness outside. "They hint at something my family tried to bury. Something sinister that connects to our current situation."

His expression shifted, curiosity mingling with concern. "Is that why you've been so distant? You've been holding out on me."

The weight of his gaze sent a flush through me. "I didn't want to drag you into it. This is personal."

"Everything we do is personal," he countered, the intensity of his stare causing my heart to race. "Especially now."

I took a breath, the air thick with unspoken tension. "The letters mention a name," I continued, my voice barely above a whisper. "A name that keeps coming up in the investigation. It's connected to the figure stalking us, and I think it's connected to my family."

"Then we need to dig deeper," Grant said, his resolve firming. "If this is about your family, it's even more important we uncover the truth."

The weight of his words lingered between us, and for a moment, the café faded into the background, leaving only the intensity of our conversation. There was a fierceness in his voice, a determination that ignited something deep within me, something that thrummed in rhythm with the chaos swirling around us. I reached across the table, grasping his hand, the warmth of his skin grounding me. "Together, then. We'll face whatever comes."

"Together," he echoed, his thumb brushing against my knuckles, igniting a spark that sent a jolt of electricity racing through me. The connection between us had deepened, becoming more than just partners in this investigation; it had morphed into something raw and powerful, something I could no longer ignore.

We spent the next hour piecing together the fragments of my family's past, weaving a narrative filled with intrigue and treachery. The café buzzed with life around us, but in our bubble, time stood still. Each revelation pushed us closer, the shared intensity forging an unbreakable bond that shifted the atmosphere from investigative urgency to something more intimate.

As the sun dipped below the horizon, the city lights flickered to life, casting a warm glow through the windows. I leaned in closer, captivated by the determination etched on Grant's face as he spoke. Suddenly, he paused, his eyes locking onto mine, and the air between us crackled with unspoken words.

"Can I kiss you?" he asked, his voice low and slightly hesitant, as if asking for permission to cross a line we had both danced around for far too long.

I didn't answer with words. Instead, I leaned forward, closing the distance between us. Our lips met softly at first, a gentle exploration that quickly ignited into a passionate kiss, fueled by the adrenaline of our shared secrets and the uncertainty that loomed ahead. It was intoxicating, the world around us fading into oblivion as we lost ourselves in that moment, the worries and shadows of our past mingling with a burgeoning hope for the future.

As we pulled away, breathless and wide-eyed, the reality of our situation washed over me. What lay ahead was fraught with danger, a sinister figure lurking just out of sight, but in this moment, under the glow of the café lights, I felt a renewed sense of strength. Together, we would face whatever darkness awaited, and perhaps, just perhaps, the connection we shared would light the way through the shadows of our past.

The coffee shop's warmth faded as we stepped back into the night, the cool air wrapping around us like a crisp, unwelcome blanket. My mind spun with the remnants of our kiss, the thrill of it still electrifying my senses, but the shadows loomed larger than ever. As we walked side by side, the city felt alive, vibrant, yet oddly foreboding, as if it were a character in our story, playing both friend and foe. The neon lights glimmered, casting colorful reflections on the slick pavement, and every passing car felt like a reminder of the urgency weighing heavy on my heart.

"Let's not linger too long," I suggested, my voice carrying a tinge of anxiety. "I'd rather not be out here with the darkness creeping in." The thought of the figure following us felt like a whisper in my ear, a reminder that safety was an illusion.

Grant nodded, his expression serious but laced with the warmth I had come to rely on. "You know, I always thought this city had a heartbeat of its own, but tonight it feels more like a pulse racing out of control." His attempt at levity brought a smile to my lips despite the heaviness in the air.

"More like a city in denial," I replied, quickening my pace. "It struts around like it owns the night, while we're the ones left picking up the pieces."

We turned down a quieter street, the bustling life of the main thoroughfare fading behind us, replaced by the occasional flicker of streetlights and the soft rustle of leaves in the wind. I felt a tug at my heartstrings—this was the kind of evening one would spend with a glass of wine, wrapped in the cozy embrace of a favorite blanket. But here we were, wrapped in the tension of a mystery that had become all too personal.

"What's next?" Grant asked, his tone steady. "Do we dig deeper into your family's history, or do we chase after this shadow lurking behind us?"

I paused, taking in the moonlight spilling over the cobblestones. "I think it's time to confront the past. The letters are a starting point, but I need to know what my family was trying to hide. There's a reason the name keeps appearing, and I'm not going to let it haunt me."

Grant's eyes darkened with a hint of concern. "What if it puts you in danger? What if we open a door that's better left closed?"

"Then I'll deal with it," I declared, a fierce determination rising within me. "I can't run from my own history. It's time I faced it head-on."

He studied me for a moment, and I could see the gears turning in his mind, weighing the risks. Finally, he relented, a slow smile breaking through his serious demeanor. "Okay, but if we're doing this, we're doing it together. I don't plan on letting you go at it alone, especially when we're up against whatever monster this is."

As we made our way to the small library that held the key to my family's past, the streets became a maze of memories—each corner, each alley stirred echoes of laughter and whispered secrets. I remembered my mother bringing me here as a child, her hand wrapped around mine as she shared tales of our ancestors, weaving a tapestry of family history that now felt more like a veil hiding dark truths.

The library loomed ahead, its façade both inviting and intimidating, the large wooden doors creaking as we pushed them open. The air inside was thick with the scent of aged paper and polished wood, a sanctuary for anyone seeking refuge in stories. We wandered down the narrow aisles, Grant's presence grounding me amidst the swirling thoughts in my mind.

"I've never been much of a bookworm," he admitted, his voice a soft murmur as he brushed his fingers along the spines of forgotten tomes. "But for you, I might just take up reading."

"Just promise me it won't be about how to catch a killer," I quipped, chuckling softly. "Unless you want to write a bestseller."

"Only if you're my co-author," he shot back, a twinkle in his eyes.

I felt a warmth spreading through my chest, the flirtation mingling with the seriousness of our mission. Together, we traversed the aisles, searching for anything that might shed light on the mysteries surrounding my family.

"Over here," Grant called, his voice echoing slightly as he gestured toward a section filled with local history. I joined him, and together we pulled down volumes, skimming through dusty pages. Each name I encountered felt like a potential piece of the puzzle, each story an echo of my lineage.

Hours passed as we delved deeper, the soft rustle of paper and the occasional sigh of the old building our only company. I stumbled upon a journal tucked between two hefty books, its leather cover worn and faded. As I opened it, a shiver ran down my spine. The entries were penned in elegant cursive, recounting tales of family gatherings, celebrations, and... a darkness that loomed in the background.

"There's something here," I murmured, scanning the pages feverishly. "Listen to this." I read aloud, my voice trembling slightly. "The shadows that lurk at the edges of our joy, they are whispers of a past we cannot escape. We must tread carefully, for the roots of our lineage intertwine with forces we cannot comprehend."

Grant leaned closer, his breath warm against my ear. "What does that mean? Are you saying your family was involved in something sinister?"

"Maybe," I replied, my voice barely above a whisper. "Or perhaps they were just trying to protect me from something they didn't understand."

Before we could delve deeper, the sound of footsteps echoed in the otherwise silent library, a shuffling that sent a jolt of adrenaline through my veins. I glanced at Grant, and we exchanged a wary glance, the weight of unspoken questions hanging heavy between us. Who else could be here? The thought of a lurking figure sent a thrill of fear skittering down my spine.

"Stay close," he murmured, his voice low and urgent. We moved quietly, the excitement of discovery now entwined with an unsettling sense of foreboding. As the footsteps drew nearer, we ducked behind a shelf, holding our breath, hearts pounding in sync. The air thickened with tension, and I could feel the electric current of anticipation crackling between us.

What were we about to uncover? The answer loomed like a shadow just out of reach, teasing us with promises of truth intertwined with danger.

The footsteps drew closer, a rhythmic cadence that reverberated off the library walls, sending a thrill of panic racing through me. I pressed against the shelves, the cool wood against my back grounding me as I focused on Grant. His eyes were wide with uncertainty, a mixture of intrigue and caution dancing in the depths. We had stumbled into a secret, and whatever was unfolding beyond the spines of dusty volumes felt more dangerous than I had anticipated.

"Do you think it's one of the librarians?" I whispered, my breath barely escaping my lips. The library was a labyrinth of stories and whispers, and while I had always loved it, tonight it felt like a breeding ground for shadows.

"Only if they're planning to start a horror movie," Grant replied, his voice laced with humor to mask the tension. "Let's hope they're just on a book retrieval mission."

Peering around the edge of the shelf, I caught sight of a tall figure moving between the aisles, their silhouette illuminated by the faint glow of a reading lamp. The low hum of a voice filled the air, but the words were muffled, as if someone was deep in conversation with the dusty tomes. It was unsettling; it felt like we were trespassing in a realm where secrets were meant to stay hidden.

"What if it's someone looking for the same thing we are?" Grant suggested, his gaze never leaving the figure. "Or worse, someone who knows what we're up to?"

My heart raced as I considered the possibilities. "We need to find out. We can't let fear hold us back." With a shared glance that communicated unspoken agreement, we cautiously made our way down the aisle, each step laden with the weight of uncertainty.

The figure paused, and I caught a glimpse of dark hair and an all-too-familiar silhouette. "Wait," I whispered, my breath catching in my throat. "Is that...?"

"Is that who I think it is?" Grant finished for me, incredulity coloring his tone. We stepped closer, my heart hammering as recognition dawned. It was someone from my past, a name that had lingered in the recesses of my memory, shrouded in mystery.

The figure turned slightly, and I could finally see the face, a familiar smile that was both inviting and dangerous. "Avery?"

The voice was soft but unmistakably the same. I stepped out from behind the shelf, caught between the thrill of reunion and the icy grip of apprehension. "What are you doing here?"

Avery's eyes sparkled with mischief, but there was an undercurrent of something darker lurking beneath the surface. "Oh, just following a hunch," she replied, the playfulness in her tone not quite matching the intensity of the moment. "I figured you'd be digging into our family's past. Didn't think you'd be so brave to come alone."

"Brave? I think you mean reckless," I shot back, my irritation flaring as Grant moved slightly behind me, his protective stance evident. "You should know better than to poke around in things that don't concern you."

"Everything concerns me," Avery said, her gaze flicking to Grant with a hint of curiosity. "Especially when it comes to family. Isn't that right, Grant?"

His expression tightened, a silent war of recognition and wariness unfolding between them. "How do you know who I am?"

Avery chuckled, a sound that sent a ripple of unease down my spine. "Word travels fast, especially in families tangled in secrets. I've seen your name come up in more than a few discussions."

"Right, and I suppose you're the expert on secrets now?" I shot back, my frustration mounting. "What are you really after, Avery?"

"I'm here to help," she said, tilting her head in mock innocence. "There's more at stake than you realize. You've opened a door, and if you're not careful, it could swallow you whole."

Her words hung in the air, thick with foreboding. "What do you mean?" I asked, the unease coiling tighter in my stomach.

"Your family has a history, one that isn't just a collection of sweet memories and old letters," she replied, her tone now serious. "It's entangled with darker forces. You're not just dealing with old ghosts; you're provoking something alive, something that doesn't want to be found."

Grant stepped forward, his presence a steadying force. "If you know something, you need to tell us. We're already in this deep."

Avery's gaze flickered between us, weighing the situation. "Fine, but you have to promise to trust me. There's a hidden vault beneath the library, filled with documents that could change everything you think you know about your family."

"A vault?" I echoed, my skepticism flaring. "And you expect us to just follow you? How do we know we can trust you?"

"Because," she replied, her voice dropping to a conspiratorial whisper, "if you don't, you'll be in danger before the night ends."

The urgency in her voice sent a shiver of apprehension racing through me. "And why would you care about our safety?"

"Because I don't want to see anyone else get hurt. I've seen what this can do to families." The weight of her words was palpable, and for a moment, a flicker of vulnerability shone through her playful facade.

"Let's go, then," I decided, my heart pounding. The mystery deepened, and with it came an undeniable sense of urgency. Grant and I exchanged a glance, the shared resolve binding us together. "Lead the way."

Avery led us deeper into the library, her confidence seeming to overshadow the tension that simmered just beneath the surface. The air felt electric, charged with anticipation as we navigated the narrow passages, each turn potentially leading us closer to the truth—and the danger.

Finally, she stopped in front of an unassuming wooden door hidden behind a bookshelf, the faded letters barely visible above the dust. "This is it," she said, her voice a mixture of excitement and dread. "Inside lies everything you've been looking for."

As she pushed the door open, a rush of cold air greeted us, sending chills racing down my spine. I stepped inside, my heart pounding, the darkness of the room swallowing me whole.

Suddenly, the door slammed shut behind us, the sound echoing ominously. Panic surged as I turned to find it locked tight, the cold realization washing over me. "Avery!" I shouted, but my voice was swallowed by the darkness.

The room was dimly lit, and I could barely make out the outlines of boxes and old furniture that seemed to loom like specters in the gloom. Grant's hand found mine, squeezing tightly as we steadied ourselves against the rising tide of uncertainty.

"Did you know this would happen?" he asked, his voice barely above a whisper.

Before I could respond, a low rumble resonated through the air, and the walls seemed to tremble as a flicker of movement caught my eye. A figure emerged from the shadows, cloaked in darkness, their presence both imposing and strangely familiar.

I gasped, recognition crashing over me like a wave. "You..."

But before I could finish, the figure stepped forward, and the darkness closed in around us, leaving only the echo of my words hanging in the air, the truth just out of reach.

Chapter 15: The Breaking Point

The air was thick with tension, a palpable energy that crackled between us as I paced the dimly lit room. Shadows flickered along the walls, cast by the meager glow of a single lamp that struggled against the darkness of the late evening. I could hear my heart thudding in my chest, each beat resonating like a war drum, drowning out the low hum of the city outside. Grant leaned against the doorframe, arms crossed, his posture deceptively relaxed, but I knew better. Beneath that calm exterior lay a storm, one that mirrored the tempest raging within me.

"Just tell me what you know," I demanded, the urgency in my voice betraying my otherwise composed demeanor. Every word hung between us like an unsheathed sword, poised for battle. I had become an unwitting player in a game far more dangerous than I had anticipated, and now the stakes were impossibly high.

Grant shifted, his jaw tightening as he took a step closer. The scent of his cologne wafted through the air—earthy with a hint of cedar. It wrapped around me, grounding and intoxicating all at once. I forced myself to focus. We were not here to reminisce about the moments that ignited our chemistry, not when the darkness loomed so large.

"I can't," he said, his voice low, laced with frustration. "You know I want to protect you, but this goes deeper than we thought. If we're right about the connections, then it's not just about us anymore."

His words sent a shiver down my spine. I'd been entangled in a web of deceit, spun by someone I had trusted. As I studied Grant's face, that chiseled jaw and the intensity of his blue eyes, I felt a pang of conflicting emotions. He was the one person I could depend on, yet every second spent together threatened to unravel the carefully woven fabric of our relationship.

"Protect me?" I scoffed, the bitterness spilling over like a shaken soda can. "Or is it to keep me from knowing the truth? Because right now, I feel like I'm standing in the eye of a hurricane, and you're the only one who knows which way the winds are blowing." I paused, taking a breath, my anger bubbling beneath the surface. "What's really going on, Grant?"

He ran a hand through his tousled hair, a gesture that was almost charming but now felt like a signal of surrender. "You have to trust me. I'm doing everything I can to find the answers. You don't know what I'm up against."

"Then fill me in!" The desperation clawed at my insides, an insatiable urge to understand and fight back against the shadow looming over us. "What's the point of this charade? We're not in a spy novel, Grant. This is real life, and I can't just sit here while you play the hero."

He took a step forward, his gaze piercing through my defenses. "You're right. This isn't a game, and I don't want to be your hero. I just want you safe. I—"

Before he could finish, the door swung open with a crash, the loud bang echoing through the room. My heart stopped. In walked Mark, my colleague, the one person I had always believed was on my side. His face was flushed, eyes wild with an emotion I couldn't decipher.

"Grant! You need to see this," he said breathlessly, holding up his phone as if it were a lifeline.

"What is it?" Grant snapped, his demeanor shifting instantly to that of a protective shield. I took a step back, uncertainty clawing at my gut as I watched the exchange unfold.

"Footage. Someone just sent me security cam clips from the alley behind your apartment. You need to see who's been lurking around."

As he played the video, I leaned closer, my pulse racing with the dawning realization that everything had escalated beyond my comprehension. There, captured on grainy footage, was a figure in a dark hoodie, moving stealthily along the side of the building. The timestamp flashed across the screen—only an hour ago.

My stomach dropped as I recognized the gait, the unmistakable way they held their shoulders, and the flick of the wrist as they glanced around, half in shadow, half in light.

"Is that…?" I couldn't finish the sentence, the words choking in my throat.

"Someone you know?" Mark asked, glancing at me, his brow furrowed.

"It can't be," I breathed, backing away from the screen as a flood of betrayal washed over me.

Grant's expression hardened as he studied the footage. "We need to confront this head-on. We can't let them get away with this."

"No," I said, my voice cracking. "I need to know who it is. I need to understand why."

But deep down, I already feared the answer. The realization began to seep into my consciousness, dark and pervasive like ink spreading through water. I could feel the threads of trust unraveling, fraying around the edges of my reality.

"Let's go," Grant said, determination replacing his earlier frustration. He stepped toward me, but I flinched, caught between my instinct to run and my urge to confront.

"No. You don't get to just take charge," I snapped, feeling the surge of anger pulse through my veins, mingling with the fear. "I'm done being in the dark. If this is a conspiracy, then I deserve to know who's behind it, even if it's someone I thought I could trust."

Grant's face fell, the resolve crumbling slightly as he registered the weight of my words. "What are you saying?"

"I'm saying I need to handle this myself."

"No! You don't understand—"

"Don't I?" I cut him off, the words spilling out before I could stop them. "Because it feels like I'm the only one here who's in the dark. You're treating me like I'm some fragile thing that can't handle the truth."

The silence that followed was heavy, charged with unsaid emotions and mounting frustration. He stepped back, gaze locked with mine, and I could see the struggle in his eyes—the battle between protecting me and the undeniable connection that sparked between us.

"I won't let you go into this alone," he said finally, his voice softening, and I could feel the sincerity behind it.

But I shook my head, the resolve solidifying within me. "You need to let me face this. Whatever it is, I can't keep hiding behind your decisions."

Grant's features twisted into something painful, a mixture of admiration and worry, but he nodded slowly, the weight of our shared silence a testament to the bond we had forged. "Fine, but I'm not letting you out of my sight."

"Then I guess we're both facing this together," I replied, my voice steadier than I felt.

With each step I took toward the unknown, I felt the ground shift beneath me, the fragile threads of trust tested in ways I could never have imagined.

The streets outside were alive with a restless energy, an undercurrent of excitement that mirrored my own tumultuous thoughts as we stepped out into the night. The cool air hit my skin like a refreshing slap, but it did little to clear the fog of uncertainty clouding my mind. Grant walked beside me, his presence both a comfort and a catalyst for the whirlwind brewing within. With every step, I felt the sharp contrast between the warmth of his body and the icy fear that gripped my heart.

"Where do we start?" I asked, glancing up at him. The streetlights flickered overhead, casting pools of golden light that struggled against the encroaching shadows. I was determined to peel back the layers of this conspiracy, yet the gnawing doubt gnawed at me. Could I really trust the people I had surrounded myself with?

"Let's hit the café on Fifth. It's open late and always buzzing with people. If anyone's seen something, it's bound to be there," he suggested, his tone purposeful, cutting through the anxiety that threatened to swallow me whole.

I nodded, though my stomach twisted at the thought of facing any familiar faces. What if they were part of it? What if everyone I had known was just playing a role in this twisted game? The notion made my skin crawl. The café came into view, its neon sign flickering cheerily, and for a moment, it felt like a beacon of normalcy in a chaotic sea.

As we entered, the familiar scent of roasted coffee beans mingled with the sweet aroma of pastries, wrapping around me like a warm embrace. I scanned the room, searching for any hint of danger lurking among the clusters of patrons. The café was alive with chatter, the clinking of cups, and the soft strains of music playing in the background, but I couldn't shake the feeling that something was off.

Grant led us to a corner booth, sliding into the seat across from me. His eyes were sharp, vigilant, a hunter scanning the landscape for threats. I couldn't help but admire the intensity that radiated from him. It was part of what drew me in, the way he took charge without being overbearing. But now, that very strength felt like a double-edged sword, cutting deeper into my doubts.

"What's on your mind?" he asked, leaning forward, his elbows resting on the table. The concern etched into his features softened the harsh reality of our situation, reminding me that beneath the chaos, I still had someone in my corner.

"Just trying to process everything," I admitted, my voice barely above a whisper. "It's hard to believe someone I know could be involved in this. Who can I trust?"

"Trust is a tricky thing," he replied, a hint of vulnerability creeping into his voice. "Sometimes it's the people closest to you who have the most to gain. But that doesn't mean you have to go through this alone."

Before I could respond, a woman in a sleek business suit approached our table, a bright smile on her face that was almost too polished. Her hair was pulled back into a tight bun, and her heels clicked assertively against the floor. "Excuse me, but aren't you Grant Harrington?"

He turned to her, his expression shifting to one of guarded interest. "Yeah, that's me."

"I thought so! I'm a huge fan of your work. I've followed your articles on investigative journalism. Fascinating stuff." She beamed, completely oblivious to the tension swirling between us. I could see the way her gaze flickered between us, curiosity dancing in her eyes.

"Thanks," he said, the polite smile not quite reaching his eyes. "What brings you here at this hour?"

"Late-night caffeine fix and some research for an article of my own," she said, her enthusiasm infectious. "You know how it is. The best ideas come at night, right?" She winked, and I couldn't help but feel a pang of annoyance.

"Absolutely," I replied, forcing a smile, my heart sinking as I felt like an intruder in a conversation that should have been ours alone. "We're just... brainstorming some ideas too."

Her gaze snapped to me, surprise evident on her face. "Oh! Are you a journalist as well? You look familiar."

"I'm—"

"Not in the industry, actually," Grant interjected, a protective edge to his tone. "Just someone caught in the crossfire of a story."

His words hung heavy, a reminder of the dangerous game we were playing.

"Ah, I see. Well, if you ever want to collaborate or share ideas, I'm always open to it," she said, her smile bright as she gave him her business card. "Let me know if you ever want to talk shop." With that, she waved and headed to the counter, her heels clicking sharply against the floor as she disappeared into the crowd.

I exhaled a breath I hadn't realized I'd been holding. "Charming," I muttered, the bite in my tone betraying my irritation. "You have admirers everywhere."

Grant chuckled softly, shaking his head. "Not everyone is an enemy, you know. She's just enthusiastic. It's refreshing."

"Right. Refreshing." I rolled my eyes, but a small smile tugged at my lips despite myself. "It feels like everyone is after something these days. How do you know she's not connected to this?"

"Trust your instincts," he replied, the gravity of his gaze anchoring me to the moment. "But also remember, it's okay to let your guard down sometimes. It's not all dark alleys and shadowy figures."

"Easier said than done."

Just then, a familiar face caught my eye across the café—Sarah, my friend from the office, sitting at a table with a group of her coworkers. She laughed, her head thrown back, and for a brief moment, the weight of our investigation faded.

"Look who it is," I murmured, unable to contain a smile. "Should we invite her over?"

"Maybe," Grant replied, his expression thoughtful. "But is that a risk you're willing to take? With everything going on?"

"Risk? Grant, she's my friend," I shot back, my irritation flaring again. "I refuse to let paranoia dictate my relationships. I won't live like that."

"Then go ahead. But just remember that I'm here, watching your back." He leaned back, his posture relaxed yet attentive, as if bracing for whatever might come next.

Taking a deep breath, I waved at Sarah, who caught my eye and grinned, her enthusiasm infectious. She waved back and made her way over, her presence like a balm to my frayed nerves. "Hey! I didn't know you were here!"

"Just taking a break from the chaos," I said, my smile widening as I gestured for her to sit. "How's work?"

"It's a whirlwind. But enough about that," she said, glancing between Grant and me. "I can't believe you two are hanging out together! What's the story here?" Her eyes sparkled with mischief.

"Just a little project we're working on," I replied, careful not to divulge too much.

"Project? You mean you're investigating something?" Sarah's eyebrows shot up, and I could see the excitement bubbling within her.

Grant interjected smoothly, "Just looking into some leads. It's nothing serious." But the look in his eyes warned me that he knew better.

"Nothing serious? Come on!" she exclaimed, leaning in closer, the thrill of intrigue sparking between us. "You know I love a good mystery. Tell me everything!"

"Not everything," I said, glancing at Grant. "But there's more to it than just an office project."

As I glanced between them, I could feel the tension shift, an unspoken understanding passing through the air. In this moment, despite the uncertainties that loomed on the horizon, it felt as though the pieces were starting to align. We were forging connections and building alliances, and maybe—just maybe—I wasn't as alone in this after all.

The conversation with Sarah flowed seamlessly, her enthusiasm wrapping around me like a comforting blanket. We filled the air with laughter, sharing stories that danced on the edge of seriousness but never quite tumbled into the abyss of our troubling circumstances. I watched as Grant leaned back, his posture relaxed yet alert, observing the interplay like a spectator in a theater, one brow slightly raised as he took in my friend's vivaciousness.

"Okay, so you have to tell me everything about your 'project' with Grant," Sarah insisted, her eyes gleaming with curiosity. "I mean, how do you go from the daily grind to... well, whatever it is you two are tangled up in?"

Grant shot me a look, the corner of his mouth twitching as if he were fighting off a smile. "Maybe I should start charging for this kind of intel," he joked, feigning a mock-seriousness that made me chuckle.

"Please, like you could put a price on this chaos," I shot back, feeling the tension in my chest ease just a little. "But honestly, we're just trying to figure out what's been happening around here. It's a lot more complicated than we thought."

"Complicated?" Sarah echoed, her tone light but her gaze searching. "Is that code for 'someone's definitely been up to no good'?"

"More like there are layers upon layers of deceit," I replied, feeling the weight of the words settle between us. "The kind that makes you question everyone you know."

She leaned closer, a spark of determination igniting in her eyes. "So, you're saying I should be worried?"

"Worried? No, you should be intrigued," Grant interjected, his expression shifting from playful to serious. "But it's best to keep this between us for now. The less people know, the safer everyone is."

"Safe is overrated," Sarah quipped, her voice full of mischief. "Especially when you have a mystery to solve. I want in."

Before I could protest, she pulled out her phone, tapping at the screen with rapid efficiency. "If you're investigating, I can help. I've got contacts, maybe some resources we can tap into. You just have to promise to keep me in the loop."

Grant glanced at me, a mixture of concern and respect crossing his features. "This could get dangerous, Sarah. We're not just talking about late-night detective work here."

"Dangerous? Please, I've survived meetings with our boss. I can handle a little suspense." Her grin was infectious, and I felt a swell of gratitude for her unwavering spirit. "Besides, I have a gut feeling about this. You guys are onto something big."

"Fine, but if we bring you in, you have to promise to play it smart," I said, feeling a flicker of excitement. There was strength in numbers, after all.

"Deal," she replied, her eyes sparkling with mischief. "Now, what's the plan?"

Just as I was about to share our ideas, a loud crash interrupted us, drawing the attention of every patron in the café. I turned, my heart racing as a figure stumbled through the entrance, breathless and wide-eyed, a wild panic in their expression. It was Mark, the very colleague whose presence had felt like a tenuous thread connecting me to normalcy.

"Guys, you need to see this!" he shouted, his voice a frantic whisper, as if he feared someone might overhear.

"What's going on?" I asked, my pulse quickening as I took in his disheveled appearance, hair tousled and shirt rumpled.

"I just came from the office," he gasped, leaning against the table for support. "You won't believe what I found on the server."

The café fell silent, the air thick with expectation as all eyes turned to us. "What do you mean?" I pressed, urgency clawing at my throat.

Mark glanced around, his gaze darting toward the exit before he continued, "I found logs—hidden logs—of transactions between some of our executives and external parties. There's a list of names... and it includes people you know."

My heart sank, the reality of his words crashing over me like a wave. "Names?" I echoed, hardly able to breathe. "Who?"

"I can't say here. We need to talk somewhere private," he urged, eyes flickering with fear.

"Let's go to my apartment," Grant said, his voice steady and authoritative. "It's nearby, and we can figure this out without drawing attention."

"Good idea," I agreed, already pushing myself up from the booth. I shot a glance at Sarah, who looked as equally worried and intrigued. "You're coming with us, right?"

"Wouldn't miss it," she replied, her eyes alight with determination.

As we hurried out of the café, I could feel the weight of the unknown pressing down on us. The streets felt different now, darker and more sinister, as if shadows danced just out of reach. My mind raced with possibilities, every step amplifying my anxiety. I was caught between the thrill of uncovering the truth and the fear of what that truth might entail.

Grant led the way, his presence both reassuring and maddening. I could feel the tension simmering between us, the attraction that had been a spark now flaring into something more substantial. Yet, we were hurtling toward a cliff, and the ground beneath us felt precarious at best.

We reached Grant's apartment, the door swinging open with a creak that echoed through the stillness. Inside, the familiar scent of fresh coffee mingled with the musty air, creating a strange blend of comfort and tension.

"Okay, spill," Grant urged Mark as we settled in, his gaze unwavering.

Mark took a deep breath, the reality of what he was about to reveal hanging heavily in the air. "I accessed the logs from the last few months. There's evidence of illicit payments—money being funneled to a shell company linked to our department. It's not just bad news; it's a full-blown scandal. And it's happening right under our noses."

"What? Who's behind it?" I asked, my voice strained.

"That's the thing," he said, glancing between us, fear etched in his features. "I don't know. But I do know that whoever it is has the power to silence anyone who gets too close."

The room grew colder, the implications of his words sinking in like a lead weight. I felt a shiver run down my spine as reality settled over me like a dark cloud. "We need to get evidence," I said, my voice steady despite the chaos in my mind. "We can't let this continue."

"I have a few leads I can follow up on," Mark offered, determination flaring in his eyes. "But we have to be careful. If they catch wind of this, they won't hesitate to take us out."

As we strategized, the air crackled with urgency, a shared understanding binding us together in this dangerous dance. But just as I began to feel a sense of purpose, a sound echoed from the hallway—heavy footsteps approaching, followed by the sharp click of a door handle turning.

"Grant," I whispered, fear creeping into my voice.

He looked at me, tension rippling through his muscles as he quietly moved toward the door, ready to confront whatever danger awaited us. The doorknob turned slowly, and my heart raced as the door creaked open, revealing a silhouette framed by the harsh overhead light.

"Looks like we're not the only ones interested in the truth."

Chapter 16: Unraveling the Truth

The rain-soaked streets glimmered under the flickering streetlights, each puddle reflecting the chaotic dance of shadows as I stepped into the heart of the city's darkest alleys. The dampness clung to my skin, a constant reminder of the urgency gnawing at my insides. With Grant's reluctant support echoing in my mind, I could hardly decide whether I felt emboldened or utterly terrified. This place was alive with secrets, every brick of the ancient buildings whispering tales of betrayal and vengeance. It was as if the city itself was a character in our story, one with a treacherous agenda, urging us to delve deeper into the abyss of its hidden truths.

I had spent weeks piecing together fragments of information, tracing a web of deception that spiraled outward like the roots of a twisted tree. Each lead had been more confounding than the last, and I was acutely aware of the stakes involved. Our target, the mastermind behind this conspiracy, remained an elusive specter, taunting me from the shadows. I could almost hear their laughter, a cold and hollow sound that echoed in the recesses of my mind. Whoever they were, their motives lay buried beneath layers of resentment and betrayal, far too close to home for comfort.

The wind whispered through the alley, rustling the remnants of yesterday's news and discarded memories. I tightened the collar of my jacket against the chill, reminding myself that courage was not the absence of fear but the determination to move forward despite it. I glanced at my phone—Grant's last text flickered on the screen, a simple message that seemed to weigh a thousand pounds: "Be careful. I'll be there soon." But would he? A flicker of doubt coursed through me.

Turning a corner, I found myself face-to-face with the entrance to an abandoned warehouse. The door, hanging askew on rusted hinges, beckoned me closer. My heart pounded in my chest as I stepped inside, the scent of mildew and decay swirling around me like a shroud. The darkness was thick, almost tangible, wrapping itself around my senses. Every creak of the floorboards beneath my feet felt like a whisper, urging me to retreat, but I couldn't. Not now, not when I was so close.

As I navigated the maze of crates and debris, my mind raced with questions. What drove someone to this kind of madness? The answer danced just out of reach, tantalizingly close yet infuriatingly elusive. I could feel it in the air, a tension crackling like static electricity, and the sensation made the hairs on my arms stand on end.

A sound, faint yet distinct, broke the heavy silence. My heart skipped as I followed it, each step echoing in the hollow space around me. There, in a dimly lit corner, I saw a figure. My breath caught as I recognized the silhouette—Grant, his broad shoulders tense, every muscle coiled like a spring. He looked up, eyes dark with concern as they locked onto mine.

"You shouldn't be here," he warned, his voice low and gravelly, yet it held a warmth that stirred something deep within me. "It's too dangerous."

"Dangerous or not, I'm not backing down," I replied, my voice steadier than I felt. "Not now. Not when I can finally confront the one pulling the strings." I stepped closer, and the air between us shimmered with unspoken words. We had come so far, but the weight of our unsaid feelings pressed against me like the walls of the warehouse.

Before he could respond, a sudden crash echoed from the far end of the building, causing both of us to jump. Instinctively, I moved closer to Grant, my heart racing in sync with the pulse of adrenaline surging through my veins. "What was that?" I whispered, trying to steady my breathing.

"Stay behind me," he commanded, taking a protective stance. I couldn't help but admire the way his resolve solidified, how the danger ignited a fierce determination within him. It made my heart flutter—this man, so strong yet so vulnerable.

The shadows shifted as we crept toward the sound, each step a silent prayer that we would find answers and not another layer of chaos. My mind flickered to the tangled emotions that had woven themselves between us, a complex tapestry of fear, longing, and an undeniable connection that neither of us had fully acknowledged.

As we reached the source of the noise, I felt the ground beneath us shift, a sense of impending confrontation swirling in the air. Then, like the curtain lifting on a long-forgotten play, a figure emerged from the shadows. It was a woman, her features sharp and hauntingly familiar, the glint of malice in her eyes unmistakable.

"Did you really think you could unearth the truth without consequences?" she sneered, her voice dripping with scorn. "You're playing a dangerous game, and you're far from the only players at the table."

I exchanged a glance with Grant, our unspoken agreement binding us tighter than any words could. This was the moment we had been preparing for, the confrontation that would either shatter our resolve or solidify our bond.

"What do you want?" I demanded, my voice stronger than I felt. The tension was palpable, thick as smoke, as we faced down the darkness that threatened to consume us both. And yet, amidst the chaos, I felt a flicker of hope—a belief that love, if harnessed in the right moment, could light the way through the shadows.

The woman's laughter, sharp and brittle, reverberated off the warehouse walls, creating an eerie echo that danced around us like the ghosts of our pasts. "You think you can confront me here?" she taunted, stepping forward with a confidence that was unsettling. Her presence seemed to dim the already sparse light, casting a shadow that felt heavy with malevolence. "You don't even know what you're getting into."

Grant's grip on my arm tightened, a silent reminder of his unwavering support, and I felt a rush of gratitude mingle with the undercurrent of fear bubbling inside me. "And yet here we are," I countered, forcing my voice to remain steady despite the tremor beneath it. "Tell us what you want, and maybe we can save ourselves the theatrics."

Her eyes narrowed, calculating, as if weighing her next move. "What I want? Oh, darling, it's not so simple. You've unraveled one thread of a much larger tapestry, and you have no idea how tangled it truly is." She paused, tilting her head as if appraising our worth. "But if you're looking for the puppet master, perhaps you should start by examining your own strings."

I exchanged a glance with Grant, our eyes locking in an unspoken agreement. We couldn't let her manipulate the situation; we had to stay one step ahead. "Then let's cut to the chase," I said, stepping forward with determination. "You can play games, but I won't play the victim. We know there's more at stake than just your little schemes. What is it you're really after?"

For a moment, silence stretched between us like a taut wire, fraught with tension. Then she leaned back, her demeanor shifting from threatening to amused, a predatory smile spreading across her face. "Ah, the fire in you, it's quite invigorating. But you still don't get it, do you? You think this is just about me?" Her voice dripped with condescension, the smirk never leaving her lips. "No, sweetie. This is about power. About control. About a legacy."

The word legacy hung in the air like a bitter aftertaste. "Your legacy is built on manipulation and fear?" I shot back, my voice rising. "You're no queen; you're a coward hiding in the shadows."

"Cowardice is a luxury I can't afford," she retorted, her expression darkening. "And neither can you. The real game has yet to begin, and you're merely pawns in this play."

Before I could formulate a response, a loud crash erupted from somewhere deeper within the warehouse, followed by the unmistakable sound of hurried footsteps. My heart raced as adrenaline surged through my veins. "What was that?" I hissed, my instincts kicking in.

Grant's brow furrowed with concern, and he edged closer, placing himself between me and the potential threat. "We need to get out of here," he said, his voice low but urgent. "This isn't the time for bravado."

"Not without knowing what she knows," I insisted, defiance igniting within me. I was tired of running; I was tired of being afraid. "We need answers."

"Answers? You think you can handle the truth?" the woman sneered, her gaze flickering to the entrance as the footsteps grew louder. "Be careful what you wish for, darling. You might just get it."

"Or maybe we'll give you what you deserve," I shot back, refusing to let her intimidate me. The stakes had been raised, and I was determined to meet them head-on.

Just then, the source of the noise emerged from the shadows—a figure I recognized instantly. It was Marcus, the elusive informant who had been a ghost in our investigation, his expression a mix of panic and resolve. "We have to move!" he shouted, his voice echoing in the cavernous space. "They're coming for you."

"Who's coming?" Grant asked, stepping forward, his protective instincts flaring.

"Those you've stirred from their slumber," Marcus replied breathlessly. "The ones who will do anything to silence you. We need to leave—now!"

Before I could respond, the warehouse door burst open with a jarring crash, revealing a group of figures silhouetted against the night, their intentions unreadable in the flickering light. My stomach dropped as dread clawed at my insides. We were outnumbered and cornered, the darkness closing in around us like a vice.

"Run!" Grant yelled, grabbing my hand and pulling me toward the nearest exit. We dashed through the maze of crates, my heart pounding like a war drum in my chest. The thrill of the chase surged through me, igniting a primal instinct to survive.

As we neared the door, the shadows seemed to stretch and reach for us, the pursuers hot on our heels. "I thought you said we'd have answers!" I shouted at Marcus as we barreled toward the dimly lit exit.

"Trust me, this is not the time for answers!" he retorted, glancing back as we sprinted. The urgency in his voice sent a chill down my spine.

We burst through the door into the cool night air, the weight of the city pressing against us. My lungs burned as we stumbled into the open, the streetlights illuminating our frantic escape. The sound of footsteps behind us echoed ominously, and I could feel the tension coiling tighter around us like a noose.

"Where to now?" Grant panted, scanning the darkened street as we veered left, adrenaline pushing us forward.

"Head to the car!" Marcus pointed, urgency etched across his features. "I'll cover you!"

"Cover us how?" I yelled, glancing back just in time to see the silhouettes spill out of the warehouse, determination etched into their every movement.

But Marcus wasn't waiting for an answer. He darted back toward the shadows, positioning himself between us and our pursuers, his resolve evident. "Go! Now!"

Without another word, Grant and I took off toward the parked car, the engine's soft purr a distant promise of safety. My heart raced not just from fear but from the tumult of emotions threatening to spill over as we raced away from the chaos. This wasn't just about survival anymore; it was about unraveling a truth that tied us all together—bonds forged in the fire of desperation, the potential for love kindling amidst the storm.

The car's engine roared to life, a welcome sound in the cacophony of chaos that surrounded us. I threw myself into the passenger seat, my heart pounding as Grant slid behind the wheel, his expression taut with concentration. The world outside blurred into streaks of darkness and neon lights as he pressed the accelerator, propelling us into the night. My breath came in sharp gasps, the adrenaline coursing through my veins, but there was something else—a spark of exhilaration interwoven with fear.

"Are you okay?" he asked, his voice low and steady despite the frantic rhythm of our escape. His eyes flicked to mine, searching for signs of distress.

"Honestly? I think I've had better days," I replied with a wry smile, trying to mask the tremor in my voice. "But I'm alive, and that's something, right?" The tension between us crackled, thick and undeniable, as if the air itself was charged with our unspoken feelings.

"Let's not celebrate just yet," he muttered, his grip on the steering wheel tightening. "We need to put some distance between us and whoever those people were. They won't stop until they find us."

I nodded, trying to wrap my mind around the gravity of our situation. "We should head to the safe house," I suggested, the thought igniting a flicker of hope. "Marcus has connections there. He'll know what to do."

Grant glanced at me, a mixture of admiration and concern playing across his features. "You really think we can trust him?"

"Right now, we don't have much choice," I countered, my resolve hardening. "If anyone can help us figure this out, it's Marcus."

The streets blurred past us, a disorienting rush of color and sound, but my mind remained anchored on our perilous situation.

Who was the woman we had confronted? What was her connection to this tangled mess? My thoughts spiraled into uncertainty, each question drawing me deeper into the labyrinth of conspiracy we had unwittingly stepped into.

"Where are we?" I asked, noticing the flicker of unfamiliar buildings through the rain-smeared windows.

"Heading toward the industrial district," Grant replied, his focus unwavering on the road ahead. "We'll take a back route to avoid any major intersections."

As he navigated the winding streets, I felt a swell of admiration for his unwavering determination. There was a strength in him, a fierce loyalty that made my heart flutter. It was crazy, but in that moment of danger, the thrill of it all only deepened my feelings. "You know," I said, attempting to lighten the mood, "if we survive this, we could write a bestseller together. 'How to Outrun a Conspiracy in Five Easy Steps.'"

He chuckled, a sound that melted the tension between us. "I think we might need a better title, but I'm in." His gaze shifted to mine, and for a brief moment, the world outside faded. In that car, it was just us—two survivors on the run, sharing a moment of levity amidst the chaos.

But that moment was short-lived. As we turned a corner, I caught a glimpse of headlights bearing down on us from the opposite direction. My stomach dropped as realization hit. "Grant! Behind us!"

He swerved just in time, narrowly avoiding a collision. The other vehicle, a sleek black sedan, matched our speed, its windows tinted, obscuring the identities of our pursuers. I could feel the weight of their intentions pressing against us like a palpable force.

"Hold on!" Grant shouted, veering into an alley that snaked between two crumbling warehouses. The tires screeched in protest as he took the sharp turn, the sound echoing off the graffiti-stained walls. I clutched the handle above the window, bracing myself as he maneuvered through the narrow passage.

"They're still on us!" I gasped, glancing back to see the sedan barreling into the alley behind us, relentless in its pursuit. The driver was skilled, navigating the tight corners with a precision that sent shivers down my spine.

"I see that!" Grant replied, his jaw set in determination. "Just keep your head down."

"Easier said than done!" I muttered, fighting the surge of panic rising within me. "What's the plan?"

"I'm working on it!" His voice was tight, each word laced with urgency. "Just hold on."

We hurtled through the alley, weaving between trash cans and debris, the sedan gaining ground with each turn. I could hear the sound of their engine roaring like a beast hungry for prey, the tension mounting as we raced toward an unknown fate. My heart pounded in rhythm with the engine, a wild drumbeat urging us forward.

Then, without warning, Grant slammed on the brakes. I barely had time to register the sudden stop before we were thrown forward, the seatbelt digging into my chest. Confusion flooded my senses as I looked around, trying to grasp the new reality unfolding before us.

"What are we doing?" I blurted, panic seeping into my voice as I struggled to catch my breath.

"Wait for it," he said, his eyes scanning the rearview mirror with the intensity of a hawk spotting its prey. I felt the tension in him, a magnetic pull of energy that held us both in a state of anticipation.

A moment later, I saw it: the black sedan skidded to a halt behind us, the driver momentarily thrown off by our abrupt stop. But that split second of confusion quickly shifted to focus. The door swung open, and a figure emerged—dark and imposing, their intentions unmistakably menacing.

"Get ready," Grant whispered, his voice a fierce whisper that sent a shiver of resolve through me.

I barely had time to nod before he shifted the car into reverse, the engine growling like a beast awakened. The rear window shattered with a resounding crash, and I instinctively ducked, my heart racing as I tried to process the chaos unfolding around us.

"Go! Go!" Grant shouted, and we lurched backward, narrowly missing the figure as they scrambled to regain their footing. The world spun, chaos colliding with a strange sense of exhilaration.

But just as we thought we had a moment to breathe, a piercing light flooded the rearview mirror—more headlights, closing in fast. Grant's eyes widened in horror as he realized we were trapped in a tightening circle of danger.

"Not again!" he roared, slamming the car into drive and veering hard to the right. But the street ahead was a blur of shadows and uncertainty, and I could feel the walls closing in, the realization that we might not escape this alive clawing at my throat.

"What do we do?" I shouted, fear coursing through me, mingling with the adrenaline.

He opened his mouth to reply, but before he could say another word, a sharp crack echoed through the air, followed by the unmistakable sound of breaking glass. I whipped around, eyes wide with dread, only to see the darkness behind us was closing in faster than I could comprehend.

"Hold on!" Grant shouted, but it was too late. The weight of what was coming crashed over me like a tidal wave, and in that moment, the car shuddered violently, the engine sputtering as if protesting against the inevitable.

A jolt shot through my body, the world tilting on its axis. I clung to the door, heart hammering in my chest, as the car spun out of control. My mind raced with the possibilities, each one more terrifying than the last, the echoes of Grant's voice fading into the chaos around us.

And just as everything seemed to blur into darkness, I caught a glimpse of the figure from the black sedan, their face illuminated by the fleeting streetlights. A familiar smirk twisted across their lips, a harbinger of doom that pierced through the chaos.

In that fleeting moment, I understood that this was just the beginning.

Chapter 17: A Fragile Truce

The city, cloaked in twilight, sprawled beneath us like a living organism, pulsating with secrets and shadows. The orange and crimson hues of the setting sun bled into one another, casting a warm glow on the cold concrete jungle. It was a deceptive beauty, a façade that hid the rot beneath. As I stood there, the weight of the betrayal still heavy in my chest, I felt the tug-of-war within me escalate. Grant, with his tousled hair and those impossibly blue eyes, stirred emotions I thought had been buried under layers of hurt and anger.

He leaned against the weathered table, his fingers drumming an anxious rhythm as he stared at the stack of documents scattered before us. Each page, each line, was an unmasking of the corruption that had seeped into the very foundations of the city hall I had once considered my home. It was infuriating and fascinating all at once. My heart raced—not just from the revelations but from the proximity of the man who had once been my greatest ally and now stood as a complicated puzzle I was desperate to solve.

"What do you think?" Grant asked, his voice low and gravelly, slicing through the thick tension like a knife through warm butter. He shifted slightly, his gaze penetrating. "Is it possible that they've been this organized for so long without anyone noticing?"

I inhaled deeply, the scent of old paper mingling with the musk of the wooden table beneath my hands. "It's not just possible; it's likely. These people are pros at hiding in plain sight. We have to tread carefully." I met his gaze, feeling the weight of my words settle between us. "You know how much I've invested in this place. I can't just stand by and watch it burn."

"Neither can I," he said, and for a fleeting moment, I saw the man I used to know, a glimpse of the soft-hearted hero who fought for what was right, even when it came at a personal cost. That shimmer of humanity was quickly extinguished, though, as he ran a hand through his hair, frustration evident in the slight furrow of his brow. "But this... this is different. We're talking about people who have nothing to lose. They'll stop at nothing to protect their interests, even if it means going after us."

I nodded, feeling the gravity of our situation wrap around me like a suffocating shroud. The walls felt like they were closing in, the darkness outside creeping into the corners of the room. "So what's the plan, then? We can't just sit here sifting through paperwork forever."

Grant sighed, leaning forward, the tension in his posture revealing the unspoken layers of his worry. "We need to go on the offensive. Gather evidence discreetly, find allies who might be sympathetic to our cause, and then—" He hesitated, glancing at me, as if testing the waters. "We expose them. We rip the curtain down, no matter what it takes."

"Exposing them won't be easy," I replied, biting my lip. The very thought sent a ripple of anxiety through me. "They'll have their eyes on us the moment we make a move. We need to be smart."

He tilted his head, a hint of a smile creeping onto his lips, the corners crinkling in a way that tugged at something deep within me. "Smart? I thought you meant reckless. You've always had a flair for the dramatic."

"Oh, please," I scoffed, rolling my eyes. "That's a trademark of yours, not mine. I prefer to think things through. It's one of the many ways I've managed to survive in this cesspool of politics."

"Touché." He chuckled softly, and for a moment, the tension melted away, replaced by a familiar banter that reminded me of late-night conversations over coffee and pastries at our favorite café. But that brief moment of camaraderie flickered out as quickly as it had come, replaced by the harsh reality of our circumstances.

"We should split up," I suggested, steeling my resolve. "You take the east side of town. I'll head to the west and see if I can find anyone who might be willing to talk. We need eyes and ears everywhere."

His brow furrowed, a flash of concern crossing his face. "Alone? I don't like the idea of you out there without backup."

"Neither do I," I admitted, feeling a knot form in my stomach. "But we're running out of time. I can't let fear dictate my choices, Grant. Not now, not when the stakes are so high."

"Okay," he relented, the resignation in his voice heavy. "But promise me you'll be careful. If things get too dicey—"

"I'll call you," I interrupted, firm in my resolve. "I promise."

His eyes searched mine, a silent agreement passing between us, the air thick with unspoken words. I didn't want to dwell on what lay ahead, the uncertainty that hung in the air like a dark cloud ready to burst. Instead, I focused on the task at hand, determined to regain my footing in a world that had shifted beneath me.

With a final nod, we stood up and gathered our things, the silence between us charged with anticipation and a hint of something else—something I dared not name. As I stepped out into the cool night air, the city enveloped me like an old friend. The streets were alive with sounds—the distant hum of traffic, the murmur of voices, the scent of rain-soaked asphalt mingling with the faint whiff of something sweet from a nearby bakery.

I took a deep breath, my heart pounding not just with apprehension but with a spark of defiance. It was time to dive back into the fray, to fight for what was right, even if it meant facing the ghosts of my past, especially the one standing just a breath away.

Navigating the city streets felt different now, each step an echo of my conflicting emotions, a mix of determination and uncertainty. The familiar pathways shimmered with new possibilities, yet every corner I turned reminded me of the stakes that lay ahead. The golden glow of streetlights flickered to life, illuminating the fading remnants of the sunset, casting long shadows that danced alongside me. I clutched my jacket tighter around me, the brisk air mingling with the scents of fresh bread and coffee wafting from nearby cafés.

As I made my way toward the heart of the city, I replayed our conversation in my mind. The ease with which we had slipped into our old dynamic felt both comforting and dangerous. Grant's presence stirred something within me, a mixture of nostalgia and longing, and I couldn't quite tell if it was the thrill of our shared mission or the lingering feelings from the past that made my pulse quicken. I shook my head, trying to focus on the task at hand.

My first stop was a small diner nestled between two towering buildings, its neon sign buzzing softly like a lighthouse guiding ships through a stormy sea. Inside, the smell of frying bacon and brewing coffee enveloped me like a warm hug. I slid into a booth at the back, my eyes scanning the room for anyone who might be an ally. The usual crowd of tired workers and late-night patrons filled the space, each lost in their own world, but I was on a mission.

The waitress approached, a whirlwind of energy with a pencil tucked behind her ear and a notepad that looked like it had seen better days. "What can I get you, hon? You look like you could use a strong cup of coffee and maybe a slice of our famous pie."

I smiled, appreciating her directness. "You know what? I'll take both. Coffee black, and make that pie a slice of your apple. I need to think."

As she hurried off, I pulled out my phone, scrolling through contacts until I landed on a name that made my heart skip. Jenna was a journalist I had worked with in the past—a fierce woman with a knack for unearthing hidden truths. She had a network of informants that could rival any secret society, and if anyone could help me expose the corruption I was up against, it was her.

"Hey, Jenna," I said when she answered, keeping my voice low, just in case. "It's me. I need your help. Can we meet?"

"Absolutely. How about the usual spot?" Her voice was a blend of enthusiasm and concern. "You sound... urgent."

I winced at the word. "You could say that. I have some intel that could blow this whole thing wide open."

"Count me in," she said without hesitation. "I'll be there in twenty."

My heart raced as I hung up, excitement coursing through me. Jenna was exactly what I needed—a partner who wasn't afraid to dive into the deep end, even if it meant ruffling a few feathers. Just as I was setting my phone down, the waitress returned with my coffee and pie, the aroma wafting up to me like a siren's call. I took a moment to savor the moment, the warmth seeping into my bones, before I allowed my mind to wander back to Grant.

The thought of him ignited a smoldering ember of anxiety. What if he was right? What if we were too late? The shadows lurking in the city seemed to whisper caution, hinting at dangers I couldn't yet see. But this was my city. I had poured my heart into making it a better place, and I wasn't about to let anyone undermine that.

As I took a bite of the pie, the sweet and tart flavors bursting in my mouth, the door swung open with a jingle, drawing my attention. Jenna strode in, her dark hair a wild halo around her determined expression. She spotted me instantly, waving as she approached the booth, her eyes scanning the room with the practiced gaze of someone accustomed to being on alert.

"Got a death wish, sitting in a booth like this," she said, sliding into the seat opposite mine. "Anyone could be watching."

"Let them watch," I replied, emboldened by the sugary pie and caffeine. "I'm ready to make some noise."

Jenna leaned forward, her voice low and conspiratorial. "So what's the scoop? What are we diving into?"

I hesitated for just a heartbeat, the enormity of what I was about to disclose pressing down on me. "There's a network of corruption tied to city hall. I've got documents, but I need someone on the inside to help me connect the dots."

Her eyebrows shot up. "You've got documents? And you're just sitting here eating pie? We need to get those into the right hands."

"I just got the intel," I said, trying to maintain my cool. "I need to make sure I'm not walking into a trap. These people are dangerous, and they've got connections everywhere."

"Dangerous doesn't even begin to cover it," she muttered, glancing around again, her instincts honed. "You know, I've heard whispers about a certain councilman who's been living a little too high on the hog. If we can tie him to this mess, it could unravel the whole thing."

I nodded, feeling the weight of her words settle into my chest. "I thought the same. We just need the right proof."

Jenna's expression shifted, determination replacing her casual demeanor. "Let's go then. We'll hit the streets, see what we can dig up. I'll make some calls, see if anyone is willing to talk."

"Perfect," I said, the excitement bubbling inside me. "But let's be smart about it. We're not the only ones searching for the truth, and we need to stay one step ahead."

We finished our coffee quickly, the urgency of our mission outweighing the simple pleasure of our meal. As we slipped out of the diner, the night air greeted us like a breath of fresh resolve. I glanced at Jenna, her eyes sparkling with the thrill of the chase.

"Ready to unearth some secrets?" she asked, a sly smile playing at her lips.

"Always," I replied, feeling the adrenaline surge through me. With Jenna at my side, I felt like I could face anything—even the ghosts of my past and the complicated history I had with Grant. We stepped into the unknown, the vibrant pulse of the city surrounding us, our footsteps echoing a new mantra: the truth was waiting, and we were determined to find it.

With the city's vibrant energy enveloping us, Jenna and I plunged into our mission, our shared determination propelling us forward. The streets felt alive, the hum of voices and laughter blending into a cacophony of excitement and urgency. We turned down an alleyway that led to a series of run-down buildings, their façades worn but resilient, like the secrets they harbored. I could feel the pulse of the city quicken beneath my feet as we neared our destination, an old warehouse rumored to be a hub for shady dealings.

"Are you sure this is the place?" Jenna asked, glancing around, her instinct for danger palpable. The light from a flickering streetlamp cast eerie shadows, making the atmosphere almost cinematic.

"Nothing says underground like a good old-fashioned warehouse," I replied, trying to keep the mood light despite the tension thrumming in my veins. "Besides, I've heard whispers that some of the city hall's less-than-savory associates meet here. If we're lucky, we might catch a glimpse of something useful."

"Lucky is the word I'd use to describe the mood around here," she said dryly, taking the lead as we crept closer. "More like foolhardy."

A rustling sound echoed from within the warehouse, and both of us froze, hearts racing in unison. We exchanged glances, the unspoken question hanging heavy in the air: had we ventured too far? But Jenna's eyes gleamed with mischief, a spark of adrenaline driving her forward. "Let's get a closer look."

As we approached the entrance, we crouched behind a stack of crates, peering into the dimly lit interior. Shadows flitted about, and the low murmur of voices reached our ears, indistinct yet charged with urgency. It was as if we had stumbled into the beating heart of a conspiracy, the thrill of discovery battling with the fear of being discovered.

"Are we really doing this?" I whispered, my heart pounding louder than the muffled voices inside. "This is definitely a bad idea."

"Bad ideas make for the best stories," Jenna replied with a grin, her eyes sparkling with excitement. "Besides, we can't leave until we find something that ties this all together."

Just then, a figure emerged from the shadows, and my breath hitched in my throat. It was a man I recognized all too well—Councilman Brooks, his expensive suit contrasting sharply with the grim surroundings. He leaned against a support beam, his voice low and conspiratorial. "You're sure no one saw you?"

"Of course," came the reply from another man, his face obscured in the shadows. "We've covered our tracks well. But we need to act fast. If they catch wind of this, it could ruin everything."

I exchanged a wide-eyed glance with Jenna, my mind racing. They were planning something big, and it was essential to get every detail we could. I leaned in closer, heart racing as I strained to hear more.

"What about the documents?" Brooks asked, his tone icy. "I want to make sure everything is in place before the meeting."

The other man chuckled darkly. "Don't worry. We have everything we need. The city is ripe for the picking, and once we execute the plan, no one will stand in our way."

"Then let's move quickly," Brooks urged, glancing over his shoulder as if sensing our presence. "We don't want to leave any loose ends."

I felt a chill run down my spine. Loose ends? What did that mean? I pulled back slightly, but a stray piece of wood cracked under my weight, and the noise shattered the fragile silence. My heart sank as Brooks's head snapped toward the sound, his expression morphing from casual confidence to cold alertness.

"Did you hear that?" he barked, moving toward the entrance, his eyes narrowing.

"Let's get out of here," I hissed to Jenna, adrenaline surging as we darted back the way we came. We bolted down the alley, my legs pumping with the fear of being caught. The pounding of my heart echoed in my ears, drowning out everything else.

As we rounded a corner, we paused to catch our breath, leaning against a cold brick wall that felt reassuringly solid. "What the hell was that?" Jenna gasped, her chest rising and falling rapidly.

"I think we just stumbled into something much bigger than we anticipated," I replied, trying to shake off the fear that had settled over me like a heavy cloak. "We need to figure out what those documents are and how they tie into everything."

Just then, the hairs on the back of my neck prickled as I sensed someone approaching. I glanced around, my heart dropping as I saw a figure emerge from the shadows. "Grant?" I called out, unsure if it was him or another threat lurking in the dark.

The figure stepped into the dim light, and relief flooded through me as I recognized his familiar silhouette. "There you are! I thought I'd lost you two," he said, a mix of concern and frustration etched across his face. "What were you thinking, sneaking off like that?"

"We heard something—Brooks is planning something big," I blurted out, urgency threading through my voice. "We have to stop him, but we need more information first."

His expression shifted, a flicker of understanding crossing his features. "Then we need to get back in there. We can't let them know we're onto them."

Jenna shook her head vehemently. "Are you insane? They'll see us coming from a mile away. We need a different approach."

Just then, a sharp noise echoed from the warehouse, a loud crash followed by the unmistakable sound of shuffling footsteps. My heart raced as I exchanged frantic looks with Grant and Jenna. We had to act fast.

"Split up," Grant said, his tone decisive. "Jenna, you take the north side of the building. I'll circle around the back. I'll try to find a way in without being seen. You, come with me."

Before I could respond, Grant grabbed my arm, pulling me into the shadows as we slipped away from the entrance. "We can't let them know we're here. Stick close to me."

The world around me faded into a blur as we moved stealthily toward the side of the warehouse, the sounds of muffled voices and footsteps echoing ominously behind us. We crept along the wall, our hearts pounding in unison, as I fought to steady my breathing. The thrill of danger mixed with a spark of determination. This was it—the moment we had been waiting for.

But just as we reached a small window, a sudden noise erupted from behind us, sharp and alarming. I turned, my breath hitching in my throat as a dark figure loomed in the shadows, silhouetted against the flickering light of the warehouse. A sense of dread washed over me, the realization sinking in that we might not be alone after all.

"Grant..." I whispered, but the words barely escaped my lips as the figure stepped closer, and I recognized the glint of a weapon in their hand. My heart raced as I grappled with the question: Were we prepared for what was about to unfold? In an instant, the stakes rose impossibly higher, and I braced myself for the storm that was surely about to break.

Chapter 18: A Dance with Danger

The evening air was electric with anticipation, a palpable current that set my heart racing as I stood in front of the mirror. The soft golden glow of the vintage chandelier danced over the crimson fabric of my gown, a breathtaking creation that hugged my curves like a second skin. It was the kind of dress that demanded attention and respect, whispering tales of power and allure. I adjusted the straps delicately, the fabric smooth and cool against my skin, a stark contrast to the heat pooling in my stomach. Tonight, I was not just a guest; I was a player in a game filled with deception, and I intended to win.

Grant entered the room with a presence that turned the air thick, a quiet confidence that made him magnetic. Dressed in a tailored suit that accentuated his broad shoulders and lean frame, he looked every bit the part of the charming rogue. I couldn't help but feel a rush of excitement as our eyes met. There was something undeniable in the way he held my gaze, a flicker of mischief mixed with a seriousness that made my pulse quicken. He sauntered closer, and as he did, I caught a hint of his cologne—a warm, woodsy scent that made my thoughts swirl.

"You look like trouble," he murmured, a smirk playing at the corners of his mouth as he held my gaze, his eyes a stormy blue that promised both danger and delight.

"And you look like the kind of trouble I'm eager to embrace," I replied, my voice steady despite the quiver of nerves fluttering beneath the surface. We were stepping into a den of thieves, and yet here, in this moment, I felt anything but afraid.

As we arrived at the venue, a grand estate sprawling against the night sky, it was clear that opulence and extravagance were the order of the evening. Glittering lights twinkled like stars strung low to the ground, illuminating the manicured gardens where elegantly dressed guests mingled, their laughter and chatter a symphony of distraction. The estate itself was a masterpiece of architecture, each stone a silent witness to the secrets buried within its walls. I felt the weight of the night pressing down on me, a mix of exhilaration and dread as we made our way through the crowd, our true intentions cloaked beneath the guise of glamour.

"Stay close to me," Grant whispered, leaning in just enough that his breath brushed my ear, sending a thrill down my spine. "We need to keep our wits about us. The host is known for keeping dangerous company."

His words hung between us like a warning, but instead of fear, they ignited a fire in my chest. The thrill of being by his side, of moving through this perilous landscape together, eclipsed any anxiety that threatened to surface. With every step, our chemistry crackled like static electricity, drawing us together in a way that was impossible to ignore.

As we wove through the crowd, the air thick with perfume and laughter, I spotted familiar faces—adversaries mingling effortlessly with the elite, masks of civility hiding their ulterior motives. I felt like an intruder in their world, but with Grant's steady hand on my back, I found strength. He led me to the bar, where glimmering crystal glasses sparkled like jewels.

"What will it be?" he asked, his eyes twinkling with amusement as he surveyed the vast selection.

"A glass of courage, if you have it," I shot back, unable to resist the playful banter.

He chuckled, a deep, rich sound that resonated in my chest. "Then I'll have two, please." He ordered a pair of martinis, and as he turned to me, I couldn't help but admire how the dim light caught the angles of his jaw, the way he seemed to command the space around him.

As we sipped our drinks, the atmosphere shifted. Laughter morphed into tense murmurs, and I felt the first prickle of unease skitter down my spine. Grant leaned closer, his voice dropping to a low murmur. "We should find a way to speak with our target discreetly. The sooner we get information, the sooner we can leave this circus."

I nodded, my heart pounding in my chest. The thrill of danger buzzed through me, mingling with the warmth of the martini. Just then, a sudden commotion erupted nearby. A group of guests gathered, their faces twisted in anticipation. Intrigued, we edged closer, weaving through the crowd, our hearts synchronizing in an anxious rhythm.

In the center stood a performer, a fire-breather whose flames danced like serpents in the night, casting flickering shadows on the faces surrounding him. The heat radiated toward us, and I felt an electric thrill surge through the air. It was a mesmerizing display, yet I couldn't shake the feeling that it was merely a distraction—a show meant to keep us entertained while darker dealings unfolded behind closed doors.

"Impressive, isn't it?" Grant said, his voice low.

"Almost too impressive," I replied, my eyes narrowing as I scanned the faces in the crowd. "What are they hiding?"

Just then, the fire-breather stepped aside, and a tall figure emerged from the shadows, his silhouette sharp against the flames. I felt the air shift around us as I caught a glimpse of the host—his smile charming, his eyes calculating.

"Now would be a good time to make our move," Grant urged, his grip tightening around my waist.

With adrenaline coursing through my veins, I nodded. We were warriors entering the battlefield of secrets and lies, and together, we would unveil the truth hidden beneath the surface of this extravagant masquerade.

We slipped through the throngs of guests, the world around us fading as we focused solely on our objective. I could feel Grant's presence beside me, a silent reassurance that pushed me forward. There was a promise in his gaze—a vow that together, we would navigate whatever darkness awaited us. With each step, the night morphed into a labyrinth of intrigue, and I couldn't help but wonder what secrets lay waiting for us, hidden behind the laughter and glamour of this dangerous dance.

The atmosphere shifted the moment we stepped away from the thrumming pulse of the crowd. The laughter faded into a hushed murmur, and the extravagant decor transformed into a maze of flickering candlelight and shadowy corners. My heart raced as Grant led me through a series of ornate archways draped with ivy and delicate fairy lights, each step drawing us deeper into the estate's hidden realms. It was as if we were escaping the polished veneer of the gala into a world where secrets simmered just below the surface, waiting for the right moment to erupt.

"Over there," Grant whispered, nodding toward a small alcove lined with velvet drapes. A flicker of urgency ignited in his eyes, and I followed his lead, the hem of my gown brushing against the polished marble floor. The world outside this sanctuary was a whirlwind of champagne toasts and glittering smiles, but here, in this dimly lit space, we could breathe.

Once hidden behind the drapes, the sound of the gala faded to a soft thrum, replaced by the sound of our quickened breaths. Grant turned to face me, his expression a blend of determination and something warmer, more intimate. "We have to stay alert. There's a reason this gathering feels like a ticking time bomb."

"Are you suggesting we play nice?" I quipped, raising an eyebrow as I crossed my arms. "I thought we were here to unmask the villain."

He chuckled softly, the sound echoing against the lush fabric surrounding us. "Nice? I thought you were here to dazzle everyone with your looks and snatch away the spotlight."

"Flattery will get you nowhere," I teased, biting back a grin. "But I'm still willing to give it my best shot."

His smile widened, and for a moment, the tension around us melted away, replaced by the warmth of shared mischief. But just as quickly, a shadow flickered across his face. "We can't let our guard down. The host is known for being ruthless, and you know how easily things can spiral out of control."

"I know," I replied, my voice dropping to a whisper. "But if we're going to do this, I want to do it with flair. Besides, it's hard to be cautious when you look this good." I twirled, the fabric of my gown swirling around me like a burst of color against the monochrome backdrop of the shadows.

"Show-off," he replied with mock exasperation, but I could see the amusement dancing in his eyes. The playful banter between us felt like a shield against the looming dangers outside.

"Just setting the stage, my dear Grant," I said, placing a hand over my heart in a dramatic gesture. "We can't let them forget who we are, can we?"

As we prepared to leave our little hideaway, a low rumble of laughter drifted in from the main hall, causing me to pause. My instincts flared, a warning that we were not alone in our pursuit. With a gentle push, Grant edged the curtain aside just enough to peek through.

"Keep your eyes peeled," he said, his voice steady but low. "I'm not sure what we're looking for yet, but I can feel the tension in the air."

I pressed close to him, our shoulders brushing, my breath hitching in anticipation. The scene unfolding beyond the drapes was a theater of deception. Guests swirled like leaves caught in a gust of wind, their laughter ringing hollow as they exchanged furtive glances. Conversations seemed to morph into conspiracies, and I strained to catch snippets of dialogue that floated through the air like smoke.

"...word on the street... dangerous alliances...," a woman with fiery red hair and a dress that sparkled like a million stars said to a man with sharp features, his eyes darting about like a predator assessing its prey.

Grant's grip tightened on my waist, and I felt the warmth radiating from him. "We need to move, now," he urged, the urgency of his tone sending a thrill through me. I nodded, the thrill of the chase invigorating my senses as we slipped back into the thrumming heart of the gala.

Navigating through the crowd felt like a delicate dance, one foot in danger and the other in deception. The laughter around us was intoxicating, yet I sensed the undercurrents of fear and anticipation. The host's presence loomed larger, an invisible specter haunting the festivities.

"Look there," Grant whispered, tilting his head toward a corner where a cluster of guests stood huddled, their voices a low murmur. "I think that's our target."

I focused my gaze on a tall man clad in an impeccably tailored suit, his smile bright but his eyes cold as ice. He moved with an air of authority, the way a king might command his court. I could see the glint of something metallic peeking out from under his jacket—a weapon or perhaps a hidden agenda. Either way, it made my pulse quicken.

"We need to get closer," I said, my voice laced with determination. "If we can overhear anything—"

"Or we can draw him out," Grant interjected, his eyes sparkling with mischief. "What if we play the distraction? I can charm the socks off anyone. And you, my fiery phoenix, can swoop in for the kill."

"Charming the socks off anyone?" I laughed softly. "Are you sure you're not confusing charm with arrogance?"

He feigned shock. "Me? Never. Besides, how else are we going to uncover the truth? You distract while I...well, I'm just going to be charming, thank you very much."

"Right, and if that doesn't work, I'll just wave my gown around and hope for the best." I rolled my eyes, but beneath the playful banter lay a sense of purpose. We were a team, partners in this chaotic ballet of intrigue.

With a subtle nod, we executed our plan. Grant moved toward the center of the crowd, his confidence infectious. I remained on the periphery, watching as he engaged the host, their laughter echoing through the sea of guests.

"Who knew Grant was such a natural?" I mused to myself, catching glimpses of their conversation through the throng. My heart raced with anticipation, my focus sharp as I searched for any hint of a slip, a crack in the armor of the host.

Just then, I noticed a familiar face lurking at the edge of the gathering—a woman with striking blonde hair and an icy demeanor, her gaze fixated on the host with a predator's intensity. I recognized her from previous encounters, an enigmatic figure who played both sides of the game.

"What are you up to, darling?" I whispered to myself, feeling the pull of the tension crackle in the air. She was the key to unraveling this web, and I couldn't let the opportunity slip through my fingers.

As I moved closer, the sounds of Grant's laughter blended with the murmurs of the crowd, the stakes rising higher. I needed to get close enough to hear the conversation, to glean any secrets that could turn the tide in our favor. The night was filled with uncertainty, but one thing was clear: I wouldn't be going home without answers—or perhaps a twist I hadn't seen coming.

The crowd pulsed around me, a living organism of ambition and illusion, each guest a carefully crafted façade. I could feel the weight of my own disguise, the crimson gown swishing around my legs like a warning flag, urging me to tread carefully. With Grant in the center of the swirl, weaving his charm, I focused my energy on the woman whose icy demeanor had snagged my attention.

As I moved closer, the blonde seemed to sense my approach, her sharp eyes locking onto mine like a hawk spotting its prey. There was something distinctly predatory in her gaze, an awareness that she was not one to be trifled with. "You shouldn't be here," she said, her voice smooth and cold, as if every word was coated in a thin layer of ice. "This isn't a place for amateurs."

"A little late for that advice," I shot back, a defiant smile playing on my lips. "I thought the party was for everyone."

She smirked, but the amusement didn't reach her eyes. "You think it's a party? This is a game, and you're just a pawn. You'd do well to remember that."

"I've always preferred to be the queen," I replied, feeling the thrill of the challenge pulse through me. It was dangerous territory, but the thrill of sparring with her was intoxicating. Behind her poised exterior, I sensed layers of insecurity, and the instinct to unravel her defenses stirred within me.

The noise around us faded, and I could see the host and Grant exchanging words, laughter mingling with the tension. My heart raced, but I couldn't let that deter me. "You're quite the strategist, aren't you?" I pressed, stepping closer, my voice low and conspiratorial. "Tell me, what's the angle? What does the host have on you?"

Her expression flickered—just for a moment—revealing a glimpse of vulnerability. "Information is currency here," she said, her voice dipping, as if revealing a secret. "And I have no intention of letting anyone in on my business."

"I might just have something of value too," I countered, my mind racing. "You don't want to find yourself on the losing side of this game."

She studied me for a heartbeat, weighing her options. The fire-breather's flames roared in the background, a fitting metaphor for the chaos swirling around us. I could feel the tension thrumming like a taut string, and I had to strike before it snapped.

"Why are you really here?" she asked, her tone shifting. "You're not just a pretty face in a fancy dress, are you?"

"Smart enough to know a dangerous game when I see one," I replied, keeping my tone light. "And clever enough to play it my way."

Before she could respond, the atmosphere shifted again. A commotion erupted at the far side of the room, and my gaze flickered to the source—a group of men had gathered, their voices rising in urgency. The blonde's expression hardened, and she took a step back, the moment of connection evaporating like mist in the sun.

"I have to go," she said abruptly, turning on her heel. "This isn't over."

I barely had time to respond before she slipped into the crowd, leaving me standing at the edge of the chaos, my heart racing. My instincts screamed at me to follow, to pry deeper into her motives, but I needed to keep my focus on Grant. He was the linchpin in this precarious scenario, and I couldn't afford to lose sight of him.

I weaved my way back toward the center, scanning the sea of faces, my pulse thrumming as I approached Grant, who was animatedly talking to the host. The man's laughter rang out, rich and deep, but I noticed the way his eyes darted over Grant's shoulder, his gaze shifting to something—or someone—behind me.

"Grant," I whispered urgently, slipping beside him. "We need to move. Something's not right."

He turned, his brow furrowing. "What did you find out?"

"Not much, but I think our friend is more dangerous than we anticipated. The blonde—she's in deep, Grant. We need to figure out her connection before it's too late."

His gaze darkened, the playful glimmer fading as he nodded, his mind clearly racing. "Let's find a quieter place to regroup. I have a few ideas of my own."

But just as we made to slip away, the crowd erupted in gasps, and I felt the air grow thick with tension. Grant and I exchanged a glance, the thrill of danger crackling between us. We turned toward the commotion, our bodies instinctively aligning as we faced the unfolding scene.

A man stood in the center of the ballroom, his face obscured by a mask that glinted like polished silver under the chandelier lights. He held a glass of champagne aloft, a darkly triumphant smile playing on his lips as he surveyed the crowd. The air shifted, an unsettling mix of fear and intrigue swirling around us.

"Ladies and gentlemen," he began, his voice smooth and velvety, yet laced with an unmistakable edge. "It seems the night has taken an unexpected turn. I believe we have a few uninvited guests among us."

My breath hitched in my throat, the reality of his words striking me like a blow. The room held its breath, anticipation hanging in the air like an unsheathed sword.

Grant's hand clenched around mine, his grip firm and protective. "We need to get out of here," he said, urgency threading through his tone.

Before I could respond, the masked man turned his gaze toward us, his eyes locking onto mine with an intensity that felt both thrilling and terrifying. "Ah, but where do you think you're going?"

he purred, his voice dripping with condescension. "The night is just getting interesting."

In that moment, the tension snapped, and chaos erupted as guests began to scatter, panic bubbling to the surface. I glanced at Grant, his expression a mix of determination and concern. We were out of time.

"Follow my lead," he said, his voice low as he pulled me through the fray, weaving expertly between terrified guests and overturned tables. The world spun around us, but his presence anchored me, an unshakeable force against the whirlwind.

As we darted toward an exit, a piercing scream sliced through the air, echoing off the walls like a death knell. My heart raced as we rounded a corner, and I caught sight of the blonde woman, her face pale and terror-stricken as she was cornered by the masked man. The scene before us was an electrifying mix of chaos and danger, and I felt my resolve strengthen, ready to face whatever lay ahead.

"Grant, we can't leave her," I urged, but the masked figure was already stepping toward her, his intentions dark and dangerous.

"Then we need to act fast," he replied, his expression steely. "We can't afford to be caught in the crossfire."

As we rushed back toward the center of the turmoil, a sharp crack echoed through the air, and the ballroom erupted into pandemonium. The masked man raised his glass once more, but this time it was not to toast; it was a declaration of war.

"Let the games begin!" he shouted, and with that, the world around us exploded into chaos, leaving only one certainty in the maelstrom: our lives would never be the same again.

Chapter 19: The Mask of Deceit

The gala shimmered like a thousand diamonds scattered across velvet, each guest a glistening figure weaving in and out of conversations that sparkled as brightly as the chandeliers overhead. I maneuvered through the crowd, my heels tapping a staccato rhythm on the marble floor, the sound nearly drowned out by the symphony of laughter and clinking glasses. I adjusted the mask on my face, a delicate creation of black lace and rhinestones, meant to conceal my identity while amplifying the thrill of the night. But I felt anything but concealed. Instead, I felt exposed, as if every secret I harbored was being laid bare beneath the scrutiny of my peers.

I had anticipated a night of revelry, of dancing until dawn and mingling with people who, up until that moment, I had believed to be allies. Yet, as I caught sight of Lena—my confidante, my rock—conversing with Victor, the host with a notorious reputation for betrayal, a chill ran down my spine. Their laughter, light and airy, echoed like an ominous bell in my ears. Something felt wrong, deeply wrong. I couldn't quite put my finger on it, but the tension coiling in my stomach signaled a storm brewing just beyond the festive atmosphere.

"Isn't it stunning?" Grant's voice pulled me from my spiraling thoughts. He stood beside me, his crisp navy suit complementing the ethereal glow of the gala. His eyes sparkled with mischief, a stark contrast to the unease that knotted my gut. I turned to him, forcing a smile despite the weight of suspicion that clung to my heart.

"Stunning, yes, if you ignore the lurking shadows," I replied, casting a glance over my shoulder toward Lena and Victor. Grant followed my gaze, his expression shifting from playful to serious.

"Keep your friends close and your enemies closer, right?" His tone was light, but the underlying tension was palpable. I could tell he sensed my discomfort. I shifted uncomfortably, the luxurious fabric of my gown suddenly feeling restrictive.

"Why do they look like they're conspiring?" I muttered, half to myself, half to Grant, as my gaze locked onto Lena's animated gestures. Victor leaned in closer, his face inches from hers, their proximity raising a dozen unwelcomed thoughts in my mind.

"They might just be sharing gossip. But you're right to be wary," he replied, his voice low, thoughtful. "Not everyone at this gala is to be trusted."

As if the universe conspired to prove him right, a sudden commotion erupted across the ballroom, drawing everyone's attention. A woman, her dress a vibrant shade of crimson, collapsed dramatically onto the floor, the sound of her heels echoing like a gunshot in the tense silence that followed. Gasps rippled through the crowd as people surged forward, instinctively drawn to the spectacle.

"Let's get some air," Grant suggested, his hand gently urging me away from the growing crowd. I nodded, grateful for the escape, and allowed him to lead me to a hidden balcony overlooking the cityscape below.

The air outside was a welcome relief, cool and fragrant with the scent of blooming jasmine. Stars dotted the inky sky like shards of glass, twinkling overhead as I leaned against the wrought iron railing, inhaling deeply. Grant joined me, standing close enough that I could feel the warmth radiating from him, a stark contrast to the chill that lingered in the shadows of the gala.

"Are you okay?" he asked, his voice a soothing balm amidst the chaos.

I hesitated, the weight of the evening pressing down on me. "I don't know," I admitted, my voice a whisper. "I thought I could trust Lena, but it feels like everything is unraveling. The moment I saw her with Victor—" I cut myself off, shaking my head. The words tasted bitter, filled with the ache of betrayal.

"People are complicated. Sometimes they make choices that don't make sense to us," Grant replied, his gaze steady and unwavering. "You're strong. Whatever's going on, you'll figure it out."

His faith in me was both comforting and disarming, stirring a longing deep within. In this moment, on the edge of a dizzying world of glitter and lies, I felt vulnerable and yet oddly safe with him. The fear that had gripped me began to dissolve, replaced by a tentative connection that shimmered like the stars above us.

"What if I can't?" I breathed, the words slipping from my lips like a confession.

He turned slightly, his expression shifting from concern to something deeper, more contemplative. "You can. We'll face it together," he said, and I believed him. There was a sincerity in his voice that wrapped around me like a protective cloak.

Just then, a rustle came from the shadows behind us, a movement so slight that it could easily have been overlooked. But I felt it—a prickling sensation on the back of my neck, the instinctual awareness that came from years of navigating treacherous waters. I glanced over my shoulder, squinting into the darkness, my heart quickening as I caught a glimpse of a figure lingering just beyond the glow of the balcony lights.

"Did you see that?" I asked, my pulse racing.

"What?" Grant turned to look, but the figure had vanished, swallowed by the night.

"Someone was watching us," I insisted, though doubt crept into my voice. The shadows had played tricks on me before, but this felt different. An unsettling weight settled in my chest, urging me to remain alert.

"Maybe just your imagination," Grant replied, though the slight furrow of his brow suggested he was considering the possibility.

"I wish it were just that," I murmured, feeling a sense of foreboding loom just beyond our haven. "I can't shake this feeling that something is off."

"Then let's not let it ruin our night. We can deal with whatever it is once we're back inside," he suggested, offering a gentle smile that almost reached his eyes.

I nodded, but as we stepped back into the gala's blinding light, I couldn't shake the sensation of eyes upon us, a shadow lurking just beyond the edges of my vision. The night was far from over, and I couldn't help but feel that this was only the beginning of a game I was unprepared to play.

The inside of the gala felt like stepping into a dream—an extravagant whirl of shimmering fabrics, elegant laughter, and music that flowed like honey. Yet beneath the polished surface, a sense of dread bubbled just out of reach, threatening to boil over. As Grant and I re-entered the ballroom, the electric atmosphere buzzed with anticipation, the air thick with whispered secrets and veiled intentions.

"Look at them," I muttered, my gaze drifting toward a group of guests huddled together, their hushed voices punctuated by occasional bursts of laughter that rang hollow. "You'd think they were plotting a heist."

"Maybe they are. Perhaps they're stealing my dance moves," Grant quipped, his smirk playful yet his eyes scanning the crowd with a hint of seriousness. I couldn't help but chuckle, the sound feeling foreign against the tension swirling around us.

"Focus, Grant. This is serious!" I replied, nudging him with my elbow, though the warmth of his presence softened my anxiety. "What if Lena is involved in something shady with Victor? I can't shake this feeling that it's more than just idle chatter."

"Then we'll confront her. Together," he said, his voice steady, as though it was the most natural thing in the world. His confidence was infectious, nudging me toward bravery I didn't feel.

As we approached Lena, she caught sight of us, her smile a veneer that seemed to flicker for just a moment before she plastered it back on. "You two look like you just escaped a horror movie," she teased, her eyes dancing with a mischief that felt unsettling.

"Just trying to make sure we weren't the main characters," I replied, a sharpness creeping into my tone. "What were you and Victor discussing? You seemed quite... chummy."

Lena's laughter was bright, but it didn't reach her eyes. "Oh, you know how it is. Just some gossip about the upcoming charity auction. Nothing scandalous," she insisted, waving her hand dismissively as if to brush away my concern.

"Right. Because Victor's charm is known for its lack of ulterior motives," I retorted, unable to mask the skepticism in my voice. Grant stood silently beside me, his expression a mix of concern and curiosity as he observed the interaction.

"Relax, will you? I thought you were here to enjoy the night," Lena said, her tone shifting slightly as if she were reprimanding a petulant child.

"Maybe I would enjoy it more if I knew my friends weren't hiding things from me," I shot back, frustration bubbling beneath the surface. "You're acting like everything is fine when I can practically feel the tension in the air."

"Perhaps you need to lighten up. Not every conversation is a conspiracy," she countered, crossing her arms defensively, and I could see the familiar fire in her eyes, the same passion that had always drawn me to her. Yet tonight, that spark felt like a double-edged sword.

Before I could respond, Victor sauntered over, his presence imposing. "Ladies, is there a problem?" His voice was smooth, dripping with a charm that felt manufactured, plastic even.

"No problem at all," I replied, forcing a smile. "Just a little friendly chat among friends." I could feel Grant shift slightly closer to me, a silent show of support as I stood my ground.

"Good to hear. Wouldn't want anything to spoil this beautiful evening," he said, his gaze lingering a moment too long on me before he turned back to Lena. "Shall we find a quieter place to continue our conversation, Lena?"

Lena's eyes flickered between Victor and me, a mixture of exasperation and intrigue playing across her features. "Sure, why not? I could use a drink." With that, she linked her arm through Victor's and they sauntered away, leaving a swirling storm of uncertainty in their wake.

"What the hell was that?" I breathed once they were out of earshot. "You think she's in over her head?"

"I don't know, but something feels off," Grant replied, his brow furrowed in thought. "We should keep an eye on them. Just to be safe."

As we made our way through the throngs of guests, the atmosphere crackled with an energy that seemed to amplify my unease. I spotted familiar faces—acquaintances from past events, all exchanging pleasantries, masks firmly in place. Each interaction felt like a performance, a masquerade that heightened my sense of isolation amidst the crowd.

"Want to grab a drink?" Grant suggested, his voice a steady anchor against the tide of my thoughts. "Something strong to cut through the tension?"

"Always a good idea." We made our way to the bar, where the bartender, a woman with a dazzling smile and deft hands, mixed cocktails with the precision of a maestro conducting a symphony.

"What's your poison?" she asked, her eyes sparkling.

"A gin and tonic, please," I said, appreciating the simple comfort of familiarity. Grant ordered whiskey neat, the amber liquid glinting like liquid gold in the dim light.

"Here's to surviving this night," he said, raising his glass, his voice light but the gravity of the situation evident in his eyes.

"To surviving and figuring out what's really going on," I added, clinking my glass against his. We took a moment to savor the drinks, the warmth of the alcohol mingling with the chaos swirling in my mind.

"Do you think Lena's in danger?" I asked, my voice lowered to a conspiratorial whisper.

Grant frowned, deep in thought. "I think she's gotten mixed up with someone she shouldn't have. Victor has a reputation, and not a good one. I'd be cautious."

"Great. Just what I need. My best friend caught up with a snake in the grass," I said, rolling my eyes. "If only she'd listen to me."

"People don't always see what's right in front of them. Sometimes they're too caught up in their own desires." His gaze drifted over the crowd, a shadow flickering across his face.

"Speaking of desires, is there a chance I'm the only one who thinks Victor is dangerously charming?" I asked, raising an eyebrow, half-joking.

He met my gaze, his expression serious. "Charm can be a mask, just like those we're wearing tonight. And sometimes, the most charming people are the most dangerous."

Before I could respond, a loud crash reverberated through the hall, silencing conversations. Glass shattered against the marble floor, and a ripple of shock coursed through the crowd.

"Let's go check that out," Grant suggested, his expression shifting to one of concern. We moved quickly, weaving through the throngs of guests as tension hung in the air like a coiled spring ready to snap.

As we reached the source of the commotion, I spotted Lena again, her face pale as she knelt by the broken glass, Victor standing over her, his expression inscrutable. A group of onlookers formed around them, some whispering while others stared in morbid fascination.

"Lena, what happened?" I asked, my heart racing as I pushed my way through the crowd.

She looked up, eyes wide, shock evident. "I don't know! One moment I was talking to Victor, and the next—" She trailed off, her voice shaking.

"Did he do something?" I asked, my voice low and urgent, glancing at Victor, who stood with a façade of calm that only fueled my suspicion.

"No! No, it wasn't him," Lena insisted, but the tremor in her voice spoke volumes.

I exchanged a glance with Grant, the unspoken concern flaring between us. The night had taken a sinister turn, and as shadows shifted around us, I felt the weight of something dark lurking just beyond our vision. Whatever was happening, I knew we had only scratched the surface.

Chaos erupted around me as I knelt beside Lena, the shards of glass glistening like jagged stars scattered across the polished floor. The guests' murmurs rose in a crescendo, a mixture of concern and curiosity, transforming the gala into a theatre of the absurd. I could feel the weight of Victor's gaze, heavy and assessing, as he stood a few feet away, arms crossed, his mask of charm slipping ever so slightly.

"What happened?" I asked again, my voice threading through the tension, desperate to anchor us to reality. "Did someone push you?"

"No, it was just a freak accident!" Lena exclaimed, her voice sharp with frustration as she brushed a strand of hair from her face, revealing the sheen of sweat forming on her brow. "I knocked it over when I was trying to grab my drink. It's not a big deal."

The way her eyes darted toward Victor betrayed her, a flicker of something unspoken hanging in the air. I didn't believe her, and I wasn't alone. Grant's posture shifted beside me, a protective stance as he observed the scene, his expression darkening.

"Are you sure it wasn't Victor? I mean, he could have—" I started, but Lena shot me a look that could have cut glass, her usual exuberance replaced by a simmering anger.

"Stop it! Just because you're suspicious doesn't mean you have to throw accusations around!" she snapped, her voice rising. "I'm fine! Look." She attempted to stand, but the movement caused her to wince, a flash of pain crossing her features.

"Lena, you just fell. You might need a minute," Grant interjected, concern threading through his words as he stepped forward, an instinctive protector.

"Can someone please get a broom?" Victor finally chimed in, a smirk tugging at the corners of his mouth as if he found the entire situation amusing. "It's not a good look for the gala, don't you think?"

The smugness in his tone ignited a fire within me. "Why don't you help instead of standing there like a statue?" I shot back, my temper flaring.

"Why would I want to get my hands dirty?" he retorted, his eyes narrowing in disdain. The tension was palpable, and I could see the crowd shifting uneasily, the murmurings now laden with suspicion, the façade of elegance cracking.

"Let's get her out of here," Grant suggested, his tone brisk as he placed a steadying hand on Lena's back, guiding her away from the broken glass and the gathering onlookers. I fell into step beside them, my heart racing, anxiety bubbling just below the surface.

"What's wrong with you? I thought we were in this together," Lena hissed as we maneuvered through the crowd, her voice laced with hurt.

"I am in this with you," I insisted, trying to reign in my frustration. "But you need to be honest. This isn't just about the drink; it's about Victor. You know he's dangerous."

"Dangerous? Or just misunderstood?" She laughed, but the sound was brittle, and I could see the uncertainty lurking in her eyes. "You're reading too much into this."

"No, I'm not! I've seen the way he looks at you," I pressed, feeling the urgency creep into my voice. "He's using you as a pawn. You have to see that!"

"I can handle myself, thank you very much!" she snapped, her tone sharp, and I recoiled slightly at the fierceness in her words.

Grant sighed, his patience unwavering. "Let's step outside for a moment, get some fresh air, and talk this through," he suggested, steering us toward a quieter exit. The distant sounds of the gala faded as we stepped into the cool night air, the stars shimmering overhead like tiny beacons of hope.

"Lena, I'm not trying to be your enemy," I said gently, my voice softer now, as I crossed my arms against the chill. "I just don't want to see you hurt. You mean too much to me for that."

She looked at me, the defenses in her eyes beginning to crack. "I know you care. I just... I thought things would be different tonight. I wanted to have fun, to let loose. Not get caught up in this mess."

"Fun is all well and good, but this isn't just a party," I replied, frustration still simmering in my chest. "We can't ignore what's happening."

"Then let's find a way to confront him," Grant suggested, his voice calm yet firm, grounding us. "I can help with that."

Lena's expression shifted as she considered our words, and the uncertainty in her eyes turned to determination. "Fine. Let's do it."

Just as I felt a flicker of hope, a rustle in the bushes nearby caught my attention, a faint rustling that didn't belong to the wind. My breath caught in my throat as I exchanged a look with Grant. The air thickened around us, laden with the sense of something lurking in the shadows, a chill creeping down my spine.

"Did you hear that?" I asked, my heart racing anew.

"What?" Lena's brow furrowed as she leaned in closer, confusion written across her face.

Before I could respond, a figure emerged from the darkness—a silhouette cloaked in shadows, moving with a predatory grace. My stomach dropped as recognition flooded me. It was the same shadow I had sensed earlier, watching us from the periphery.

"Run!" Grant shouted, grabbing Lena's arm and pulling her back toward the entrance. The figure lunged forward, a flash of white catching the moonlight, and panic surged through me.

I stumbled, the ground uneven beneath my feet, but instinct kicked in, urging me to follow them. I could hear the sound of my heartbeat pounding in my ears, drowning out the cacophony of the gala behind us.

"Don't look back!" Grant shouted, urgency threading through his voice. We darted toward the entrance, weaving through the thinning crowd as the figure chased us, its presence an ominous shadow in the chaos.

My mind raced, questions spiraling. Who was this person? Why were they after us? The weight of uncertainty wrapped around me like a vice, squeezing the air from my lungs.

As we burst through the doors, I felt a surge of adrenaline propel me forward, a primal instinct to survive overwhelming every other thought. We raced down the street, the cool night air invigorating as we fled into the darkness.

"Where do we go?" Lena gasped, her breath coming in quick, shallow bursts as we turned a corner.

"There's a café a few blocks down," Grant suggested, glancing over his shoulder. "We can hide there until we figure this out."

I barely had time to process his words before a shout rang out behind us, sharp and demanding. "Stop!" It echoed through the night, a chilling command that sliced through the chaos.

My heart raced as we dashed down the alley, urgency fueling every stride. The world around us faded, the music and laughter replaced by the echoing footsteps behind us. We were being hunted, and I had no idea what fate awaited us at the end of this night.

But I knew one thing: whatever came next would change everything.

Chapter 20: The Depths of Despair

The air hung thick with the scent of damp earth and rain-soaked asphalt, mingling into a familiar perfume that brought back memories I'd rather forget. It was the smell of desperation, the kind that clung to the bones of a place where hope was just another word for vulnerability. I stood at the edge of the alley, half-hidden in the shadows, the weak glow of the streetlamp illuminating just enough of my surroundings to make them both comforting and foreboding. This was my world now, one that pulsed with unspoken secrets and whispered dangers, and I was all too aware that I was playing a part in a story much larger than myself.

Grant leaned against the graffiti-clad wall, his silhouette a stark contrast against the vivid chaos of colors. He was a beacon in this darkness, an anchor I desperately needed as we ventured deeper into the labyrinth of lies and betrayals that had ensnared us both. His eyes, usually a vibrant blue, were shadowed with concern, reflecting a turmoil that mirrored my own. "Are you ready for this?" he asked, his voice low, laced with the tension of a coiled spring.

"Ready? I'm not sure that's the right word." I chuckled softly, trying to mask the tremor in my voice. "But it's not like we have much of a choice, do we?" The bravado in my words felt flimsy, like the delicate paper-thin wall between courage and fear. I had always been good at pretending, but the stakes had risen beyond my wildest imaginings. It felt as though we were diving into the very depths of despair, where each revelation threatened to pull us under, away from everything we cherished.

The two of us slipped into the alley, our footsteps muffled by the damp ground, the echoes of our movements swallowed by the oppressive silence. The neon lights of the city pulsed like distant stars, reminding me of the vibrant life just beyond the shadows. I thought of my mother, her laughter echoing in my mind like a soothing balm, and I couldn't help but feel a pang of guilt. I had dragged her into this mess. My quest for the truth had unwittingly endangered everything she held dear.

As we rounded a corner, the alley widened, revealing a hidden courtyard. The remnants of an abandoned warehouse loomed before us, its windows shattered like teeth missing from a grin. Vines twisted their way up the concrete walls, nature attempting to reclaim what humanity had forsaken. "This is where it all began, isn't it?" Grant mused, stepping closer to inspect the rotting door at the base of the structure.

"More like where it all went wrong," I replied, the weight of my words hanging heavy in the air. It was the nexus of our nightmare, the birthplace of the conspiracy that threatened to engulf us. We had uncovered fragments of the truth, each piece revealing a darker layer of the world we thought we knew. The more we learned, the closer we came to an uncomfortable reality that sent chills racing down my spine.

With a cautious push, Grant forced the door open, the creaking sound resonating through the stillness. The air inside was stale, thick with the dust of neglect. I followed him inside, my heart pounding like a drum echoing through an empty hall. "Stay close," he whispered, the words a shield against the unseen threats lurking in the shadows.

The interior was a maze of debris and forgotten memories, remnants of a time when this place had purpose. Broken crates lay strewn about, their contents long since looted or decayed. A faded mural of what once was clung to the wall, depicting a vibrant scene of life, laughter, and hope. Now, it felt like a cruel joke, a ghost of a time I yearned to return to but knew was lost forever.

We moved cautiously, our whispers the only sound as we navigated through the detritus. Each step brought us closer to a revelation that could shatter the delicate balance we had built around us. I felt the weight of every choice I had made pressing down on my shoulders, each one a thread in the tapestry of my life, pulling tighter with each passing moment.

"Over here," Grant called softly, motioning me toward a doorway at the back of the room. My heart raced, a mix of excitement and dread swirling within me. As we stepped through, the flickering light of a single bulb illuminated a long-forgotten office, its walls lined with yellowed newspapers and a heavy layer of dust. The air felt electric, charged with anticipation.

"What are we looking for?" I asked, my voice barely above a whisper. I could feel the tension coiling around us, the sense that we were on the precipice of something monumental.

"Anything that links back to the organization," Grant replied, his brows furrowed in concentration as he scanned the room. "Documents, names—something that ties them to the... events."

As he rummaged through the scattered papers, I couldn't shake the feeling of being watched, a prickling sensation dancing along my spine. It was a familiar instinct, honed by a lifetime of navigating through the treacherous waters of trust and betrayal. Just when I thought the quiet might be our ally, the distant echo of footsteps reached my ears, sending a jolt of panic coursing through me.

"Grant, someone's coming," I hissed, my heart racing. The unease that had been a whisper in the back of my mind now roared to life, demanding my full attention.

He froze, his expression shifting from determination to alarm. "We need to hide," he said, urgency spilling into his tone. We quickly ducked behind a desk, the wood splintering under our weight. The sounds of approaching footsteps echoed louder, a rhythmic thud that matched the frantic beating of my heart.

As we crouched there, shadows dancing in the flickering light, I couldn't help but wonder if this was it—the moment everything would unravel. The air grew heavy with tension, each breath a reminder of the precarious line we walked. I glanced at Grant, his jaw clenched, eyes steely with resolve, and in that fleeting moment, I understood that we were in this together. Whatever lay ahead, we would face it as partners in this chaotic dance of danger and discovery.

The footsteps grew louder, reverberating off the concrete walls like a sinister heartbeat. I held my breath, straining to hear through the thrumming pulse in my ears. Grant's hand brushed against mine, grounding me even in the midst of our frantic reality. His fingers were warm and steady, a reminder that we weren't alone in this chaos, even if the world outside threatened to tear us apart.

"Any ideas?" I whispered, glancing at him through the dim light. I had spent too long in this place of shadows; the dark corners were starting to feel like home, an unsettling thought that made my stomach churn.

"Just hold tight," he replied, his voice barely above a murmur, infused with a fierce determination that sent a spark of courage through me. "If they find us, we'll be outnumbered."

With every heartbeat, the footsteps grew closer. They were almost upon us, a rhythmic march that seemed all too confident. I squinted into the darkness, desperate to catch a glimpse of our pursuers. Were they part of the organization we had been hunting? Or were they something worse?

A sliver of light sliced through the room as the door swung open, illuminating the faces of two figures silhouetted against the brightness. My breath hitched in my throat. I could barely make out their features, but the air around us thickened with the chill of danger.

"Where is he?" one of them growled, the deep timbre of his voice cutting through the silence like a knife. "He has to be here somewhere."

"Keep looking," the other replied, scanning the room with an intensity that made me shudder. "We don't leave without him."

As they advanced, the realization hit me like a tidal wave. They weren't searching for us specifically; they were hunting Grant. The weight of that knowledge settled in my stomach, a leaden mass that threatened to pull me under. "Grant," I whispered, panic rising in my chest. "They're after you."

"I know," he replied, his expression steely, though I could see the flicker of concern in his eyes. "We need to move—now."

Before I could protest, he nudged me to the side, and we ducked further behind the desk, pressing our backs against the cool, rough surface. The two men entered the office, the tension radiating from them palpable. I could feel the electricity in the air, a charged moment where everything hung in the balance, and I feared that a single breath could shatter the fragile stillness.

"Do you think he came this way?" the second man asked, a hint of irritation in his tone.

"I wouldn't doubt it," the first replied, his voice dripping with disdain. "He's always been reckless. He thinks he can outsmart us."

My heart raced as I considered the implications. Grant had clearly been embroiled in something far more dangerous than I had realized. I felt a pang of guilt mixed with admiration; he was fighting a battle I had only scratched the surface of. "We can't let them find you," I said, my voice quaking with urgency.

"Just keep quiet," he whispered back, but there was a warmth in his tone, a subtle reassurance that sparked a flicker of hope in my heart.

As the men rummaged through the scattered papers, my mind raced. We needed a distraction, something to shift their focus long enough for us to escape. The thought of confronting them head-on sent a chill of dread through me, but we had no choice. The fear of losing Grant was a weight I couldn't bear.

I took a deep breath, my fingers brushing the edge of the desk as I surveyed our surroundings. The room was cluttered, but it also held potential. A few old crates lay against the wall, and one was precariously teetering. If I could tip it over...

"Grant," I whispered, gauging his reaction as I edged toward the crates. "I'm going to create a diversion."

He shot me a look that was equal parts admiration and concern. "Are you sure that's a good idea?"

"Do we have a better one?" I retorted, a determined fire igniting in my chest.

Without waiting for a response, I reached for the nearest crate and pushed with all my might. The wood creaked, and for a moment, I feared it wouldn't budge. But finally, it tipped over, crashing to the floor with a thunderous bang. Dust and debris erupted into the air, swirling around me like a storm.

"Hey!" one of the men shouted, whirling around, and in that instant, I dashed back toward Grant. "What was that?"

"Go!" Grant urged, his voice sharp as he pulled me to my feet, and we sprinted toward the far corner of the office. The door was still ajar, the path to freedom shimmering just ahead, but the space between us and the exit felt like an eternity.

The men were shouting now, their voices a chaotic mix of confusion and rage, and I couldn't help but feel a rush of exhilaration mixed with fear. We were moving, we were alive, and somehow, we had a chance.

We burst through the door, skidding to a halt in the dim hallway beyond. The fluorescent lights flickered overhead, casting eerie shadows that danced against the cracked walls. My heart hammered in my chest, each beat a reminder of the danger looming behind us.

"Which way?" Grant asked, glancing back toward the noise. The urgency in his voice sent a chill racing through me.

"Down the stairs, I think," I said, pointing toward the narrow staircase at the end of the hall. "If we can get to the street, we can find somewhere to hide."

"Let's go!" He took my hand, and together we raced down the stairs, each step echoing in the confined space, reverberating with the tension of our flight. As we reached the bottom, the smell of damp concrete mingled with the faintest hint of freedom wafting through the open doorway ahead.

Just as we crossed into the open, the sunlight hit us like a wave, blinding but invigorating. The street stretched out before us, bustling with life, and for a moment, I felt a rush of hope. But the sound of pounding footsteps echoed behind us, shattering the illusion of safety.

"Quick!" I urged, scanning the street for any sign of sanctuary. "We can't let them catch us!"

We darted into a narrow alley between two buildings, the shadows swallowing us once more. My heart raced, not just from fear but from the thrill of the unknown, the intoxicating mix of adrenaline and danger that surged through my veins.

"This way," Grant whispered, tugging me to the left. The alley narrowed, and I could feel the walls closing in, but we pressed on, driven by the urgency of escape. Each footfall felt like a countdown, a reminder that time was slipping through our fingers.

The world outside faded, the noise and chaos replaced by the echo of our breaths and the distant sounds of the city. As we rounded a corner, a flicker of movement caught my eye—a door ajar, its peeling paint offering a glimmer of refuge. "In there!" I shouted, pointing.

We slipped inside just as the footsteps grew louder, the shadows of our pursuers creeping closer. The door closed with a soft click behind us, sealing us in a sanctuary of forgotten memories.

Inside, the room was dimly lit, lined with shelves of dusty books and boxes long neglected. The air was thick with the scent of aged paper and a hint of something floral, reminiscent of a garden long abandoned. I glanced around, searching for anything that might aid our escape, my heart pounding in my ears.

"Do you think they'll find us?" I asked, the reality of our situation settling heavy in my chest.

"Not if we stay quiet," Grant said, his expression intense. "Just keep your head down."

As we crouched behind a stack of crates, the tension between us shifted, filled with unspoken words. I could feel the warmth of his presence, a tether anchoring me to reality. The pounding of my heart began to synchronize with the muted sounds of the outside world, the chaos fading to a dull thrum as we sat in the silence, hoping against hope that we could ride out this storm together.

The room was heavy with the musty scent of dust and forgotten dreams, a hidden sanctuary that felt both claustrophobic and oddly comforting. As Grant and I crouched behind the stack of crates, every creak of the floorboards above seemed magnified, the echoes of our pursuers a relentless reminder of the danger lurking just outside. My heart raced, each thud resonating like a drumbeat, a stark contrast to the suffocating silence that enveloped us.

"Do you think they'll find us here?" I whispered, the weight of uncertainty hanging between us like a dense fog.

"They shouldn't," Grant replied, his brow furrowed in concentration. "But we can't stay too long. If they come in—"

I cut him off, "Then we'll just have to be faster than they are." My bravado felt like a thin veil over my fear, but I couldn't let him see the doubt creeping in. "You've survived worse, right? This is just another day at the office for you."

A ghost of a smile crossed his lips, and I could see the tension easing slightly in his shoulders. "Oh, absolutely. Just your average

Tuesday," he replied, his tone teasing despite the dire circumstances. "Just me, my partner in crime, and a couple of heavy-hitters looking to end us."

"Let's make it a memorable Tuesday then," I shot back, grateful for the moment of levity in the oppressive atmosphere. But beneath the surface, I was acutely aware of the stakes. This wasn't just about us anymore; it was about uncovering the truth and exposing the web of deceit that had ensnared us.

As the footsteps faded away, the quiet wrapped around us like a thick blanket, muffling the outside world. I could hear the faint hum of the city, a reminder that life went on even in the face of our chaos. "What now?" I asked, pulling my knees up to my chest, suddenly feeling vulnerable.

Grant leaned back against the crates, his eyes scanning the room. "We need to find something—anything—that can help us piece together what's happening. There must be records, files...something that connects the dots."

I nodded, determination hardening my resolve. "Let's do it."

We moved cautiously, the floorboards creaking beneath us as we rose from our hiding spot. I felt a flicker of excitement as I stepped into the dim light, a sense of purpose igniting within me. The room was cluttered, its surfaces covered in layers of dust that danced in the air like tiny fireflies.

Grant began rifling through the scattered papers, his fingers deftly sifting through the remnants of a bygone era. "Look for anything that mentions the organization," he instructed, his voice steady despite the anxiety simmering beneath the surface.

I nodded and approached a dusty old desk in the corner, its surface strewn with yellowing documents. Each paper I turned held a whisper of secrets, and I couldn't help but feel a thrill at the prospect of uncovering something significant. "What if we find nothing?" I murmured, glancing at Grant. "What if this leads us to a dead end?"

"Then we keep searching," he replied, his confidence bolstering my own. "There's always a way forward."

I sifted through old contracts and invoices, the names blurring together until one caught my eye. "Wait," I said, my pulse quickening. "This one mentions a payment to a shell company—look at this." I held up the paper, pointing to the line that detailed an unusual transaction.

Grant stepped closer, his brow furrowing in concentration. "This is tied to the organization, isn't it?"

"I think so." My fingers trembled slightly as I traced the details. "This looks like a cover-up. They're funneling money through various fronts."

"Good find." He smiled, the warmth of his approval wrapping around me like a comforting blanket. "If we can prove that they're laundering money, we might have enough to expose them."

As we poured over the documents, I felt a swell of hope. Maybe this was our way out, our chance to turn the tide in this relentless game of cat and mouse. But just as the light of possibility brightened the corners of my mind, the sudden crash of a door being kicked open shattered the moment, sending a shockwave of fear coursing through my veins.

"Search everywhere!" a voice roared, the threat vibrating in the air like an electric charge.

My heart dropped. "They're here!" I hissed, panic rising like bile in my throat.

"Back!" Grant urged, pulling me behind the desk just as two figures stormed into the room. My heart raced, adrenaline flooding my system as I pressed against the cold wood, willing myself to remain silent.

The men moved with purpose, their eyes scanning the room, searching for any sign of us. "He has to be here," one of them grunted, frustration seeping into his voice. "I know he wouldn't just disappear."

I exchanged a frantic glance with Grant. We were trapped, our escape thwarted by the very thing we had hoped to avoid. I could feel my pulse racing, each beat echoing in my ears like a death knell.

"What now?" I whispered, desperate for a plan.

"Wait," he said, his gaze narrowing as he assessed the situation. "If we stay quiet, they might miss us."

I held my breath, every fiber of my being attuned to the tense atmosphere. The men continued to search, rummaging through the documents, their frustration mounting as they found nothing of value.

"It's like looking for a needle in a haystack," one of them muttered, tossing a stack of papers aside. "He can't have gotten far."

"Then let's check the other rooms," the second man replied, his tone low and dangerous. "If we find him, we end this."

I felt a shiver run down my spine at the implication of those words. "Grant, we can't let them find us," I whispered urgently, my mind racing for options.

"I know," he replied, his voice barely a breath. "We'll wait until they leave, and then we'll find another way out."

The tension in the room grew thick as molasses, every second stretching into eternity. I could feel the sweat pooling at the nape of my neck, the anxiety curling in my stomach like a live wire. Just when I thought we might get through unscathed, the first man turned, his eyes narrowing as he caught sight of something out of place—a faint glimmer of light reflecting off the edge of the desk.

"What's that?" he asked, stepping closer.

"Damn it," Grant muttered under his breath, his expression hardening.

Before I could react, the man reached for the edge of the desk, and my heart lurched. "We need to move!" I urged, adrenaline surging as the gravity of our situation became abundantly clear.

In one fluid motion, Grant and I bolted from our hiding spot, darting toward the back of the room. The men shouted, their voices a cacophony of chaos that sent a fresh surge of panic coursing through my veins.

"We're running out of time!" I yelled, my breath coming in quick gasps as we neared the far wall, searching for any exit. Just as hope began to flicker, we were met with an unexpected sight—a small, windowed door, slightly ajar, revealing a narrow path beyond.

"Over there!" Grant pointed, his eyes gleaming with urgency.

We raced toward the door, my heart pounding against my ribcage as I pushed it open, the hinges creaking in protest. The narrow corridor was dimly lit, and the air felt heavier, charged with the promise of danger lurking around every corner.

"Keep going!" Grant urged, shoving me forward as we darted into the hallway.

The sound of footsteps echoed behind us, a reminder that we were still being hunted, and with every step we took, the walls seemed to close in tighter. I could hear the men shouting, their frustration palpable as they realized we had slipped through their grasp.

"Where are we?" I panted, glancing around frantically.

"I don't know," Grant admitted, his expression serious. "But we have to keep moving."

Just as we turned a corner, a sudden crash reverberated through the corridor, followed by a series of shouts that sent a chill racing down my spine. The men were closing in, their determination palpable as they hunted us like prey.

As we raced forward, my thoughts churned with uncertainty. What would happen if they caught us? What secrets lay hidden in the shadows of this place? The walls felt like they were closing in, a trap set to ensnare us at every turn.

And then, as if in a cruel twist of fate, the lights flickered and went out, plunging us into darkness. The sudden absence of light was suffocating, disorienting, leaving only the frantic beating of my heart and the sound of our breaths in the oppressive silence.

"Grant?" I called out, the panic creeping into my voice. "Where are you?"

"Right here," he replied, the warmth of his presence a comforting anchor. "Just stay close. We'll find a way out."

I could hear the distant sounds of footsteps echoing in the darkness, and dread settled deep within me. The walls were no longer just barriers; they were closing in, ready to trap us in a nightmare we might never escape.

Just as I felt the first tendrils of despair

Chapter 21: Into the Abyss

The night draped itself over the city like a heavy velvet curtain, dimming the flickering streetlights and casting long shadows that slithered across the pavement. Each breath I took felt labored, heavy with the weight of uncertainty and dread that coiled tightly in my stomach. The world outside our makeshift headquarters pulsed with an anxious energy, a silent acknowledgment that something monumental was on the horizon. I could almost taste the tension in the air, sharp and metallic, as it mingled with the scent of old paper and stale coffee that permeated our cramped space.

"Okay, let's lay this out one more time," Grant said, his voice a steady anchor amid the chaotic storm brewing in my mind. His brow was furrowed, and I could see the faint sheen of sweat tracing the contours of his temples, a testament to the hours we'd spent poring over maps and documents that seemed to multiply with each passing moment. The city's conspiracy reached deeper than I'd ever imagined, wrapping itself around powerful figures like ivy clinging to a crumbling wall.

I glanced up from the pile of papers, meeting his gaze, and for a brief moment, the room fell silent. "It's like trying to untangle a ball of yarn with a thousand knots," I replied, forcing a smile that didn't quite reach my eyes. "And every time we pull on one string, another one seems to tighten."

His lips twitched in what could have been a smirk, but it faded quickly as he glanced back at the maps spread before us. The glow of the desk lamp illuminated his strong jawline, making him appear rugged and determined—everything I admired about him. Yet, as I watched him, I felt the familiar pang of something more. It was terrifying to confront the truth about my feelings, especially with the stakes this high.

"Maybe we need a new approach," he said, tapping his finger on a particularly convoluted map of the city's underground tunnels. "These routes could give us an advantage, but we have to be strategic."

A flicker of defiance sparked within me. "Or maybe we need to stop playing their game altogether. They think they know the rules, but what if we flipped the board?" The words spilled out before I could reconsider, igniting something in the atmosphere, a sense of rebellion against the looming threat.

"Flipping the board could get us killed," he replied, a wry smile breaking through his earlier seriousness. "But it's the kind of chaos I could get behind."

His humor eased some of the tension coiling in my chest. I took a moment to gather my thoughts, allowing myself to imagine the possibility of turning the tables on our adversaries. "If we can't beat them at their own game, maybe we can expose them. Force their hand."

Grant's eyes gleamed with interest, and I could see the wheels turning in his mind. "I like where you're going with this. If we can gather enough evidence to make a public spectacle, it might just shake things up."

A rush of adrenaline surged through me, the thrill of planning a counteroffensive invigorating my senses. Together, we poured over the documents once more, piecing together fragments of information like a jigsaw puzzle that would, hopefully, reveal a complete picture. With every minute that ticked by, the walls of our safe haven felt more like a cage, and the world beyond beckoned with a chaotic allure.

As the hours waned, fatigue washed over me, and I rubbed my eyes, trying to shake off the weight of exhaustion. Grant, ever perceptive, leaned back in his chair, studying me with an intensity that made my heart race. "You okay?" he asked, his voice low, genuine concern threading through his words.

"Just tired," I replied, brushing off his concern even as I felt the tendrils of weariness tugging at me.

"Not just tired," he pressed, his brow creasing. "You look—"

"I look what?" I snapped, surprising myself with the sharpness of my tone. The last thing I wanted was to lash out at him, especially when he had been my constant support.

"Like you're carrying the weight of the world," he replied, his voice gentle now, like he was coaxing a frightened animal from its hiding place. "You're not alone in this, you know. Whatever happens, we face it together."

Those words struck a chord deep within me, resonating with a truth I had been too scared to fully acknowledge. I wanted to believe him, to trust that we could conquer this nightmare side by side. But fear, that insidious creature, curled tighter around my heart, whispering doubts that gnawed at my resolve.

"I know," I said, my voice barely above a whisper. "It's just... everything is so uncertain. I feel like we're walking into an abyss."

"Then let's shine a light into it," Grant replied, a fierce determination in his gaze. "We're going to expose them for who they really are, and we'll come out stronger on the other side."

In that moment, I realized that my feelings for him were more than just an inconvenient distraction—they were the lifeline I desperately needed. They anchored me, grounding me in a storm that threatened to sweep me away. I could see the flicker of hope in his eyes, and with it, a possibility of a future not just surviving the abyss, but thriving beyond it.

And as we dove back into our plans, the flicker of connection between us burned brighter, pushing the shadows back just a little. In that instant, the looming dread felt less like an impending doom and more like an invitation—a chance to forge our path through the darkness together, no matter what awaited us on the other side.

The next morning dawned with a relentless grayness that seeped into the very bones of the city, casting everything in a muted palette that matched my mood. Raindrops pattered against the window like tiny fingers tapping impatiently, each one echoing my own rising anxiety. I wrapped my arms around myself, wishing I could conjure warmth from the cool air that nipped at my skin. Grant had already retreated into his world of plans and possibilities, his mind a fortress fortified against the uncertainty we faced. But beneath the layers of strategizing and plotting lay an undercurrent of tension that thrummed like an unplayed string, waiting for someone to strike it.

"Coffee?" Grant asked, his voice cutting through the silence as he walked in, a steaming mug in hand. His disheveled hair stuck up in various directions, a wild halo that made him look both endearing and fiercely determined. The sight of him ignited a small spark of warmth within me, a reminder of the bond we shared even in the darkest moments.

"Yes, please," I replied, taking the cup he offered and inhaling the rich aroma that wafted upwards. The warmth seeped into my palms, a small comfort amid the brewing storm outside. "Any breakthroughs?"

He leaned against the doorframe, crossing his arms as he regarded the chaos spread across the table. "Nothing concrete, but I'm convinced we're missing something. The way those reports are connected... it's like a tangled web. We just need to figure out where the center is."

"Or cut the web altogether," I suggested, taking a sip of the coffee, its bitterness awakening my senses. "We're chasing shadows here, Grant. What if the real power lies somewhere else—somewhere unexpected?"

"Like?" His eyebrows arched, his curiosity piqued.

I set my mug down, my thoughts racing. "What if our enemy isn't just some shadowy figure in an office, but someone we least suspect? Someone right under our noses?"

A glimmer of recognition flickered in his eyes. "You think it could be someone in the city council?"

"Or higher. What if this goes all the way to the top?" My heart pounded as I imagined the implications of my words. "We need to widen our scope. Gather intel on people we haven't even considered."

The storm outside escalated, rain lashing against the window like a chorus of anxious whispers. I could feel the tension crackling between us, the gravity of our situation sinking deeper into my consciousness. If we were going to unearth the truth, we had to tread carefully, like dancers on a tightrope suspended over an abyss.

As the day wore on, we delved into research mode, poring over documents, cross-referencing names, and digging into the city's public records. Hours blurred into an unrecognizable haze, the clock ticking relentlessly as the rain continued to drum against the glass, an insistent reminder of the time slipping away.

"Here," Grant called out, his voice a mix of excitement and apprehension. "This might be worth looking into." He pointed to a name that seemed to stand out like a sore thumb amidst a sea of familiar faces.

"What about him?" I asked, leaning closer to the screen. The name belonged to a councilman known for his philanthropic efforts but rumored to have dubious connections.

"The fundraisers he hosts are too lavish for the donations he claims," Grant replied, his fingers flying over the keyboard as he pulled up more information. "And look at this. He has connections to several businesses involved in the projects we've been investigating."

A thrill ran through me, a surge of adrenaline fueled by the prospect of uncovering something tangible. "This could be it! If we can link him to the larger conspiracy..."

Before I could finish, the sound of a heavy thud reverberated through the room. We both froze, eyes darting toward the door. "What was that?" I whispered, my heart racing.

"Not sure," Grant replied, his tone serious as he reached for a nearby baseball bat, a relic from his college days.

"Do you think...?" My voice trailed off as I considered the worst-case scenario, my imagination spinning vivid tales of infiltration and betrayal.

"Stay behind me," he instructed, his eyes narrowing with focus. I nodded, clenching my fists as the familiar rush of anxiety twisted in my stomach. Together, we approached the door cautiously, the tension palpable in the air like static electricity.

As Grant opened the door, the hallway beyond lay shrouded in shadow, illuminated only by the dim light from the room. I held my breath, listening intently for any sound, any indication of what might lie beyond.

Suddenly, a voice broke the silence. "Grant? Are you in there?"

It was Sam, one of our allies, his voice laced with urgency. Relief flooded through me as I stepped back, allowing him to enter. "What's going on?" I asked, my heart still racing.

"I came as soon as I heard. There's been a development—things are getting dangerous. People are talking." Sam's face was pale, his eyes wide with alarm. "We need to move. Now."

Grant exchanged a glance with me, the weight of the situation settling like a stone in my gut. "What do you mean, 'dangerous'?"

"There are whispers of a crackdown. They're not just watching; they're preparing to silence anyone who knows too much." Sam's voice trembled with urgency. "You two are on their radar."

"What do you suggest?" I asked, my voice steadier than I felt.

"Lay low for a while. I know a place where you can hide. It's off the grid, but it'll keep you safe until we figure out our next move."

Grant nodded slowly, processing the information. "We can't abandon this lead, Sam. We're so close."

"Close?" Sam shook his head, his frustration palpable. "Close isn't good enough anymore. They're moving fast, and if we don't act now, we could lose everything."

In that moment, I felt the threads of our plan fraying, unraveling beneath the weight of impending danger. The abyss loomed larger, darker, and I realized that our fight wasn't just for the truth but for our lives.

"Fine," I said, my voice steady despite the turmoil inside. "Let's regroup and strategize, but we need to keep digging while we're hiding."

Grant's eyes sparkled with agreement, and I could see the determination etched into his features. Together, we would navigate this treacherous terrain, every twist and turn only deepening the resolve that anchored us in the face of the unknown.

The rain had transformed the city into a tapestry of shimmering reflections, glistening puddles creating a mosaic of light and shadow on the streets below. As we piled into Sam's nondescript car, the hum of the engine felt like a low heartbeat, a pulse that matched the nervous energy thrumming through me. Grant sat in the front, his expression resolute, while I leaned back against the worn leather seat, staring out at the blurred scenery. Each drop of rain that hit the window echoed my thoughts—a symphony of uncertainty, fear, and an undercurrent of exhilaration.

"Where are we heading?" I asked, my voice barely rising above the sound of the rain.

"A safe house," Sam replied, his eyes flicking to the rearview mirror. "Trust me, it's remote and secure. No one will think to look for you there."

"Remote sounds ominous," I said with a wry smile, attempting to lighten the heavy air in the car. "I hope it comes with a decent Wi-Fi signal, or I might just wither away."

Grant turned in his seat, amusement dancing in his eyes. "If it doesn't, we'll set up a makeshift network. Who knows? We could become the world's first underground hackers, fighting for justice and good coffee."

"Great, now I can add 'cyber vigilante' to my resume," I teased, grateful for the fleeting moment of levity.

Sam's lips twitched, but the humor faded quickly as he focused on the road, tension threading through his shoulders. "Just stay alert. This isn't a game anymore. They're watching us."

The gravity of his words sank in as the car turned down a narrow road, flanked by trees that loomed like sentinels, their branches swaying gently in the wind. The world outside transformed from the city's chaos into an enveloping embrace of nature, where the rain fell softly, almost like a soothing lullaby. I took a deep breath, the air crisp and filled with the earthy scent of wet foliage. It felt like a different world, one far removed from the shadows we had been navigating.

As we pulled up to a quaint cabin nestled between the trees, I couldn't help but let out a small sigh of relief. The rustic exterior, with its wooden beams and inviting porch, exuded a warmth that seemed welcoming, a stark contrast to the turmoil swirling within. "You really brought us to a cabin in the woods?" I asked, trying to hide my surprise. "Is this where I'm supposed to become a lumberjack?"

"More like a survivalist," Grant countered, stepping out of the car. "But hey, if things go south, I've always wanted to learn how to chop wood."

"Let's not put the cart before the horse, shall we?" I replied, trying to mask my unease with humor.

As we entered the cabin, I was struck by the cozy atmosphere—wooden beams overhead, a stone fireplace, and large windows that framed the view of the sprawling forest. Despite the circumstances, it felt like a temporary refuge. Sam set about securing the doors and windows, while Grant and I unloaded the few supplies we had managed to grab in our hasty escape.

"We should set up a plan for communication," I said, dropping a duffel bag onto the table. "We can't just sit around waiting for something to happen."

"Agreed," Grant said, rifling through the contents of the bag. "We'll need to establish a way to contact our allies and keep an eye on the councilman. The last thing we want is for him to catch wind of our presence here."

The fireplace crackled to life, casting flickering shadows on the walls as I found a seat on a plush couch, sinking into the cushions as fatigue washed over me. "What's the plan, then?" I asked, hoping for clarity in the swirling storm of uncertainty.

"First, we lay low and gather intel. We can use Sam's contacts to get updates on the councilman's movements," Grant said, his brow furrowing in thought. "Then we decide when to strike."

The weight of his words settled heavily in the room, filling the air with tension. I could feel the enormity of our mission pressing down on us, the walls closing in as the reality of our situation sank in. "And if they find us here?"

Sam's face grew serious. "We need to trust in the safety of this place. If they find us, we'll already have a plan to escape."

"What about you?" I asked, concern creeping into my voice. "You can't put yourself at risk just for us."

"It's too late for that," Sam replied, his gaze steady. "I'm in this with you."

Silence enveloped us as we absorbed the gravity of our situation, the camaraderie solidifying in the unspoken promises we made to one another.

Hours passed in a blur, the rain drumming against the cabin, wrapping us in a cocoon of sound. The shadows lengthened, and the dimming light created a surreal atmosphere. I found myself staring into the flames, my thoughts flickering like the firelight.

Suddenly, Grant's phone buzzed, shattering the tranquility. He answered it, his brow furrowing with each word spoken. "What do you mean they're here?" His voice sharpened, and I felt my heart race as I leaned closer, trying to catch every detail.

"Who's here?" I asked, anxiety clawing at my throat.

"Sam, you need to get to the back," Grant said, his tone commanding as he hung up.

"What? What's going on?" I pressed, dread pooling in my stomach.

"Authorities are doing a sweep of the area," he said, his voice low. "They're searching for us. We need to move. Now."

Panic surged through me as I jumped to my feet. "Where do we go?"

"Out the back. There's a small path that leads deeper into the woods. It'll give us a head start," Sam instructed, urgency lacing his words.

As we rushed toward the back door, I felt my heart pounding in my chest, each beat echoing the reality that we were on the run, fugitives in our own fight for justice. Grant grabbed my hand, and the warmth of his grip grounded me, reminding me that I wasn't alone in this chaos.

The door swung open to reveal a darkened path that seemed to stretch into the unknown, the shadows inviting yet foreboding. We darted into the woods, the sounds of pursuit echoing behind us, urgency propelling us forward.

Branches snagged at my clothes, the underbrush clawing at my legs as we ran deeper into the wilderness. The rain drizzled softly now, a haunting lullaby that mingled with the sound of our ragged breaths.

Suddenly, a loud shout rang out from behind us, followed by the crack of branches snapping. "They're gaining on us!" Sam yelled, panic in his voice.

"Keep going!" Grant urged, his grip tightening around my hand as he pulled me forward.

But just as we reached a clearing, a bright light burst through the trees, illuminating our path. I turned, heart racing, to see figures emerging from the shadows, their expressions grim and determined.

"Stop! You're surrounded!" a voice commanded, echoing through the night.

The realization hit me like a slap to the face. We were trapped, cornered like prey before the hunt. The abyss was no longer a distant threat; it loomed before us, and as the light closed in, I understood that we were about to confront the darkness head-on.

Chapter 22: The Breaking Dawn

The world around us felt almost unreal, as though the dawn had brushed a soft haze over everything, blurring the edges of my reality. Shadows clung to the corners of the warehouse like whispered secrets, and I could almost taste the metallic tang of adrenaline on my tongue. The cracked concrete underfoot was littered with the remnants of neglect—discarded pallets and rusted scraps that spoke of forgotten days and abandoned hopes. Yet, here we stood, poised on the precipice of a confrontation that could very well alter the course of our lives forever.

I exchanged a glance with Mia, whose usual warmth was replaced by a steely determination. Her hair, usually cascading in effortless waves, was pulled back in a tight bun that framed her face like a warrior preparing for battle. There was a fierceness in her green eyes that I had never seen before, a spark that hinted at the depths of her resolve. We had come too far, sacrificed too much to turn back now. Every breath felt heavy with the weight of our choices, our dreams intertwined in a tapestry woven with both hope and trepidation.

"Ready?" she whispered, her voice barely rising above the echo of our footsteps. I nodded, though my heart threatened to leap from my chest. The plan was simple in theory, but theories often crumbled under the pressure of reality. The enemy was cunning, a master manipulator who had pulled the strings of our lives from the shadows. The secrets we had unearthed hinted at a depth of corruption that went far beyond anything we had anticipated.

The air inside the warehouse was stale, tinged with the faint odor of mildew and something far more sinister that I couldn't quite place. It wrapped around us like a shroud, suffocating yet strangely comforting in its familiarity. We were intruders in a world that had long since lost its innocence, and every step drew us closer to the heart of darkness.

As we ventured deeper into the cavernous space, I felt a shiver dance down my spine. It was not merely the chill of the early morning; it was the unsettling realization that we were not alone. The sound of muffled voices reached my ears, a low rumble that sent a wave of unease washing over me. I glanced at Mia, who held a finger to her lips, signaling me to remain silent. Our training had taught us the importance of stealth, the necessity of patience, yet the urgency of the moment gnawed at my resolve.

"What if we're too late?" I whispered, fear threading through my words.

Mia's eyes hardened. "We won't be. We can't afford to be."

She pressed forward, her body tense with anticipation. I followed, my heart hammering in my chest like a war drum, each beat echoing the rallying cries of our collective resolve. With each step, the cacophony of voices grew clearer, each syllable a piece of a puzzle that we were desperate to solve.

Then, there it was—the dim glow of a flickering bulb illuminating a circle of figures huddled together in the distance. I strained to catch snippets of their conversation, piecing together the fragments like a jigsaw puzzle. The mention of names—names that sent jolts of recognition through me—fueled the fire of determination within.

"This is our chance," I breathed, the words barely escaping my lips.

Mia nodded, her grip tightening around the small device tucked in her pocket—the key to unraveling the web of deceit that had ensnared us for so long. We edged closer, using the shadows to cloak our movements, adrenaline surging through my veins as we prepared for the final act.

Suddenly, the atmosphere shifted. Laughter erupted from the group, harsh and mocking, slicing through the tension like a knife. The sound sent a ripple of dread coursing through me. I leaned in closer, straining to catch the words that followed, and my stomach twisted as realization dawned.

"I told you, it's just a matter of time before they figure it out," one voice scoffed, dripping with disdain.

"They'll never see it coming. Too busy playing the heroes," another chimed in, and the others chuckled in agreement, their voices blending into a chorus of arrogance.

My heart sank as the weight of their confidence settled upon me. They believed we were merely pawns in their game, naive enough to underestimate the depth of their plans. But they didn't know us—not the fire that burned in our chests, the unity that forged our resolve.

Mia glanced back at me, her expression fierce and unyielding. "This is it. We confront them now."

With a deep breath, I stepped forward, the shadows falling away as I emerged into the light of their circle. The laughter ceased abruptly, eyes turning to me, wide with surprise and something darker—recognition.

"Well, well, if it isn't the duo of delusion," the mastermind smirked, leaning casually against a rusted support beam, his presence radiating a toxic blend of charisma and menace.

"Surprised to see us?" I challenged, forcing my voice to remain steady despite the storm brewing inside me.

The air crackled with tension, an electric charge that could ignite at any moment. The moment hung between us, an unspoken acknowledgment of the battle to come.

"Not surprised, just disappointed," he replied, his tone smooth like silk, hiding the steel beneath. "You think you can unravel what's been meticulously crafted over years? How quaint."

Mia stepped forward, her voice strong and unwavering. "We're not just here to talk. We're here to end this."

A dangerous smile spread across his face, a wolf among sheep. "Then come, let's see how this little game of ours plays out."

As the weight of his words settled around us, I knew in my heart that this was the moment we had prepared for. The breaking dawn had arrived, illuminating the path ahead, one filled with uncertainty but also the promise of liberation. Our resolve crystallized; there was no turning back now.

The air crackled with unspoken words, heavy and electric, as we stood facing our adversary. The dilapidated warehouse, with its peeling paint and rusted beams, felt like an unwilling witness to the unfolding drama. Shadows danced on the walls, twisting and contorting like the secrets we were about to uncover. I could hear the rapid thump of my heart, each beat a reminder of the stakes that loomed larger than life itself. It wasn't just about us anymore; it was about everyone who had suffered under the weight of our enemy's schemes.

"Is this really how you want to play this?" the mastermind taunted, his voice dripping with disdain. He stepped forward, and the dim light caught the sharp angles of his face, revealing a mix of charm and danger that made my skin prickle. "So eager for a showdown? You must be aware of how this usually ends for the heroes."

Mia, her resolve unyielding, shot me a glance that radiated confidence. It was a look that said we were in this together, come what may. I took a deep breath, anchoring myself in the moment. "The heroes don't always win, but they don't quit either," I replied, surprising even myself with the steadiness of my voice.

A flicker of annoyance crossed his features, quickly masked by a smug grin. "A commendable sentiment, but misguided. Let me enlighten you. Every hero has a weakness, and I assure you, I'm well acquainted with yours."

I could feel the sweat trickle down my back, but I held my ground. "You think you know us, but you don't. You've underestimated us from the start."

His laughter echoed around us, sharp and mocking. "Underestimating you was my greatest mistake, indeed. But tell me, what makes you think you can topple an empire built on years of deception?"

At that moment, the atmosphere shifted, thickening with tension. I glanced at Mia again, her eyes alight with a spark of mischief. "Because," she said, stepping forward, "we've already toppled the first domino. You just haven't realized it yet."

Before he could react, Mia activated the small device she had kept hidden, and a holographic projection illuminated the room, casting our enemy in stark relief against the swirling images. Data, photographs, and snippets of incriminating conversations burst forth like a digital fireworks display, each frame punctuating our resolve.

"Do you see this?" Mia declared, her voice unwavering. "This is your downfall. Every crime you thought was hidden, every deal you made in darkness, it's all here. You may have thought you were playing chess, but we've been playing checkers, and you've just moved into our trap."

The arrogant smirk on his face faltered, eyes narrowing as the implications sank in. "You think this is enough to take me down?"

"Let's see how your friends react when they see the truth," I countered, my pulse quickening. "You've made enemies everywhere, and they're about to find out what you've been up to."

The atmosphere shifted again, uncertainty creeping into his demeanor. "You've been clever, I'll give you that. But you've also made a grave mistake. This is my domain, and I will not be taken down so easily."

"Famous last words," Mia quipped, her confidence unwavering despite the palpable tension.

Suddenly, the sound of footsteps echoed from the far end of the warehouse, heavy and purposeful. A group of shadowy figures emerged from the gloom, their faces obscured but their intentions clear. I felt a knot of panic tighten in my chest as the realization hit: we were surrounded.

"Seems like reinforcements have arrived," I said, trying to mask the rising anxiety in my tone.

Mia's expression hardened as she assessed our new predicament. "We've got to stay focused. Remember the plan."

With a nod, I shifted my attention back to our opponent. "Looks like you're not as invincible as you thought. Your allies may be here, but they won't shield you from the truth."

The figures drew closer, revealing familiar faces—some of our former allies, corrupted by greed and fear. My stomach twisted at the betrayal. "You?" I exclaimed, disbelief tinging my words. "You've sided with him?"

"Not just side," one of them sneered. "We're ready to take what's ours. You think you can disrupt everything we've built?"

Mia took a step forward, eyes blazing. "You're making a mistake. He's using you. Do you really want to be on the wrong side of this?"

Their laughter was harsh, echoing off the concrete walls. "We've made our choice, and it's too late for you to change it."

In that moment, time seemed to stand still. Everything felt amplified—the whispers of doubt, the heartbeats of the determined, the ticking clock of our fate. I glanced at Mia, and in her gaze, I found a strength I hadn't known I needed. We weren't just fighting for ourselves; we were fighting for everyone who had been wronged, everyone who had suffered at the hands of this tyranny.

"Let's show them what we're made of," I whispered, adrenaline surging through me.

With that, we sprang into action, the energy of our collective resolve electrifying the air. I lunged forward, aiming for the nearest ally-turned-enemy, and the world erupted into chaos. Bodies collided, a flurry of movement as we fought not just against the men who had betrayed us, but against the dark undercurrents of fear that had bound us for too long.

"Is this all you've got?" I shouted, dodging a blow that grazed my shoulder. "I expected more from the so-called 'elite.'"

"Elite, yes," one of them retorted, a flash of anger in his eyes. "But we're also human."

Mia's laughter rang out, sharp and defiant. "Human? Then you should know that we're not backing down. You've made your choices, and now it's time to live with them."

As fists flew and chaos ensued, I felt a surge of exhilaration—this was our moment, the culmination of every sleepless night and every sacrifice. The air was thick with the smell of sweat and fear, and the sound of our hearts pounding in our chests matched the chaos around us. In that swirling vortex of uncertainty, we fought not just for victory but for the very essence of who we were.

The tides of battle shifted with each blow, and I could feel the weight of our combined determination propelling us forward. With every strike, every defiant shout, we forged our own path through the darkness, driven by an unyielding hope that would not be extinguished.

In the pale light of dawn, the world outside held its breath, shrouded in a fragile silence that only the truly reckless would dare to disturb. Inside the warehouse, dust motes danced lazily in the weak light filtering through broken windows, a cruel mockery of the urgency that throbbed in our veins. Each creak of the floorboards beneath our feet whispered warnings of impending chaos, a dark premonition that resonated with the echoes of our hurried breaths. The air, heavy with the scent of rust and betrayal, tasted bitter on my tongue as I exchanged glances with my companions, their faces etched with determination and fear, the perfect amalgam of warriors prepared for the storm.

We moved with purpose, an unspoken agreement guiding our steps, but the closer we drew to the heart of the hideout, the more the atmosphere thickened with tension. My heart raced not just from the fear of what lay ahead, but also from the adrenaline that coursed through my veins, an intoxicating blend of dread and excitement. As we rounded a corner, the shadows deepened, cloaking our enemy in an aura of menace, yet there was a flicker of something else—vulnerability hidden beneath layers of deceit. It made me pause, just for a heartbeat, an instinctual recognition of the man behind the mask.

"Are we really ready for this?" My voice, barely above a whisper, cut through the silence, and for a moment, I felt like a child standing at the edge of an abyss, unsure of the leap before me.

"Ready or not, we don't have a choice." Marcus's tone was gravelly, laced with the kind of conviction that both soothed and stoked the fires of my anxiety. He was the brawn of our group, all sharp edges and unwavering loyalty, but even he seemed on edge, his usual bravado dimmed under the weight of uncertainty.

I nodded, forcing my breathing to steady, though my mind spun with possibilities. What if this man—this monster—wasn't the villain we envisioned? What if, underneath the layers of corruption, there was a story begging to be told? But I quickly brushed aside the thought, focusing instead on the mission, the plan we had meticulously crafted over sleepless nights fueled by caffeine and desperation.

With renewed resolve, we pressed on, weaving through the maze of crates and shadows, our footsteps a chorus of impending confrontation. Then, like a scene drawn from the depths of a nightmare, we stumbled upon the inner sanctum of our enemy. The sight that met our eyes was surreal: a makeshift throne of discarded boxes and splintered wood, and perched atop it, the man who had pulled the strings of our misery.

"Ah, my little avengers," he purred, his voice smooth as silk, a stark contrast to the jagged tension in the air. He was unassuming in appearance—slender and sharply dressed, his facade almost charming if it weren't for the calculating glint in his eyes. "What a delightful surprise. I wasn't expecting visitors this early."

His demeanor was disarming, a calculated move designed to throw us off balance. "Cut the theatrics," I snapped, stepping forward, the weight of my words bolstered by the support of my comrades. "We know what you've done."

A slow smile curled his lips, twisting my stomach into knots. "What I've done? Or what you think I've done?" His eyes sparkled with mischief, as if he were amused by our naive belief in justice. "Let me enlighten you."

"Don't play games with us," Marcus growled, stepping protectively in front of me, muscles coiled like springs ready to explode. "You think you can manipulate us into doubting our purpose?"

"Oh, sweet boy," the man replied, amusement lacing his tone, "it's not manipulation; it's a simple fact. You have no idea what you're up against."

Just then, a loud crash reverberated through the warehouse, the sound echoing ominously as metal clanged against metal. Instinctively, we turned, hearts pounding in unison as a shadow moved against the far wall. "What was that?" I whispered, a knot of dread twisting in my gut.

"Backup," he said, eyes narrowing. "I did promise my associates a front-row seat to this little drama."

"Why would you even need them?" I countered, trying to maintain a facade of control. "You're the mastermind; you should be able to handle us yourself."

He chuckled, a dark, melodic sound that sent shivers down my spine. "Handling you? Oh, my dear, it's not about handling. It's about showing you just how misguided your little crusade is."

Before I could retort, the door burst open, and chaos unfurled as figures clad in dark clothing swarmed into the space, a tsunami of bodies moving with precise intent. "Fall back!" I shouted, gripping Marcus's arm as we began to retreat, but the realization hit us simultaneously: we were cornered.

"Stay together!" Marcus yelled, his voice cutting through the rising panic. But as we huddled together, the reality of our predicament crashed over us.

"Do you really think you can escape?" our enemy taunted, his smirk now a malevolent grin. "You see, this is where the story takes an unexpected twist. The fun is just beginning."

In a heartbeat, the air grew electric, charged with the kind of tension that could spark a fire. We were outnumbered, our resolve tested against a tide of uncertainty. But in that moment of impending chaos, I felt a surge of something unexpected—a flicker of hope. Perhaps we were not just fighting against the darkness; perhaps we were fighting for something greater than ourselves.

And as the darkness loomed closer, it was clear that this confrontation was merely the beginning of a far more intricate game, one that would unravel in ways none of us could foresee.

Chapter 23: Confrontation

The air was thick with tension, a palpable electricity that crackled between us like a storm gathering its strength. I stood in the cavernous expanse of the old factory, the shadows deepening as the sun dipped below the horizon, casting long fingers of darkness across the cracked concrete floor. Each creak of the building echoed in my ears, amplifying my pulse as it raced in sync with the distant rumble of thunder. Grant was at my side, his presence a steadying force, yet the uncertainty hung heavy, threatening to pull us under.

"Are you ready for this?" he asked, his voice a low rumble that seemed to reverberate through the walls. His eyes, usually so warm and inviting, were now pools of steel, reflecting the seriousness of the moment. I could see the flicker of worry dance behind them, but I couldn't afford to dwell on that. Not now.

I swallowed hard, my throat dry as the desert sun. "As ready as I'll ever be. We can't back down now." My words came out stronger than I felt, but resolve surged within me. The secrets that had swirled around my family like a suffocating fog were finally about to be dragged into the light, and I was determined to face them head-on.

The sound of footsteps echoed through the empty space, each thud a countdown to the confrontation we'd been dreading. I turned to Grant, my heart racing, the heat of his body grounding me in the chaos. "We can do this," I murmured, though I couldn't shake the feeling that I was stepping into a trap, one carefully laid out by unseen hands.

"Together," he said, a promise etched in the determination on his face. His fingers brushed against mine, and in that brief connection, I felt a surge of courage. Whatever lay ahead, I wouldn't face it alone.

The factory loomed like a sentient being, its cracked walls whispering tales of past struggles and victories. I could almost see the ghosts of those who had fought and bled within these walls, their spirits echoing my own rising determination. I took a deep breath, inhaling the scent of rust and forgotten dreams, and stepped forward.

As we approached the makeshift stage at the center of the factory, a flickering light illuminated the figure waiting there—Julian. He was a specter of arrogance, his sharp features framed by the low light, a smirk playing on his lips. My breath hitched. There was something unsettling about the way he watched us, like a cat toying with a mouse before the final strike. The air grew denser, charged with unspoken challenges.

"Ah, the fearless duo," Julian drawled, his tone dripping with mockery. "How quaint. Did you come here to surrender, or is this just a last-ditch effort to save face?"

Grant stepped forward, his posture radiating strength, but I could see the tension in his jaw. "We're here to end this, Julian. Once and for all."

I felt a rush of adrenaline surge through me, and the gravity of the moment took hold. My fingers curled into fists at my sides. "You don't get to dictate our lives anymore," I declared, my voice steady despite the storm raging inside. "We know the truth now. Your reign of manipulation ends here."

Julian's laughter echoed around us, a sharp, slicing sound that sent chills down my spine. "Oh, but you have it all wrong. You're merely pawns in a game much larger than yourselves. Your precious truths won't save you."

"Maybe not," I shot back, emboldened by a sudden rush of defiance. "But I refuse to be a pawn any longer. You've twisted everything, but the truth always finds a way to surface."

His expression darkened, and for a moment, the playful façade slipped away, revealing the predator lurking beneath. "You think you're brave, don't you? But bravery can often lead to folly."

With a swift motion, he revealed a glimmering object—a family heirloom I recognized instantly, a pendant that had hung around my mother's neck during my childhood. The room seemed to shrink, the air growing heavier as he held it aloft like a trophy. "Did you really think you could unearth secrets without consequence?"

I felt the floor shift beneath me as the weight of his revelation settled in. The implications crashed over me like a tidal wave, and I glanced at Grant, who was visibly straining against the swell of tension. "You've played with our lives long enough, Julian. That pendant doesn't define us!"

"Ah, but it does," he purred, stepping closer, his eyes gleaming with a predatory delight. "Your family is entangled in this mess, whether you want to believe it or not. You think you're fighting for a future, but what if I told you that your past is the real monster?"

The room fell silent, the air thick with disbelief. I felt like I was standing on the edge of a precipice, and beneath me lay a chasm filled with the secrets I had tried so hard to escape. My heart thundered in my chest, a relentless drum urging me to fight, to reclaim what was rightfully mine.

Grant moved to stand beside me, a silent affirmation that we were in this together. "Whatever you think you know, Julian, you're wrong. We've come too far to be intimidated by your games."

Julian's laughter rang out, but it was laced with something darker, a chilling undertone that sent shivers racing down my spine. "Then let the games begin."

With that, the world around us exploded into chaos.

The air crackled with tension, a storm of emotions swirling around us as Julian's laughter faded into the oppressive silence. I could feel the weight of his words settling in like a thick fog, wrapping around my mind and clouding my judgment. He held that pendant like a puppet master, and I was the marionette, strings pulled taut, ready to dance at his command. But I refused to be that puppet.

Grant stood resolute beside me, his presence a fortress against Julian's dark influence. "You're right about one thing," he said, his voice steady and firm, "this is a game. But you're not the one in control anymore."

Julian's smile faltered for just a moment, revealing the sliver of uncertainty beneath his bravado. I seized the opportunity, drawing in a breath to steady my racing heart. "You've used fear to manipulate us for far too long. But no more. If you think you can scare me with relics of the past, you've underestimated my resolve."

"Oh, darling," he replied, a mocking lilt creeping into his voice. "It's not fear I'm relying on. It's the truth. The truth that binds you to the very chaos you're trying to escape." He gestured with the pendant, its surface glinting in the dim light like a serpent poised to strike. "Your mother's choices have consequences, and those consequences are about to unfold in ways you cannot imagine."

The words hit me like a slap, a harsh reminder of the family legacy I had fought so hard to distance myself from. My mother's past was a labyrinth of secrets, and as much as I wanted to believe I could carve out my own path, Julian was determined to drag me back into her tangled web.

I could feel Grant's steady gaze on me, a reminder that I wasn't alone in this fight. "Whatever your game is, Julian," he said, stepping forward, "we're ready to play. Just remember—there are rules, and we know how to bend them."

Julian's eyes narrowed, the playful demeanor shifting to something more predatory. "Ah, but rules are for the naïve. You should know that by now."

Before I could retort, a loud crash erupted from behind us, shattering the tension like glass. My heart leaped into my throat as I turned to see a figure stumbling through the entrance, silhouetted against the fading light. The newcomer was disheveled and breathless, but even from a distance, I recognized the fierce determination etched into her features. It was Zoe, my best friend, and she had barged into our storm with all the subtlety of a tornado.

"Just in time for the drama, huh?" she quipped, raising an eyebrow at the unfolding chaos. "I thought I'd missed the fireworks."

"Zoe!" I exclaimed, relief flooding through me, dispelling the darkness that Julian's words had cast. "What are you doing here?"

She shrugged, an irreverent smile tugging at her lips. "Couldn't let you face this psycho alone. You know me—I'm always up for a little family reunion."

"Family reunion?" Julian echoed, his voice dripping with sarcasm. "How quaint. You think you can simply waltz in here and join the party?"

"Waltzing is overrated," Zoe shot back, her tone light, but the steel behind it was unmistakable. "I'd rather dance with my friends."

With that, she stepped forward, her presence an unexpected ally amidst the swirling tension. The shifting dynamics in the room momentarily caught Julian off guard, and I seized the moment. "You don't own us, Julian. You may have some power, but we have something you'll never possess: loyalty and love."

"Oh, how touching," he sneered, but there was a flicker of concern in his eyes, a realization that perhaps the game was shifting. "But love won't protect you from the consequences of your family's past."

Zoe's expression hardened. "And neither will your threats. We're not backing down. Not now, not ever."

Julian stepped closer, his voice lowering to a menacing whisper. "You think you can simply defy me? You have no idea how deep the roots of this conflict run."

"Then enlighten us," Grant challenged, taking a protective stance beside me. "Let's lay it all on the table. No more shadows, no more whispers. Just the truth."

A flicker of surprise crossed Julian's face, quickly masked by a mask of indifference. "You truly believe you're prepared for that? Very well. The truth it is."

He lowered the pendant, letting it dangle from his fingers like a pendulum ticking down to our doom. "Your mother was not the innocent victim you've been led to believe. Her choices—her alliances—have bound you to a legacy of darkness that you cannot escape."

Each word dripped with venom, and I felt a tight knot of anxiety coil in my stomach. "Stop trying to twist my mother's choices into weapons," I spat back, refusing to let him erode my confidence. "Her life is not yours to control."

"Ah, but it already is," Julian countered, his tone chilling. "You're here because of her. Every decision she made, every person she deceived—it all leads back to you. You're caught in a web of her making, and you'll never break free."

The room felt colder, shadows creeping closer as doubt began to seep into my resolve. Grant must have sensed my hesitation because he leaned closer, his shoulder brushing against mine. "Don't listen to him," he urged softly. "He's trying to sow discord. We're stronger than this."

Julian chuckled, a sound that sent shivers down my spine. "Strength? You think you possess strength when your foundation is built on lies? You'll crumble, just like the rest."

Before I could respond, Zoe stepped in, her eyes blazing with fierce determination. "We're not going anywhere. You may think you have all the pieces, but you're forgetting one crucial detail: we're not defined by our past. We shape our own future."

The fervor in her voice ignited something deep within me. I straightened, feeling the warmth of resolve wash over me. "We're here to reclaim what's ours. You might think you're holding the cards, but we're changing the game."

Julian's expression shifted, the confidence faltering as he realized that the tide was turning. The balance had shifted, and he could no longer rely on intimidation alone. The game was about to evolve into something far more unpredictable, and I felt the thrill of empowerment coursing through me.

"Then let's see how well you play with your newfound courage," he challenged, his voice dark and low. "But remember—every move has its price."

The storm clouds gathered, and with each moment, the stakes grew higher, the air thick with a tension that promised an explosive climax.

The tension in the factory swelled to a breaking point, each breath I took heavy with the weight of Julian's accusations. He stood there, a silhouette of menace, the pendant swinging slowly like a pendulum counting down our fate. The flickering light danced across his face, illuminating the twisted satisfaction that played upon his lips. I had to push back against the encroaching darkness, the specters of doubt threatening to pull me under.

"Enough with the theatrics, Julian," I said, forcing my voice to remain steady despite the tremor beneath. "You may think you hold the truth, but I refuse to be defined by anyone else's narrative. My mother's choices are her own, and I'm forging my own path."

Grant shifted beside me, his presence a protective shield as he took a step closer, grounding me in the moment. "You can try to tear us apart, but you won't succeed. We're not afraid of you."

Julian's smile faltered, just a fraction, but it was enough for me to see the uncertainty simmering beneath his bravado. "Fear is the least of your worries," he retorted, his tone sharp as a knife. "What you should truly fear is the truth. It's a ravenous beast, and it won't stop until it consumes everything you care about."

Zoe stepped forward, the fierce glint in her eyes rivaling the sharpest blade. "If the truth is a beast, then we'll tame it together. You may have your secrets, Julian, but so do we."

His gaze flicked between us, calculating, and for a brief moment, I saw the flicker of panic in his eyes. "Secrets? What secrets could you possibly possess that would compare to the ones I wield?"

Without a moment's hesitation, Zoe replied, "How about the truth that we're not as alone as you think? The connections we've made go deeper than you can imagine."

The air crackled with the potential for confrontation, and I could feel the tension rising like steam. "What do you mean?" I demanded, unable to suppress the urgency in my voice. "What are you hiding?"

A flicker of uncertainty crossed Julian's face before he quickly masked it with disdain. "You think you've built a fortress of friendships? Those alliances are as fragile as glass, and when the pressure mounts, they'll shatter, leaving you to pick up the pieces."

"You underestimate us," I shot back, my anger igniting a fire within me. "We've faced worse than you, and we've come out stronger. You won't divide us."

"Stronger?" Julian mocked, but his bravado was waning. "Strength is a fleeting thing. You'll learn that soon enough."

The air was electric with the threat of conflict, a storm brewing just beneath the surface. I could sense the shift, the way the energy in the room morphed, as if we were all drawn into a whirlwind of fate that threatened to consume us. I glanced at Grant, his expression fierce and unwavering, the steadfast ally I needed most in this moment.

Suddenly, a loud bang echoed from the far end of the factory, startling us all. The door swung open with a violent creak, and a group of figures emerged, shadows slicing through the dim light like knives. My heart raced as I recognized their silhouettes: the very people who had spun their own webs of deceit, tangled in the very drama we were trying to escape.

"Looks like the party's gotten bigger," Julian sneered, his confidence returning like a tide. "And I suspect they're here for the same reason as you."

"What do you want?" I shouted, my voice breaking through the rising chaos. "You don't have to be part of this!"

One of the newcomers stepped forward, a woman with fierce eyes and an icy demeanor. "We're here for the truth, just like you," she replied, her voice low and dangerously calm. "But we have our own agenda, and you're in our way."

"What do you think you can accomplish?" Grant asked, his stance shifting to a protective barrier between me and the looming threat. "You think you can walk in here and dictate the terms? You don't know who you're dealing with."

"On the contrary," the woman replied, a slow smile creeping across her lips. "We know exactly who we're dealing with. We know everything about your little family drama, and it's time to expose it all."

A wave of panic swept over me, and I exchanged a frantic glance with Zoe. "What do you mean?" I demanded, fear clawing at my throat. "What do you know?"

Before she could respond, Julian cut in, the glint of amusement returning to his eyes. "Oh, isn't this rich? You think you can just demand answers? The truth is a currency, my dear. And it's one you can't afford."

The woman leaned in closer, her voice dropping to a whisper. "What if I told you your mother's choices were not merely misguided? What if they were part of a much larger scheme, one that involves us all?"

I felt my stomach drop. "What are you talking about?"

Julian laughed, a sound that reverberated like thunder. "You're about to find out just how deep the rabbit hole goes, and trust me, it's not a pretty sight."

The weight of his words pressed down on me, a shroud of dread encasing my heart. As the shadows gathered, swirling like a tempest, I couldn't help but feel that we were standing on the precipice of something monumental—something that would change everything.

In that moment of uncertainty, I felt the ground shift beneath me. My past loomed larger than life, and with it, the secrets I had tried so hard to bury threatened to rise up and swallow me whole.

Just as I opened my mouth to demand more answers, the lights flickered ominously, casting everything into darkness. I heard shouts and chaos erupting around me, the sound of glass shattering, and I felt a sharp pain slice through the tension. A voice broke through the turmoil, crystal clear amid the confusion, leaving me teetering on the edge of despair.

"Don't let him win!"

But before I could comprehend the full weight of those words, the darkness consumed everything, and I was plunged into uncertainty, teetering on the brink of revelation and chaos.

Chapter 24: A New Horizon

The sun crested over the skyline, casting a warm, golden light that danced playfully across the cobblestone streets, illuminating the remnants of yesterday's turmoil. I stood on the weathered steps of city hall, the cool stone grounding me against the flurry of emotions swirling within. Grant stood beside me, his presence a steady anchor in the choppy waters of change. The air buzzed with energy, a vibrant mix of hope and resolve, and I could almost taste the promise of a new beginning.

Around us, the community had gathered, faces animated and eager, each person a thread in the rich tapestry of our city. Conversations flowed like the nearby river, laughter rising above the murmur, punctuated by the occasional cheer. Children ran through the crowd, their shrieks of joy mingling with the rich aroma of freshly baked bread from a nearby vendor. The scent wafted over, enticing me, and I realized I hadn't eaten since breakfast—a lifetime ago, it felt. My stomach grumbled, a rude reminder that even in the midst of revolution, one's appetite doesn't pause.

"Want me to grab you something?" Grant's voice was low, soft against the lively backdrop, his eyes crinkling with concern. I could see the warmth in his gaze, a flicker of mischief as if he were trying to coax me into smiling amidst the chaos.

"No, I'm fine," I replied, the words tumbling out with a practiced nonchalance that didn't quite match the flutter in my chest. "Besides, I wouldn't want to miss any of this." I gestured grandly toward the sea of faces—neighbors, friends, even the occasional local celebrity trying to lend their star power to the movement.

"Right, can't have you distracted from the monumental task of changing the world one pastry at a time," he teased, a smirk dancing on his lips.

"Exactly! I'll let the others handle the heavy lifting," I shot back, a playful glimmer in my eye. The banter felt familiar, grounding me even as I contemplated the weight of the day's events.

As we watched the crowd, I noticed an older woman, her silver hair gleaming like a halo, stepping forward with a megaphone clutched in her trembling hands. I recognized her from the neighborhood council meetings—Mrs. Hargrove, the firebrand who had fearlessly rallied the residents when our community faced a housing crisis last summer. Today, her fierce spirit seemed ready to ignite the very air around us.

"Listen up, everyone!" she called, her voice ringing out with the strength of a trumpet. "We have fought too long in the shadows, and today we step into the light!" The crowd erupted into cheers, a chorus of determination echoing through the square. I felt the thrill of solidarity prickling at the back of my neck, and Grant's hand found mine, fingers interlacing in a gesture of shared commitment.

As she spoke, I absorbed every word, feeling the pulse of the crowd resonate with my own heartbeat. Mrs. Hargrove painted a picture of the future, a future where our community thrived—not just survived. Her voice surged and fell like a tide, washing over us with stories of resilience, of neighbors banding together, of hopes rising like the sun that now hung high above us.

"In every corner of this city, we have a choice," she proclaimed, her voice piercing through the ambient noise. "We can either remain passive spectators, or we can be the architects of our destiny!" The crowd roared in response, and for a fleeting moment, the remnants of my earlier anxiety faded like mist in the sunlight.

In that charged atmosphere, I turned to Grant, his gaze fixed on the crowd, and I could see the same fire ignited in his eyes. "It's happening," I murmured, the weight of it filling the air between us. "We're actually doing this."

He nodded, his expression serious yet imbued with a hint of awe. "And to think, just a few weeks ago, we were at each other's throats." A soft laugh escaped his lips, and I couldn't help but join him, the absurdity of our past grievances a far-off echo now.

"Who knew a little chaos would bring us closer together?" I quipped, elbowing him gently. The laughter between us felt like a lifeline, a thread that tethered me to sanity amidst the frenetic energy swirling around us.

As the speeches continued, punctuated by laughter and impassioned shouts, I caught sight of a familiar face weaving through the crowd. Emily, my best friend and an ever-enthusiastic advocate for social change, waved energetically, her auburn hair bouncing as she approached.

"Did I miss the revolution?" she exclaimed, her cheeks flushed with excitement. "You should have seen me trying to find parking; I nearly got into a duel with a parking meter!"

"Ah, the age-old battle: one woman versus the city's parking regulations," I replied, grinning at her theatrical entrance. "You really know how to make an entrance."

She beamed, the light in her eyes contagious. "This is amazing, isn't it? Just look at everyone! It's like a sea of hope."

I glanced around, taking in the passion on display—the laughter, the shared stories, the smiles. It was infectious, wrapping around us like a comforting blanket. "It really is. We've turned a corner, Em."

"Let's keep turning, shall we?" she said, her voice rich with determination. "I can't wait to see what we can build together."

As I stood there, surrounded by the vibrancy of life and the promise of a new dawn, I realized that today marked not just a community's awakening but my own as well. I felt the echoes of fear and uncertainty fading into the background, replaced by a newfound clarity that filled me with purpose. The future stretched out before us like an open road, ripe with possibilities, and I was ready to step forward—together with Grant, with Emily, with all of us—into whatever awaited.

As the laughter of the crowd swirled around us like a joyous symphony, I felt an unexpected surge of confidence rising within me. I turned to Emily, who was already scanning the bustling crowd, her eyes twinkling with mischief. "I think we should organize a march for better parking, right after this," she suggested, her voice dripping with playful sarcasm. "It could be our next big community project. I can already envision the posters: 'No More Meters, Just Smiles!'"

I chuckled, imagining the colorful signs adorned with glitter and slogans that would elicit both laughter and exasperation from our local council. "Only if you promise to wear a tiara while leading the charge. It's the only way to ensure our demands will be taken seriously."

"Done! A tiara it is!" she declared, her laughter ringing out like a bell. With Emily around, even the gravest of matters felt lighter, a constant reminder that humor could pierce through any tension.

Our banter was interrupted when a familiar figure emerged from the throng, striding toward us with a determined gait. It was Eric, the head of the community outreach program, a man whose presence seemed to draw energy from the crowd. With his well-worn leather jacket and an enthusiasm that could light up the darkest corners of the city, he was a force of nature.

"Hey! You two!" he called, waving enthusiastically as he approached. "You're not going to believe this! We've got a chance to partner with the local university for a series of workshops on community activism. Imagine it—training sessions for anyone interested in making a change!"

"That sounds incredible!" I exclaimed, my pulse quickening at the thought of gathering passionate people to forge paths for our community's future. "But what's the catch? You know there's always a catch."

Eric rubbed the back of his neck, the gesture indicating he was about to unleash something complicated. "Well, they want to film a documentary on the process. You know, for educational purposes and all that jazz."

Emily's eyes sparkled with excitement, a gleam that suggested she was already drafting ideas for how we could utilize that exposure. "A documentary? Count me in! Just imagine: the two of us starring in a community action flick. We could be the next big thing!"

"Sure, but do you think we'll need a dramatic backstory? Maybe I should get a pet iguana or something to spice things up," I added, suppressing a grin.

"Only if I can name it—Sergeant Scaley," she shot back, laughter spilling from her lips. The three of us stood there, our spirits buoyed by the possibilities. But beneath the surface of the lighthearted exchanges, I felt the faintest tremor of apprehension. What if this documentary unveiled more than just our triumphs? What if it caught the moments of vulnerability we worked so hard to disguise?

"Let's do it!" Eric said, clearly unaware of the sudden chill I felt. "I'll coordinate a meeting next week, and we can hash out the details. This is our chance to showcase the spirit of our community, to inspire others!"

I nodded, forcing enthusiasm into my voice, "Absolutely! Count me in." But as the words left my mouth, I couldn't shake the nagging sensation that this would be more than we bargained for.

As the day unfolded, we embraced the energy around us, our conversations weaving a tapestry of ideas and dreams. The sun dipped lower in the sky, casting a warm glow that transformed the city into a painting of amber and gold. I caught Grant watching me, an expression of pride mingling with something deeper—a sense of shared purpose that felt almost sacred.

"Let's take a walk," he suggested, his voice low and inviting. I didn't need a second invitation; I craved a moment away from the fervor, a chance to reflect on the day's whirlwind. We slipped away from the crowd, our hands clasped together as we strolled down a shaded pathway lined with blooming cherry blossoms, their petals fluttering like whispers in the gentle breeze.

"I can't believe how far we've come," I said, looking up at him. The pink blossoms danced overhead, casting soft shadows on his face. "Just a few weeks ago, everything felt so... uncertain."

Grant nodded, his gaze serious yet warm. "And now? Now, we're standing at the precipice of something real. I can feel it in the air, like the calm before a storm."

"Or the thrill before an adventure," I countered, a smile creeping onto my face. "What if we're like those explorers in old tales? Setting sail for uncharted waters, forging a path through the wild?"

He chuckled, the sound rich and full. "Then I hope you're ready to hoist the sails and navigate the rough seas ahead. Because I'm not letting go of your hand."

We walked on, the weight of his words settling in my heart. The thought of navigating the unknown with him felt exhilarating and terrifying all at once. What awaited us beyond the horizon? New friendships, unexpected challenges, perhaps even deeper connections—both with the community and each other.

But just as I began to bask in the warmth of possibility, a commotion interrupted our tranquil moment. From a distance, the sounds of shouting pierced the air, jagged and sharp, slicing through the serenity like a knife. I exchanged a worried glance with Grant, his brow furrowing in concern.

"What's that?" I asked, my heart quickening as we hurried toward the source of the noise.

As we rounded a corner, we were met with a chaotic scene. A group of protesters clashed with a smaller group of counter-protesters, their chants rising in a cacophony of anger and frustration. A sense of dread settled in my stomach as I recognized some faces among the crowd—neighbors and friends, people I'd seen rallying for change, now divided.

"Stay close," Grant murmured, his grip tightening around my hand as we maneuvered through the throng. I felt the tension crackling in the air, like static before a storm, and it was evident that the fragile harmony we'd forged was already beginning to fray.

The words exchanged were sharp, laden with misunderstandings and emotions running high. I could see Mrs. Hargrove at the forefront, her voice raised as she attempted to mediate, but the frenzy only escalated. I had a sinking feeling that our moment of unity was slipping away, and the impending storm would require more than just passion to weather it.

We pushed our way closer, desperate to restore a sense of order before it spiraled further out of control. In the midst of the turmoil, I realized that not only was our community on the brink of a new chapter, but I was also standing at a crossroad in my own life—one where my voice would need to rise above the chaos if we were to reclaim the hope we had nurtured just moments before.

The tension in the air was palpable, thick enough to slice through with a knife. The crowd pulsed like a living organism, voices rising and falling in a discordant symphony of anger and confusion. I could see Mrs. Hargrove still attempting to mediate, her arms outstretched like a seasoned referee in a ring of heavyweights. "Everyone, please! This isn't helping!" she shouted, but her pleas were drowned out by the escalating clamor.

"Maybe if they weren't so stubborn!" a voice shouted from the crowd, igniting a fresh wave of discontent. "We're fighting for what's right!"

Grant squeezed my hand tighter, his expression a mix of concern and determination. "We need to help her," he said, pulling me closer to the fray. "If we can't get them to listen to her, this could turn ugly."

"Or messy, and I just got my favorite shoes clean," I replied, trying to inject some humor into the anxiety bubbling beneath the surface.

"Priorities, right?" he chuckled, but I could see the seriousness in his eyes. We navigated the shifting crowd, maneuvering past passionate faces twisted in frustration. As we got closer, I could make out a few familiar figures—neighbors whose voices I had heard at countless meetings, now standing resolutely on either side of the growing divide.

"Let's just hear each other out!" I shouted, hoping to pierce through the noise. "We're all in this together!" My words barely made a dent, but I pressed on, bolstered by a surge of conviction. "If we can't talk to one another, how can we expect to change anything?"

As if my words were a key, the crowd momentarily hushed, heads turning toward me. I felt a mixture of dread and hope wash over me as eyes locked onto my face. I had always preferred the sidelines, a supportive cheerleader rather than the main event. But today, as uncertainty crackled around us like electricity, it felt like the moment to step into the light.

"Listen, we all want what's best for our community. But division won't get us there!" I continued, emboldened. "We have a chance to build something new, but it requires us to listen, to compromise. We can't forget why we started this fight in the first place."

There was a flicker of recognition in the faces around me, a glimmer of hope that threatened to break through the tension. I took a breath, heart racing, knowing that every word counted. "Remember what we've achieved together? We've turned this community into a place of strength. Let's not lose sight of that!"

In the tense silence, someone shouted, "And what if the other side is wrong?"

"Then we need to show them why!" I replied, feeling the fire of conviction ignite further. "But we won't do that by shouting over one another. We need to meet them where they are."

Grant stood beside me, nodding in agreement. "Exactly! We're stronger together, and when we stand united, we can challenge anything." He stepped forward, his voice steady and unwavering. "We have the power to make change, but that power comes from collaboration, not conflict."

A ripple of murmurs passed through the crowd. The tension shifted, transforming from hostility into contemplation. It was a tiny victory, but a victory nonetheless.

Just as hope began to bloom like flowers breaking through winter's frost, a loud crash echoed nearby, the sound of something shattering against the pavement. The crowd turned, shock rippling through them like a wave. I strained to see through the throng, but panic set in as I caught sight of the source: someone had thrown a rock through the window of the old diner that had been a cornerstone of our community for decades.

"Enough!" a deep voice bellowed from the back. I turned, my heart plummeting as I recognized the figure emerging from the shadows. It was Keith, a local businessman who had been openly critical of our community efforts. He pushed through the crowd, his expression thunderous, a volatile mix of rage and disdain.

"This is what happens when you coddle the weak!" he shouted, pointing an accusing finger at the assembly. "You think compromise will save this city? Look around! It's falling apart!"

The crowd erupted, the earlier unity fracturing as people began to shout in anger and disbelief. The atmosphere grew electric with hostility, and I could feel my pulse racing, the sense of hope I had kindled threatened to extinguish under the weight of chaos.

"Keith, this isn't the way!" I called out, my voice strained but unwavering. "We're trying to unite, not tear each other apart! You can't just—"

"Can't what? Speak the truth?" he shot back, his eyes flashing with indignation. "You think we can just sit down and sing Kumbaya while our city crumbles? You've been blinded by idealism!"

His words landed with the force of a sledgehammer. I glanced at Grant, who looked equally taken aback, then back at Keith, feeling the heat of anger rising in my chest. "Your truth isn't everyone's truth, Keith! You're just adding fuel to the fire!"

"Maybe we need a little fire," he sneered, his tone dripping with sarcasm. "Sometimes, things need to burn down before they can be rebuilt!"

The shouts escalated, voices climbing over one another, creating a cacophony that threatened to swallow us whole. A few individuals moved toward the diner, their expressions wrought with fury, some clutching makeshift signs as if they could physically challenge Keith's tirade.

"Everyone, stop!" I shouted, my heart racing as I felt the world around me tilt. I had to do something. I stepped forward, drawing in a deep breath, channeling every ounce of resolve I could muster. "If we don't come together, we're going to lose everything we've worked for!"

But my voice was a whisper against the storm. The crowd surged forward, angry voices echoing around me, and I felt Grant's hand slip away as he moved to block an escalation that threatened to devolve into chaos. I looked around, realizing that the moment of unity was slipping away faster than I could grasp it. The fire I had felt moments ago flickered uncertainly, swallowed by the rising tide of anger and frustration.

In that chaos, a shrill scream cut through the air, piercing the tumult like a siren. I turned just in time to see a figure falling to the ground, clutching their leg—a woman who had been in the front row of the protests, now crumpled in pain. Gasps filled the space, the crowd recoiling, stunned into silence for a heartbeat.

Time seemed to freeze, the scene shifting into slow motion. A wave of dread washed over me as I realized that we were teetering on the edge of a precipice, the delicate balance of hope and despair threatening to tip into the abyss. I had fought to ignite a flame of unity, only to find it extinguished in an instant.

Then, from the chaos, I heard a familiar voice rising above the din, calling my name, desperate and frantic. I turned, and my heart dropped as I saw Emily, her face a mask of fear, pointing into the distance.

And as I followed her gaze, I felt a shiver run down my spine—a shadow looming just beyond the throng, watching us with an intensity that sent a jolt of foreboding through my very core. The sun dipped low on the horizon, casting an ominous glow that left the figure shrouded in mystery.

In that moment, the chaotic symphony of voices faded into a haunting silence, the world narrowing down to that solitary figure watching us, and I couldn't shake the feeling that the real battle was only just beginning.

Milton Keynes UK
Ingram Content Group UK Ltd.
UKHW031121081124
450926UK00001B/88